A TRACE OF VICE

(A KERI LOCKE MYSTERY—BOOK 3)

BLAKE PIERCE

ISBN: 978-1-64029-012-9

BOOKS BY BLAKE PIERCE

RILEY PAIGE MYSTERY SERIES
ONCE GONE (Book #1)
ONCE TAKEN (Book #2)
ONCE CRAVED (Book #3)
ONCE LURED (Book #4)
ONCE HUNTED (Book #5)
ONCE PINED (Book #6)
ONCE FORSAKEN (Book #7)
ONCE COLD (Book #8)
ONCE STALKED (Book #9)

MACKENZIE WHITE MYSTERY SERIES
BEFORE HE KILLS (Book #1)
BEFORE HE SEES (Book #2)
BEFORE HE COVETS (Book #3)
BEFORE HE TAKES (Book #4)
BEFORE HE NEEDS (Book #5)
BEFORE HE FEELS (Book #6)

AVERY BLACK MYSTERY SERIES
CAUSE TO KILL (Book #1)
CAUSE TO RUN (Book #2)
CAUSE TO HIDE (Book #3)
CAUSE TO FEAR (Book #4)

KERI LOCKE MYSTERY SERIES
A TRACE OF DEATH (Book #1)
A TRACE OF MUDER (Book #2)
A TRACE OF VICE (Book #3)
A TRACE OF CRIME (Book #4)

PROLOGUE

Even though Sarah Caldwell was just sixteen, she had a good head on her shoulders and a keen sense of when things felt off. And this felt off.

She almost didn't go. But when Lanie Joseph, her best friend since elementary school, called and asked her to hang out at the mall this afternoon, she couldn't think of a convincing reason not to go.

But ever since they met up, Lanie seemed jumpy. Sarah couldn't understand what about wandering around the Fox Hills Mall could be so anxiety inducing. She noticed that when they were trying on cheap necklaces at Claire's, Lanie's hands shook as she tried to fasten the clasp.

The truth was that Sarah didn't really know what made Lanie nervous anymore. They'd been incredibly close all through elementary school. However, once Sarah's family had moved from south Culver City to the still working-class but less-dangerous neighborhood of Westchester, they'd slowly drifted apart. The communities were only a few miles apart. But without cars, which neither girl had, or a serious commitment to stay connected, they'd lost touch.

As they tried on makeup at Nordstrom, Sarah stole glances at Lanie in the mirror. Her friend's light blonde hair was streaked with blue and pink. She already had on so much dark eye makeup that there was really no reason to test anything out at the counter. Her fair skin seemed even paler when contrasted with her multiple tattoos and the black tank top and Daisy Dukes she wore. Amid the intentional body art, Sarah couldn't help but notice some bruises mixed in.

She looked back at her own reflection and was stunned by the contrast. She knew she was pretty too, but in a more subdued, almost sensible way. Her shoulder-length brown hair was pulled back in a ponytail. Her own makeup was subtle, highlighting her hazel eyes and long lashes. Her olive skin was tattoo free and she wore faded jeans and a cute but far from risqué teal top.

She wondered if she'd stayed in the old neighborhood, would she look like Lanie did now? Almost certainly not. Her parents would never have allowed her to start down that path.

If Lanie had moved to Westchester, would she still look like she was a teen prostitute working a truck stop?

1

Sarah felt her face turn crimson as she shook the thought from her head. What kind of person was she, to think such awful thoughts about someone she'd played Barbies with as a girl? She turned away, hoping Lanie wouldn't see the guilt she felt sure was plastered all over her face.

"Let's get a snack at the food court," Sarah said, trying to change the dynamic. Lanie nodded and they headed out, leaving the disappointed saleslady behind.

As they sat at a table munching on pretzels, Sarah finally decided to find out what was going on.

"So you know I always love to see you, Lanie. But you sounded so upset when you called and you seem so uneasy…is there something wrong?"

"No. Everything's cool. I just…my boyfriend is stopping by to say hi and I guess I'm nervous about you meeting him. He's a little older and we've only been together for a few weeks. I kind of feel like I might be losing him and I thought that you could talk me up a little, that if he saw me with my oldest friend, it would make him see me differently?"

"How does he see you now?" Sarah asked, concerned.

Before Lanie could answer, a guy approached their table. Even before the introductions, Sarah knew this must be the boyfriend.

He was tall and super-skinny, with tight jeans and a black T-shirt that set off his own pale skin and multiple tattoos. Sarah noticed that he and Lanie had the same small skull and crossbones image on top of their left wrists.

With his long, black, spiky hair and penetrating dark eyes, he wasn't so much handsome as beautiful. He reminded Sarah of the lead singers of those hair metal bands from the 1980s her mom always swooned over with names like Skid Row or Motley Row or something Row. He was easily twenty-one.

"Hey, babe," he said casually and leaned in to give Lanie a surprisingly passionate kiss, at least for a mall food court. "Did you tell her?"

"I didn't get a chance yet," Lanie said sheepishly, before turning to Sarah. "Sarah Caldwell, this is my boyfriend, Dean Chisolm. Dean, this is my oldest friend in the world, Sarah."

"Nice to meet you," Sarah said, nodding politely.

"The pleasure is all mine," Dean said, taking her hand in his and doing a deep, playfully exaggerated bow. "Lanie talks about you all the time, how she wishes you guys could hang out more. So I'm really glad you could get together today."

"Me too," Sarah said, impressed by the unexpected charm of the guy, but wary nonetheless. "What didn't she get a chance to tell me?"

Dean's whole face broke into an easy smile that seemed to melt away her suspicions.

"Oh that," he said. "I'm having some friends over to my place this afternoon and we thought it might be fun for you to join us. Some of them are in bands. One of them needs a new lead singer. Lanie thought you might like to meet them. She says you're a really good singer."

Sarah looked at Lanie, who smiled back but said nothing.

"Is that what you want to do?" Sarah asked her.

"It could be fun to try something new," Lanie said. Her tone was casual but Sarah recognized the look in her eyes, which pleaded for her friend not to say anything to embarrass her in front of her hot new boyfriend.

"Where is it?" Sarah asked.

"Hollywood adjacent," he said, his eyes glimmering with anticipation. "Let's head out. It's gonna be fun."

*

Sarah sat in the back seat of Dean's old Trans Am. The relic was well maintained on the outside but the interior was littered with cigarette butts and rolled up McDonald's wrappers. Dean and Lanie sat up front. With the loud music, it was impossible to have a conversation. They passed through Hollywood in the direction of Little Armenia.

Sarah looked at her friend in the front passenger seat and wondered whether she was even helping her by coming. Her thoughts drifted back to the mall ladies' room before they'd left, where Lanie had finally come somewhat clean with her.

"Dean is super passionate," she'd said as they checked their makeup one last time in the bathroom mirror. "And I'm worried that if I don't keep up, I'm going to lose him. I mean, he's so sexy. He could have his pick of girls. And he doesn't treat me like some teenager. He treats me like a woman."

"Is that why you have those bruises, because he treats you like a woman?"

She tried to catch Lanie's eye in the mirror but her friend refused to look at her directly.

"He was just upset," she said. "He said I was ashamed of him and that's why I didn't introduce him to any of my respectable girlfriends. But the truth is, I don't really have any friends like that anymore. That's when I thought of you. I figured if you two met, it would be a double whammy. He'd know I wasn't hiding him and you'd make me look good because I have at least one friend who's, you know, got a future."

They hit a pothole and Sarah's thoughts were ripped back into the present. Dean was pulling into a parallel parking spot on a seedy street with a row of small houses, all with bars on the windows.

Sarah pulled out her phone and tried for the third time to send a quick text to her mom. But she still couldn't get any reception. It was weird because they weren't in the boonies or anything; they were in the heart of Los Angeles.

Dean parked the car and Sarah put her phone back in her purse. If reception was still bad in his house, she'd use his landline. After all, her mom was pretty understanding, but going hours without giving a courtesy call was definitely against family rules.

As they walked up the path to the house, Sarah could already hear the thumping beat of music. A tingle of uncertainly coursed through her body but she ignored it.

Dean banged loudly on the front door and waited while someone inside undid what sounded like multiple separate locks.

Finally, the door opened a crack to reveal a guy whose face was hidden under a mass of long, unkempt hair. The strong smell of pot wafted out and hit Sarah so unexpectedly that she started coughing. The guy saw Dean and gave him a fist bump, then opened the door wide to let them all in.

Lanie stepped in and Sarah stayed close behind her. Blocking the foyer from the rest of the house was a large red velvet curtain, like something out of a cheesy magician's act. As the long-haired guy relocked the doors behind them, Dean pulled back the curtain and directed them into the living room.

Sarah was shocked by what she saw. The room was packed full with couches, love seats, and beanbag chairs. On each of them were couples making out and in some cases, doing much more. All of the girls looked to be Sarah's age and most looked drugged up. A few even appeared to be passed out, which didn't stop the guys, all of whom looked older, from doing their thing. The vaguely unsettled feeling she'd had walking up to the house returned, but much stronger now.

This is not a place I want to be.

The air was thick with pot and something sweeter and stronger that Sarah didn't recognize. Almost on cue, Dean handed Lanie a joint. She took a long drag before offering it to Sarah, who declined.

4

She decided she'd had enough of this place, which looked like the set of an old porno.

She took out her phone to order an Uber but found she still had no reception.

"Dean," she shouted over the music, "I need to call my mom to let her know I'll be late but I can't get a connection. Do you have a landline?"

"Of course. There's one in my bedroom. I'll show you," he offered, once again flashing that broad, warm smile before turning to Lanie. "Babe, would you get me a beer from the kitchen? It's that way."

Lanie nodded and headed in the direction he'd pointed and Dean motioned for Sarah to follow him down a hall. She wasn't sure why she'd lied about needing to call her mom. But something about this situation made her feel like it wouldn't be well received if she said she wanted to bail.

Dean opened a door at the end of the hall and stepped aside to let her enter. She looked around but didn't see a phone.

"Where's your landline?" she asked, turning back to Dean as she heard a door lock. She saw that he'd already turned the deadbolt and was attaching the chain lock near the top of the bedroom door.

"Sorry," he said, shrugging but not sounding apologetic at all. "I must have moved it to the kitchen. I guess I forgot."

Sarah weighed how aggressive she needed to be. Something was very wrong here. She was in a locked bedroom in what appeared to be something close to a brothel in a seedy part of Little Armenia. She wasn't sure how effective calling him out would be under the circumstances.

Be sweet. Act ignorant. Just get out.

"That's okay," she said perkily, "let's just go to the kitchen then."

As she spoke she heard a toilet flush. She turned to see the bathroom door open, revealing a huge Hispanic guy wearing a white T-shirt that rode up on his enormous, hairy belly. His head was shaved and he had a long beard. Behind him on the linoleum floor of the bathroom lay a girl who couldn't have been more than fourteen. She had on only panties and appeared to be passed out.

Sarah felt her chest tighten and her breathing get shallow. She tried to hide the growing panic she felt.

"Sarah, this is Chiqy," Dean said.

"Hi, Chiqy," she said, forcing her voice to remain calm. "Sorry to cut this short but I'm just headed to the kitchen to make a call. Dean, if you could just unlock the door for me."

5

She decided that instead of trying to find the kitchen, where she doubted she'd see a phone anyway, she was heading straight for the front door. Once outside, she'd flag someone down for a ride. Then she'd call 911 to get help for Lanie.

"Let me get a better look at you," Chiqy ordered in a gravelly voice, ignoring what she'd said. Sarah turned to see the massive man eyeing her up and down. After a moment, he licked his lips. Sarah felt the urge to vomit.

"What do you think?" Dean asked him eagerly.

"I think we put her in a sundress with pigtails and we got a solid earner here."

"I'm going to go now," Sarah said and hurried over to the door. To her surprise, Dean stepped aside, looking amused.

"You used the dampener so she couldn't call or text?" she heard Chiqy ask from somewhere behind her.

"Yep," Dean answered. "I watched her real close. She tried a lot but never seemed to get a connection. Did you, Sarah?"

She fumbled with the chain lock and almost had it off when a huge shadow suddenly blocked out the light. She started to turn but before she could, she felt a sharp thud on the back of head and then everything went black.

CHAPTER ONE

Detective Keri Locke's heart was pounding. Even though she was in the middle of a huge police station, she tuned out everything around her. She could barely think straight as she stared at the email message on her phone, refusing to believe it was real.

willing to meet if you follow the rules. will be in touch soon.

The words were simple but their meaning was colossal.

For six long weeks, she'd been waiting for this, hoping against hope that the man she suspected had abducted her daughter five years ago would reach out. And now he had.

Keri slid her phone away on the desk and closed her eyes, trying to stay composed as she attempted to wrap her head around the situation. When she'd first uncovered the contact information for the man known only as the Collector, she'd set up a meeting. But he never showed up.

She reached out to him to find out what happened. He indicated that she hadn't followed the rules but hinted that he might get in touch in the future. It had taken all of her discipline and patience not to try to contact him again. She wanted to desperately but worried that if she came on too strong, he would get skittish and dump the email address completely, leaving her no way of ever finding him, or Evie.

And now, after all those torturous weeks of silence, he'd finally gotten in touch again. Of course, he didn't know he was communicating with Evie's mother or even that it was a woman. All he knew was that this was a potential client interested in discussing an abduction for hire.

This time she would come up with a better plan than before. The last time, she had less than an hour to get to his assigned meeting place. She tried to set up a decoy to go in her place and survey the situation from afar. But somehow he knew the decoy wasn't legitimate and he didn't come. She couldn't let that happen again.

Stay cool. You've held out this long and it's paid off. Don't ruin it by doing something impulsive. There's nothing you can do right now anyway. The ball's in his court. Just give a basic response and wait to hear back.

Keri typed one word:

understood

Then she put the phone in her purse and stood up from her desk, too nervous and excited to sit still. Knowing there was nothing more she could do, she tried to force the Collector from her mind.

She headed for the break room to get a bite to eat. It was after 4 p.m. and her stomach was growling, although she wasn't sure if it was because she'd skipped lunch or due to general anxiety.

When she arrived, she saw her partner, Ray Sands, rifling through the refrigerator. He was notorious for snagging any food not properly marked. Luckily her chicken salad, with her name clearly taped to the container, was hidden in the lower back corner. Ray, a 6-foot-4-inch, 230-pound black man with a bald head and a heavily muscled frame, would have to really be desperate to navigate himself down there just for a salad.

Keri stood in the doorway, silently enjoying watching Ray's butt wriggle as he maneuvered. In addition to being her partner, he was also her best friend and lately, maybe something more. They both felt a strong attraction to each other and had admitted as much to one another less than two months ago, when Ray was recovering from a gunshot wound he'd sustained when they took down a child kidnapper.

But since then, they'd only taken baby steps. They flirted more openly when they were alone and there had been several semi-dates, where one of them would come to the other's apartment to watch a movie.

But they both seemed afraid to make the next move. Keri knew why she felt this way and suspected Ray felt the same. She was worried that if they decided to really go for it and it didn't work out, both their partnership and their friendship could be put at risk. It was a legitimate concern.

Neither of them had a great romantic track record. Both were divorced. Both had cheated on their spouses. Ray, a former professional boxer, was a notorious ladies' man. And Keri had to admit that since Evie was taken, she'd been one big pulsing nerve, constantly on the verge of spinning out of control. Match.com wouldn't be putting either of them on posters anytime soon.

Ray sensed that he was being watched and turned around, half of an unclaimed sandwich in his hand. Seeing that there was no one in the room but Keri, he asked, "Like what you see?" and winked.

"Don't get cocky, Incredible Hulk," she warned. They loved to tease each other with pet names that highlighted their substantial size difference.

"Who's using the double entendres now, Miss Bianca?" he asked, smiling.

Keri saw his face darken and realized she hadn't done a good enough job of hiding her nervousness about the Collector. He knew her too well.

"What's wrong?" he asked immediately.

"Nothing," she said as she brushed past him and bent down to grab her salad. Unlike him, she had no problem navigating tight spaces. While she wasn't as small as a fictional mouse nickname might suggest, compared to Ray, her 5-foot-6-inch, 130-pound body was Lilliputian.

She could feel his eyes on her but pretended not to notice. She didn't want to discuss what was on her mind for a couple of reasons. First of all, if she told him about the email from the Collector, he'd want to break it down in detail with her. And that would undermine her efforts to keep sane by not thinking about it.

But there was another reason. Keri was under surveillance by a shady lawyer named Jackson Cave, who was notorious for representing pedophiles and child abductors. To get the information that led her to find the Collector, she'd broken into his office and copied a hidden file.

The last time they'd seen each other, Cave had hinted that he knew what she'd done and said outright that he had his eye on her. It was clear to her what he'd meant. Ever since, she'd done regular sweeps for listening devices and been careful to only discuss the Collector in secure environments.

If Cave knew she was on to the Collector, he might warn him. Then he'd disappear and she'd never find Evie. So there was no way she was going to mention anything about it to Ray here.

But he didn't know any of that, so he pressed her.

"I can tell something's up," he said.

But before Keri could diplomatically shut him down, their boss burst through the door. Lieutenant Cole Hillman, their immediate supervisor, was fifty but looked significantly older, with a deeply wrinkled face, uncombed salt-and-pepper hair, and a growing potbelly he couldn't hide with his oversized dress shirts. As usual, he wore a jacket and tie but the former was ill-fitting and the latter was ridiculously loose.

"Good. I'm glad you're both here," he said, skipping any kind of greeting. "Come with me. You've got a case."

They followed him back to his office and both took seats on the weathered loveseat against the wall. Knowing she likely wouldn't have a chance to eat later, Keri scarfed down her salad while Hillman read them in. She noticed that Ray had already finished the sandwich he'd stolen before they sat down. Hillman dove right in.

"Your possible victim is a sixteen-year-old girl from Westchester, Sarah Caldwell. She hasn't been seen since lunchtime. Parents called her multiple times, saying they couldn't reach her."

"They're freaking out because their teenage daughter didn't call them back?" Ray asked skeptically. "Sounds like pretty much every family in America."

Keri didn't reply despite her natural inclination to disagree. She and Ray had argued this point many times. She thought he was too slow to sign onto cases like this. He felt that her personal experience made her far too likely to jump in prematurely. It was a constant source of friction and she didn't feel like getting into it at this moment. But Hillman apparently was willing.

"I thought so too at first," Hillman said, "but they were very convincing that their daughter would never go this long without checking in. They also tried to check her location using the GPS on her smartphone. It was turned off."

"That's a little weird, but still," Ray reiterated.

"Listen, it may be nothing. But they were insistent, panicked even. And they noted that the policy of being missing for twenty-four hours before starting a search doesn't apply to minors. You two don't have any pressing cases right now so I told them you'd stop by to take their statement. Hell, the girl may be home by the time you get there. But it won't do any harm. And this keeps our asses covered on the off chance something is up."

"Sounds like a plan to me," Keri said, standing up to go with her mouth full of her last bite of salad.

"Of course it sounds good to you," Ray muttered as he took the address from Hillman. "Another wild goose chase for you to drag me on."

"You know you love it," Keri said, walking out the door ahead of him.

"Could you two please be a little more professional when you get to the Caldwells'?" Hillman shouted through the open door after them. "I'd like them to think we're at least pretending to take them seriously."

Keri tossed her salad container in the trash and headed for the parking lot. Ray had to jog to keep up with her. As they reached the exit, he leaned in and whispered to her.

"Don't think you're off the hook on whatever it is you're keeping secret from me. You can tell me now or you can tell me later. But I know something's going on with you."

Keri tried not to visibly react. There *was* something going on. And she did plan to fill him in when it was safe to do so. But she needed to find a more secure location to tell her partner, best friend, and potential boyfriend that she might be on the verge of finally catching her daughter's abductor.

CHAPTER TWO

As they pulled up in front of the Caldwell house, Keri's stomach suddenly clenched up.

No matter how often she met with the family of a potentially abducted child, she was always taken back to that moment when she first saw her own little girl, just eight years old, being carried across the bright green grass of a park by a malevolent stranger in a baseball cap pulled low to hide his face.

She felt the same familiar panic rising in her throat now that she'd experienced as she chased the man through the gravel parking lot and saw him toss Evie into his white van like a rag doll. She relived the horror of seeing the teenager who'd tried to stop the man get stabbed to death.

She winced at the memory of the pain she'd felt as she ran barefoot on the gravel lot, ignoring the sharp bits of rock that embedded in her feet as she tried to catch up to the van that was peeling out and driving off . She recalled the sense of helplessness that had overcome her as she realized the van had no license plates and she had almost no description to offer the police.

Ray was familiar with how much she was always affected by this moment and sat quietly in the driver's seat while she worked through the cycle of emotions and gathered herself for what was to come.

"You good?" he asked, when he saw her body finally relax slightly.

"Almost," she said, pulling down the visor mirror and giving herself one last check to make sure she wasn't a total mess.

The person staring back at her looked much healthier than she had just a few months ago. The black circles she used to have under her brown eyes were no longer there and they weren't bloodshot. Her skin was less blotchy. Her dirty blonde hair, while still pulled back in a utilitarian ponytail, wasn't greasy and unwashed.

Keri was closing in on her thirty-six birthday but she looked better than she had at any point since Evie was taken five years earlier. She wasn't sure if it was because of the sense of hope she'd had since the Collector had hinted all those weeks ago that he'd be in touch.

Or maybe it was the real possibility of romance with Ray on the horizon. It could also have been recently moving out of the ratty houseboat she'd called home for several years into a real apartment.

Or it might have had to do with her reduced consumption of large quantities of single malt scotch.

Whatever it was, she noticed more men than usual turning their heads when she walked by these days. She didn't mind it, if only because for the first time in forever, she felt like she had some power over her often out-of-control life.

She flipped the visor back up and turned to Ray.

"Ready," she said.

As they walked up to the front door, Keri took in the neighborhood. This was the northernmost part of Westchester, adjacent to the 405 freeway and just south of the Howard Hughes Center, a large retail and office complex that dominated the skyline in this part of town.

Westchester had a reputation as a working-class neighborhood, and most of the homes were of the modest, one-story variety. But even those had exploded in cost in the last half dozen years. As a result, the community was a mix of old-timers who'd lived here forever and young, professional families who didn't want to live in cookie-cutter developments but somewhere with personality. Keri guessed these folks were the latter.

The door opened before they even got to the porch and out stepped a clearly worried couple. Keri was surprised at their age. The woman—petite, Hispanic, with a no-nonsense pixie cut—looked to be in her mid-fifties. She wore a nice but well-worn women's suit and old but immaculately maintained black shoes.

The man was easily half a foot taller than her. He was white, balding with tufts of grayish-blond hair, and spectacles hanging around his neck. He was at least as old as her and probably closer to sixty. He was more casually dressed than she was, in comfortable slacks and a crisp, buttoned-down plaid dress shirt. His brown loafers were scuffed and one of his laces was undone.

"Are you the detectives?" the woman asked, reaching out her hand to shake theirs even before getting confirmation.

"Yes, ma'am," Keri answered, taking the lead. "I'm Detective Keri Locke of LAPD's West Los Angeles Pacific Division Missing Persons Unit. This is my partner, Detective Raymond Sands."

"Good to meet you folks," Ray said.

The woman beckoned them in as she spoke.

"Thank you for coming. My name is Mariela Caldwell. This is my husband, Edward."

Edward nodded but didn't speak. Keri sensed that they didn't know how to begin so she took the initiative.

"Why don't we have a seat in the kitchen and you can tell us what has you so concerned?"

"Of course," Mariela said, and led them through a narrow hallway adorned with photos of a dark-haired girl with a warm smile. There had to be at least twenty photos covering her entire life from birth until now. They came to a small but well-appointed breakfast nook. "Can I offer you anything—coffee, a snack?"

"No thank you, ma'am," Ray said as he tried to squeeze against the wall to maneuver around and into a chair. "Let's all just sit down and get as much information as possible as quickly as we can. Why don't you start by telling us what has you worried? My understanding is that Sarah has only been out of touch for a few hours."

"Almost five hours now," Edward said, speaking for the first time as he sat down across from Ray. "She called her mother at noon to say she was meeting up with a friend she hadn't seen in a while. It's almost five p.m. now. She knows she's supposed to check in every couple of hours when she goes out, even if it's only a text to say where she is."

"She doesn't ever forget?" Ray asked, keeping his tone neutral so that only Keri caught his underlying skepticism. Neither of the Caldwells spoke for a moment and Keri worried that Ray had offended them. Finally Mariela answered.

"Detective Sands, I know it may be hard to believe. But no, she doesn't ever forget. Ed and I had Sarah later in life. After many failed attempts, we were blessed by her arrival. She is our only child and I admit that we are both a little, what's the word, hovering?"

"Helicopter parents," Ed added with a wry smile.

Keri smiled too. She could hardly blame them.

"Anyway," Mariela continued, "Sarah knows that she is our dearest love in the world and amazingly, she doesn't resent it or feel stifled. We bake together on weekends. She still loves to go to 'take your daughter to work' days with her father. She even came with me to a Motley Crue concert a few months ago. She dotes on us. And because she knows how precious she is to us, she is very diligent about keeping us in the loop. We established the 'text where you are' policy. But she's the one who chose the two-hour rule."

Keri watched both of them closely as they spoke. Mariela's hand was in Ed's and he was gently stroking the back of hers with his thumb. He waited until she was done, then spoke up.

"And even if she did forget, for the first time ever, she wouldn't have gone this long without getting in touch or replying to any of our texts or calls. Between us, we've texted her a dozen times and called half a dozen. In my last message I told her I was calling the police. If she had received any of those, she would have reached out. And as I said to your lieutenant, the GPS on her phone is turned off. That's never happened before."

That unsettling detail hung in the room, threatening to overwhelm everything else. Keri tried to squelch any movement in the direction of panic by quickly asking the next question.

"Mr. and Mrs. Caldwell, may I ask why Sarah wasn't in school today? It is a Friday."

Both of them looked at her with surprised expressions. Even Ray appeared taken aback.

"It's the day after Thanksgiving," Mariela said. "There's no school today."

Keri felt her heart drop into her gut. Only a parent would know that kind of detail and for all practical purposes, she no longer was one.

Evie would be thirteen now. Under normal circumstances, Keri would have been negotiating how to ensure child care for her daughter so she could work today. But she hadn't had normal circumstances in a long time.

The rituals associated with school breaks and family holidays had faded away in recent years to the point where something that used to be obvious to her no longer registered.

She tried to respond but it came out as an unintelligible cough. Her eyes got watery and she lowered her head so no one could see. Ray came to her rescue.

"So Sarah had the day off but you didn't?" he asked.

"No," Ed answered. "I own a small paint store in the Westchester Triangle. It's not like I'm rolling around in money. I can't take many days off—Thanksgiving, Christmas, New Year's—that's about it."

"And I'm a paralegal for a big law firm in El Segundo. Normally I'd be off today but we're prepping a huge case for trial and they needed all hands on deck."

Keri cleared her throat and, confident that she had control of herself, rejoined the conversation.

"Who is this friend Sarah was meeting?" she asked.

"Her name is Lanie Joseph," Mariela said. "Sarah used to be friends with her in elementary school. But when we moved here from our old neighborhood, they lost touch. Frankly, I wish it had stayed that way."

"What do you mean?" Keri asked.

Mariela hesitated, so Ed jumped in.

15

"We used to live in South Culver City. It's not very far away from here but that area is much more hardscrabble. The streets are rougher and so are the kids. Lanie had an edge that always made us a bit uncomfortable, even when she was young. It's gotten worse. I don't mean to be judgmental, but we think she's headed down a dangerous road."

"We scrimped and saved," Mariela jumped in, clearly uncomfortable at casting aspersions among strangers. "The year Sarah started middle school we moved here. We bought this place just before the market exploded. It's small but we'd never be able to buy it now. It was tight even then. But she needed a fresh start with different kids."

"So they lost touch," Ray prodded gently. "What made them reconnect recently?"

"They'd see each other a couple of times a year but that was about it," Ed answered. "But Sarah told us that Lanie texted her yesterday and said she really wanted to meet—that she needed her advice. She didn't say why."

"Of course," Mariela added, "because she's such a sweet, caring girl, she agreed without hesitation. I remember her telling me last night, 'What kind of friend would I be, Mama, if I didn't help someone when they needed it most?'"

Mariela broke off, overcome with emotion. Keri saw Ed give her hand a little squeeze of support. She envied these two. Even in a moment of near-panic, they were a united front, finishing one another's sentences, backstopping each other emotionally. Somehow their shared devotion and love was keeping them from falling apart. Keri remembered a time when she thought she'd had the same thing.

"Did Sarah say where they were meeting?" she asked.

"No, they hadn't decided as of noon. But I'm sure it was somewhere close—maybe the Howard Hughes Center or Fox Hills Mall. Sarah doesn't drive yet so it would have to be somewhere with easy bus access."

Can you give us a few recent photos of her?" Keri asked Mariela, who immediately got up to get some.

"Is Sarah on social media?" Ray asked.

"She's on Facebook. Instagram, Twitter. I don't know what else. Why?" asked Ed.

"Sometimes kids will share details on their accounts that are helpful to investigations. Do you know any of her passwords?"

"No," Mariela said as she pulled a few pictures from their frames. "We've never had cause to ask for them. She shows us posts on her accounts all the time. She never seems to be hiding anything.

16

We're even Facebook friends. I just never felt the need to ask for that kind of thing. Is there no way you can get access to those?"

"We can," Keri told her. "But without the passwords, it takes time. We have to get a court order. And right now we don't have probable cause."

"What about the GPS being off?" Ed asked.

"That helps make the case," Keri answered. "But at this point everything's circumstantial at best. You've both made a compelling argument for why this situation is so unusual. But on paper, it might not look that way to a judge. But don't let that upset you too much. We're just starting out here. This is what we do—investigate. And I'd like to start by going to Lanie's house and speaking to her folks. Do you have her address?"

"I do," Mariela said, handing Keri several photos of Sarah before pulling out her phone and scrolling through her contacts. "But I don't know how much help it will be. Lanie's father is out of the picture and her mother is...uninvolved. But if you think it will help, here it is."

Keri wrote down the information and everyone made their way to the front door. They shook hands formally, which struck Keri as odd for people who'd just been discussing something so intimate.

She and Ray were halfway down the path to his car when Edward Caldwell called out after them with one last question.

"I'm sorry to ask this but you said you were just getting started. That makes it sound like this might be a long process. But my understanding is that in the case of a missing person, the first twenty-four hours are crucial. Is that wrong?"

Keri and Ray looked at each other and then back at Caldwell. Neither was sure who should answer. Finally Ray spoke.

"That's not wrong, sir. But we don't yet have any indication that anything suspicious has happened. And in any case, you reached out to us quickly. That helps a lot. I know this is hard to hear but try not to worry. I promise we'll be in touch."

They turned and walked back to the car. When Keri was sure they were out of earshot, she quietly muttered, "Good lying."

"I wasn't lying. Everything I said was true. She could turn up back home any minute and this will be over."

"I guess," Keri conceded. "But all my instincts are telling me this one isn't going to be that easy."

CHAPTER THREE

Keri sat in the passenger seat on the way to Culver City, quietly flagellating herself. She tried to remind herself that she hadn't done anything wrong. But she was wracked by the guilt of forgetting something as simple as today not being a school day. Even Ray hadn't been able to hide his surprise at it.

She was losing touch with the parent part of her and it scared her. How long would it be before she forgot other, more personal details? A few weeks ago, she'd been given anonymous clues which led to a photo of a teenage girl. But Keri, much to her shame, hadn't been able to tell if it was Evie.

True, it had been five years and the picture was grainy and taken from far away. But the fact that she just didn't immediately know if the photo was of her daughter or not had shaken her. Even after the unit's resident tech guru, Detective Kevin Edgerton, had told her that his digital comparison of the picture to photos of Evie at eight years old was inconclusive for a match, her sense of shame lingered.

I should have just known. A good mother would have known if it was real right away.

"We're here," Ray said quietly, snapping her out of her reverie.

Keri looked up and realized they were parked just up the street from Lanie Joseph's house. The Caldwells had been right. This area, while less than five miles from their home, was much rougher-looking.

It was still only 5:30, but the sun had already mostly set and the temperature was dropping. Small groups of young men in gang attire were gathering in driveways and on stoops, drinking beers and smoking what didn't look like cigarettes. Most of the lawns were more brown than green and the sidewalks were cracked everywhere, with weeds fighting their way through the spaces. Most of the residences on the block looked to be townhouses or duplexes and all of them had bars on the windows and heavy metal screen doors.

"What do you think—should we call Culver City PD for backup?" Ray asked. "Technically, we're out of our jurisdiction."

"Nah. It'll take too long and I want to stay low profile, get in and out. The more formal we make this, the longer it's going to take. If something did happen to Sarah, we don't have time to waste."

"Okay, then let's get to it," he said.

They got out of the car and walked briskly to the address Mariela Caldwell had given them. Lanie lived in the front of a two-unit townhouse on Corinth, just south of Culver Boulevard. The 405 freeway was so close that Keri could identify the hair color of passing drivers.

As Ray knocked on the outer metal door, Keri glanced two houses over at five men huddled around the engine of a Corvette sitting on blocks in the driveway. Several of them cast suspicious looks at the interlopers but no one said anything.

The sound of multiple kids screeching came from inside. After a minute, the inner door was opened by a small blond boy who couldn't have been more than five. He wore holes-pocked jeans and a white T-shirt with a homemade Superman-style "S" scrawled on it.

He stared up at Ray, his neck craning all the way back. Then he looked over at Keri, and apparently viewing her as less threatening, he spoke.

"What you want, lady?"

Keri sensed that the kid didn't get a lot of sweetness and light in his life, so she knelt down to his level and spoke in as gentle a voice as she could muster.

"We're police officers. We need to speak to your mommy for a minute."

The kid, unfazed, turned and shouted back into the house.

"Mom. Cops are here. Want to talk to you." Apparently this wasn't the first time he'd had a visit from law enforcement.

Keri saw Ray glance over at the guys around the Corvette and without looking herself, asked him quietly, "We got a problem over there?"

"Not yet," Ray answered under his breath. "But we could soon. We should make this quick."

"What kind of cops are you?" the little boy demanded. "No uniforms. You undercover? You detectives?"

"Detectives," Ray told him and apparently deciding the boy didn't need to be coddled, asked his own question. "When's the last time you saw Lanie?"

"Oh, Lanie's in trouble again," he said, a gleeful grin consuming his face. "No surprise there. She left at lunchtime to see her smart friend. I guess she was hoping some of it would rub off on her. Don't bet on it."

Just then a woman wearing sweatpants and a heavy, gray sweatshirt that said "Keep Walking" appeared at the end of the hall. As she lumbered toward them Keri took her in. She was about Keri's height but weighed well over 200 pounds.

Her pale skin seemed to merge with the gray sweatshirt, making it impossible to clearly tell where one ended and the other began. Her grayish-blonde hair was pulled back in a loose bun that was in danger of falling apart completely.

Keri guessed that she was younger than forty but her exhausted, worn face could have passed for fifty. She had bags under her eyes and her puffy face was dotted with gin blossoms, possibly alcohol-induced. It was clear that she had once been quite attractive but the weight of life seemed to have drained her and you could only see flashes of pretty around the edges now.

"What's she done now?" the woman asked, even less surprised than her son to see police at her door.

"You're Mrs. Joseph?" Keri asked.

"I haven't been Mrs. Joseph for seven years. That's when Mr. Joseph left me for a massage therapist named Kayley. Now I'm Mrs. Hart, although Mr. Hart cleared out without a proper goodbye about eighteen months ago. But it's too much trouble to change the name again so I'm stuck with it for now."

"So you're Lanie Joseph's mother," Ray said, trying to get her on track. "But your name is…?"

"Joanie Hart. I'm the mother of five hellions, including the one you're here about. So what exactly did she do this time?"

"We're not sure she's done anything, Ms. Hart," Keri assured her, not wanting to create unnecessary conflict with a woman who was clearly comfortable with it. "But the parents of her friend Sarah Caldwell haven't been able to reach her and they're worried. Have you heard from Lanie since about noon today?"

Joanie Hart looked at her like she was from another planet.

"I don't keep tabs like that," she said. "I was working all day; 7-Eleven doesn't close just cuz yesterday was Thanksgiving, you know? I only got back about a half hour ago. So I don't know where she is. But that's not special. She's gone half the time and she never tells me where she's going. That one loves to keep secrets. I think she's got some guy she doesn't want me to know about."

"Did she ever mention this guy's name?"

"Like I said, I don't even know if he exists. I'm just saying I wouldn't put it past her. She likes to do things to piss me off. But I'm too tired or busy to get angry so that pisses *her* off. You know how it is," she said, looking at Keri, who had no idea how it was.

Keri felt her anger rising at this woman who didn't seem to know or care where her daughter was. Joanie hadn't asked about her well-being or expressed any concern at all. Ray seemed to sense how she was feeling and spoke before she could.

"Can we get Lanie's phone number and a recent photo of her, please?" he asked.

Joanie looked put out but didn't say so.

"Give me a second," she said and wandered back down the hall.

Keri looked at Ray, who shook his head in shared disgust.

"You mind if I wait in the car?" Keri said. "I'm worried I'm going to say something...unproductive to Joanie."

"Go ahead. I got this. Maybe you can call Edgerton and see if he can bend the rules to access their social media accounts."

"Raymond Sands, my stars," she said, rediscovering a bit of her sense of humor. "You seem to be adopting some of my more questionable law enforcement methods. I think I like it."

She turned on her heel and walked off before he could respond. Out of the corner of her eye, she saw that the men two doors down were all watching her. She zipped up her jacket, suddenly aware of the cold. Late November in Los Angeles was pretty tame, but with the sun gone, the temperature was in the low fifties. And all those eyes on her added an extra shiver.

When she got to the car, she turned and leaned with her back against it so she could maintain a good view of both Lanie's house and her neighbors as she dialed Edgerton's number.

"Edgerton here," came the enthusiastic voice of Kevin Edgerton, the unit's youngest detective. He may have been only twenty-eight, but the tall, lanky kid was a tech genius who was responsible for cracking many cases.

In fact, he'd been instrumental in helping Keri get in touch with the Collector while shielding her own identity. Keri imagined that right now, he was brushing the longish brown bangs out of his eyes. Why he didn't just get his sloppy, millennial hair cut was beyond her, as were most of his technical abilities.

"Hey, Kevin, it's Keri. I need a favor. I want you to see if you can access a couple of social media accounts for me. One is for Sarah Caldwell from Westchester, age sixteen. The other is Lanie Joseph, Culver City, also sixteen. And please don't give me a hassle over warrants and probable cause. We're dealing with exigent circumstances here and—"

"Got it," Edgerton interrupted.

"What? Already?" Keri asked, stunned.

"Well, not Caldwell. All her accounts are password-protected and require her approval to view. I can crack them if you need. But I'm hoping we can avoid any sticky legal situations just using Joseph's stuff. She's an open book. Anyone can look at her pages. I'm doing it now."

"Do they say anything about where she was today after about noon?" Keri asked, as she noticed three of the men from the Corvette driveway walking toward her.

The two other men remained behind, their focus on Ray, who was still standing at the Hart front door, waiting for Joanie to find a recent photo of her daughter. Keri readjusted herself slightly so that even though she was still leaning against the car, her weight was more evenly distributed in case she had to move suddenly.

"She hasn't posted on Facebook since last night but there are a bunch of posts on Instagram of her with another girl, I'm assuming Caldwell. They're from the Fox Hills Mall. One's in a clothing store. Another's at a makeup counter. The last one is of her at what looks like a food court table, eating a pretzel. The caption says 'yummy.' It's from two oh six p.m."

The three men were crossing into the Harts' yard now and were less than twenty feet from Keri.

"Thanks, Kevin. One last thing—I'm going to send you cell phone numbers for both girls. I'm betting the GPS was shut off in both of them but I need you to track their last known location before that happened," she said as the men came to a stop in front of her. "I've got to go. I'll get back to you if I need more."

Keri hung up before he could respond and slid the phone into her pocket. Along the way, she inconspicuously unsnapped the holster of her weapon.

Glancing at the men but not saying a word, she still leaned against the car but lifted her right leg so that her foot rested against the vehicle. That way she would have extra power if she needed to propel herself forward.

"Evening, gentlemen," she finally said in a firm, friendly tone, "a little nippy out tonight, don't you think?"

One of them, clearly the alpha, sniggered and turned to his friends. "Did this bitch just say it was nipply?" He was Hispanic, short, and a little paunchy in the face, but his bulky flannel shirt hid his frame, making it hard for Keri to tell what she might be up against. The other guys were both tall and skinny with the shirts hanging off skeletal frames. One was white and the other was Hispanic. Keri took a moment to appreciate the racial diversity of this particular street gang before deciding to exploit it.

"You guys letting white boys in these days?" she asked, nodding at the odd man out. "What? Hard to find enough brown-skinned members willing to take orders from you?"

Keri didn't love playing this card but she needed something to create division among them and she knew a lot of these gangs were very particular about membership requirements.

"That mouth is gonna get you in trouble, lady," the Alpha hissed.

"Yeah, trouble," repeated the tall white guy. The tall Hispanic guy remained silent.

"You always go around repeating what your boss says?" Keri asked the white guy. "You pick up any trash he drops on the ground too?"

The two men glanced at each other. Keri could tell she'd hit a sore spot. Behind them, she saw that Ray had gotten the photo of Lanie and was walking back toward them. The two remaining guys by the Corvette started to step in his direction but he gave them a sharp glare and they stopped in their tracks.

"This bitch is rude," the white guy said, apparently unable to come up with anything more clever.

"We may have to teach you some manners," Alpha said.

Keri noticed the tall, quiet Hispanic guy with them tense up at that. And suddenly she understood the dynamic among these three. Alpha was the hothead. White was the follower. Quiet was the peacemaker. He hadn't come over to join in any trouble. He was trying to prevent it. But he hadn't found a way in yet and that was partly Keri's fault. She decided to throw him a lifeline and see if he'd use it.

"You two twins?" she asked him as she nodded at White.

He looked at her for a second, clearly unsure what to make of the comment. She gave him a wink and the tension seemed to seep from his body. He almost smiled.

"Identical," he answered, taking the opening.

"Yo, Carlos, we ain't twins, man," White said, not sure whether to be confused or angry.

"No, man," Alpha jumped in, temporarily forgetting his anger. "Bitch is right. It's hard to tell you two apart. We need to pin some tags on you, right?"

He and Carlos laughed and White joined in, although he still looked perplexed.

"How we doing over here?" Ray asked, startling all three of them. Before they could get riled again, Keri jumped in.

"I think we're good," she said. "Detective Ray Sands, I'd like to introduce you to Carlos and his twin brother. And this is their dear friend…what's your name?"

"Cecil," he said willingly.

23

"This is Cecil. They like Corvettes and chatting older ladies up. But unfortunately, we're going to have to leave you to the car repair, gentlemen. We'd like to stay, but you know how it is with LAPD— always working. Unless, that is, you'd like us to stick around and discuss manners a little more. Would you like that, Cecil?"

Cecil took a look at all 230 pounds of Ray, then back at Keri, seemingly unruffled by his insults, and apparently decided he'd had enough.

"Nah, it's aight. Y'all go on and do your LAPD thing. We busy with car repair, like you said."

"Well, you guys have great night, okay?" Keri said with a level of enthusiasm that only Carlos noticed bleeding into mockery. They nodded and headed back to the Corvette as Keri and Ray got in their car.

"That could have gone worse," Ray said.

"Yeah, I know you're still not a hundred percent from that gunshot wound. I figured I shouldn't get you involved in an altercation with five gang members if I could help it."

"Thanks for looking out for your invalid partner," Ray said as he pulled out into the street

"Don't mention it," Keri said, ignoring the sarcasm.

"So did Edgerton have any luck with the social media stuff?"

"He did. We need to go to Fox Hills Mall."

"What's there?"

"I'm hoping those girls," Keri said, "but I've got a feeling we aren't going to be that lucky."

CHAPTER FOUR

The second Sarah woke up, she felt like she needed to vomit. Her vision was blurry and so was her head. There was a bright light shining down on her and it took a second to realize she was lying on a threadbare mattress in a small, otherwise nearly empty room.

She blinked a couple of times and her eyesight cleared up enough for her to see a small plastic garbage can lying on the floor beside the mattress. She leaned over and pulled it to her, retching into it for a full thirty seconds, ignoring her watery eyes and even more watery nose.

She heard a noise, looked in that direction, and saw that someone had pulled back a black curtain to reveal that she wasn't actually in a small room at all. She was in a cavernous warehouse. As far as the eye could see, there were other mattresses. And on almost all of them were girls her age, all scantily clad or naked.

Some were alone, either sleeping, or more likely passed out. Others were with men, who were having their way with them. Some of the girls struggled, others lay there helplessly, and a few didn't seem to even be conscious while they were being violated. Sarah's mind was foggy but she guessed there were at least twenty girls in the warehouse.

Someone stepped into view. It was Chiqy, the huge guy with the long beard from Dean's room. Suddenly, Sarah's head cleared and the observational distance she'd felt while taking in her surroundings disappeared. Her heart began to pound and she felt a creeping terror take hold of her.

Where am I? What is this place? Why do I feel so weak?

She tried to sit upright as Chiqy moved closer but her arms collapsed under her and she slumped back onto the mattress. That made Chiqy chuckle.

"Don't try to get up," he said, "the drugs we gave you make you clumsy. You might fall and break something. And we can't have that. It would be bad for business. Clients prefer that if any bones get broken, they're the ones doing it."

"What did you do to me?" she demanded hoarsely, trying to sit up again.

Before she knew what was happening, Chiqy backhanded her across the face, knocking her back onto the mattress and sending an explosion of pain from her cheekbone to her ear. As she gasped for air and tried to regain her equilibrium, he leaned over and whispered in her ear.

"You gonna learn, little miss. You don't raise your voice. You don't talk back unless a client wants it. You don't ask questions. Chiqy in charge. You follow my rules, you'll be okay. You don't, then not so okay. We clear?"

Sarah nodded.

"Good. Then listen up cuz here come the rules. First, you're my property. I own you. I may loan you out but never forget who you belong to. You understand?"

Sarah, her cheek still throbbing from his slap, nodded meekly. Even as she tried to wrap her head around the situation, she knew that openly challenging Chiqy in her current condition was unwise.

"Second, you gonna satisfy my clients' needs. You don't gotta love it, although who knows, maybe you'll take to it. That don't matter. You do what the client says, no matter what. If you don't, I'll beat you 'til your insides bleed. I have ways of doing that so you still look pretty for the clients. On the outside, you'll look like angel. But on the inside, you'll be all pulp. We clear?"

Again Sarah nodded. She tried to prop herself up again and squinted in the bright light, hoping to get her bearings. She didn't recognize any of the other girls. Suddenly a cold chill ran up her spine.

Where's Lanie?

"Can you tell me what happened to my friend?" she asked in what she hoped wasn't a challenging voice.

Before she knew what was happening, Chiqy had slapped her again, this time on the other cheek. The force of it slammed her down against the mattress hard.

"I wasn't done," she heard him say despite her ringing ears. "The last rule is you don't speak unless I ask you a question. Like I said, you're gonna learn fast that being uppity doesn't pay around here. You got it?"

Sarah nodded, noticing her head throb as she did.

"But that question I'll answer," Chiqy said with a cruel smile on his face. He pointed at a mattress about fifteen feet away.

Sarah looked over and saw a man who looked to be in his sixties on top of a girl whose head was slumped to the side. Just then, the man grabbed her chin and lifted her face so he could kiss her.

Sarah nearly gagged again as she realized it was Lanie. She was naked from the waist down and her black tank top was up around her neck, revealing her bra. When the man lost interest in her lips, he let go and her head lolled in Sarah's direction.

She could tell that her friend was conscious, if only barely. Her heavy-lidded eyes were barely slits and she didn't seem to be aware

26

of her surroundings. Her body was limp and she didn't physically react to the things being done to her.

Sarah took it all in but somehow the horror of the moment seemed like it was happening far away, on a distant planet. Maybe it was the drugs. Maybe it was getting hit in the face twice. But she felt numb.

Maybe I should be grateful for that.

"She was hard to handle so we had to calm her down a lot," Chiqy said. "That could be you. Or if you don't fight so much, we won't have to give you the sleepy shot. It's up to you."

Sarah looked at him and started to answer but then remembered the rules and bit her tongue. Chiqy saw it and smiled.

"Good. You're a quick learner," he said. "You can talk."

"No sleepy shot," she pleaded.

"Okay, we'll try it clean. But if you…struggle, it's the needle for you. Understand?"

Sarah nodded. Chiqy, a satisfied smile on his face, nodded back and stepped out, pulling the curtain closed behind him.

Not knowing how long she had, Sarah looked around desperately, trying to take stock of her situation. She was still wearing her jeans and teal top, which suggested nothing had been done to her yet. She checked her pockets for her phone, change purse, and ID but they were all gone. No shock there.

A loud female groan from somewhere nearby snapped her out of her numbness and she felt something approaching panic seep in. She welcomed it as it came with a jolt of adrenaline that sharpened her mind and gave her greater control over her limbs.

Think, Sarah, while you still can. You've been gone awhile. People are looking for you. There is no way Mom and Dad would wait this long for you to get in touch without calling the cops. If they're looking for you, you have to give them some kind of clue, something to let them know you were here, in case something happens.

She glanced down at her shirt. Had she told her mom what she was wearing today? No, but she had FaceTimed with her this morning so she'd seen her outfit. She'd remember it for sure. After all, they'd bought it together at the Cabazon outlet mall.

She reached down and tore off a strip about two inches long at the seam near the waist, where it was weakest. She was debating where to leave it when she heard two male voices approaching. Just as the curtain was yanked open again, she shoved the fabric under the mattress so that only a small piece was visible.

27

Trying to act as casual as possible, she looked over at the men. One was Chiqy. The other was a short white guy in his forties, wearing a suit and tie. He had on glasses, which he took off and placed on top of his shoes after he slid them off and placed them near the curtain.

"How old is she?" he asked.

"Sixteen," Chiqy answered.

"A little mature for my taste but she will most definitely do," he said as he approached the mattress.

"Remember what I told you," Chiqy warned her.

She nodded. He seemed satisfied and started to head off when the man said, "A little privacy please."

Chiqy reluctantly pulled the curtain closed. The man stood over her and stared down, his eyes wandering everywhere. She felt ill.

He began to undress and Sarah used the time to decide her next move. She wasn't going to let this happen. Of that she was sure. If they killed her so be it. But she was not going to end up some sex slave. She just had to wait for an opening.

It didn't take long.

The man had taken off his pants and boxers and was crawling toward her. He was squinting slightly and she could tell that without his glasses, he was slightly uncertain. Soon he was right above her on his hands and knees.

No time like the present.

In one swift motion, Sarah brought her right leg up to her chest and thrust her foot forward, slamming the ball of her shoe into the man's crotch. He immediately grunted and collapsed on top of her.

She had been expecting that and rolled his crumpled torso off her. Then she scurried to her feet and hurried to the curtain. The man was behind her moaning and trying to speak. She poked her head out and looked around.

At the far end of the warehouse, she saw the main door. But between her location and freedom were countless occupied mattresses and at least half a dozen men walking around, keeping tabs on things. There was no way she could make it that far.

But maybe she could find a back door if she kept in the shadows close to the wall. She was about to step out when she heard the man's voice, strangled and pained, but clear.

"Help!"

She was out of time. Stepping out from behind the curtain, she dashed to the left, looking for anything that resembled a door. She made it about twenty feet before a guy appeared, blocking her path.

28

She spun around and started in the other direction but ran directly into Chiqy, who wrapped a huge arm around her. She could barely move.

Several feet away, she saw the man who'd been wearing the suit. He was doubled over, but standing up. He was still pantsless. Reaching up his hand, he pointed at her.

"I want her for half-price after this."

Sarah saw Chiqy pull something from his pocket and realized what it was—a syringe. She tried to break free but it was no use. She felt a sharp prick in her arm.

"I warned you we'd have to use the sleepy shot if you were bad," he said, sounding almost apologetic.

She sensed his grip loosening but realized that it was only because she was losing all muscle control. Chiqy felt it too and let her go. By the time she slumped to the floor, she was completely unconscious.

CHAPTER FIVE

Keri was jumpy and nervous as she sat in the waiting room of the Fox Hills Mall security office. For the fourth time in the last fifteen minutes the same thought went through her head: this is taking too long.

One of the security guards was searching for footage of the food court from around 2 p.m., when Lanie had posted her last Instagram photo. It was taking forever, either because the system was old or the guard was inept.

Ray sat in the chair beside her, chowing down on a chicken wrap he'd picked up when they had visited the food court. Keri's wrap sat in her lap, mostly untouched.

Despite the fact that it was 6:30 and the girls had only been out of touch for about four and a half hours, Keri had the creeping sensation that something was very off with this case, even if she didn't yet have the evidence to prove it.

"Do you have to swallow that thing all in one go?" she asked Ray sourly.

He stopped in mid-chew and gave her a quizzical look before asking, with his mouth full, "What's eating you?"

"I'm sorry. I shouldn't yell at you. I'm just frustrated that this is taking so long. If these girls really were abducted, all this fiddling about is wasting valuable time."

"Let's give the guy two more minutes. If he doesn't have it by then, we'll bring down the hammer. Fair?"

"Fair," Keri replied and took a small bite of her wrap.

"I know you're annoyed about this," Ray said, "but there is clearly something else going on with you. I think it has to do with whatever you were holding back at the station. We've got a little time now. So fill me in."

Keri looked at him and could tell that even with the piece of lettuce in his teeth making him look ridiculous, he wasn't joking around.

You're closer to this man than anyone else in the world. He deserves to know. Just tell him.

"Okay," she said. "Hold on though."

She pulled out the small bug and camera detector she'd been keeping in her purse and motioned for Ray to follow her into the hall.

The contraption was recommended to her by a security and surveillance expert she'd once helped out on a case. He said that it was a good combination of portability, reliability, and decent price, and so far, he seemed to be right.

In the weeks since the lawyer Jackson Cave hinted that he'd be keeping close tabs on her, she'd found several eavesdropping devices. One bug had been put in the lamp on her office desk. She suspected a member of the cleaning staff had been bribed to place it there.

She had also found both a camera and an audio bug in her new apartment. The bug was in the living room and the camera had been set up in the bedroom. She had also found a bug inside her car's steering wheel and another in the sun visor of Ray's car.

Edgerton had added extra protections on her office desktop to specifically hunt for tracking software. So far, nothing had been discovered. But she played it safe and avoided using it for anything other than official business.

Her cell phone was clean so far, probably because it never left her side. It was the only device through which she'd communicated with the Collector and was therefore the one she was most protective of.

When they reached the hall, Keri swiped herself, then Ray. She pointed to his phone. He held it out and she swiped it as well.

Ray had been through this routine many times before in the last few weeks. He was initially resistant but after Keri discovered the bug in his car, he no longer balked. In fact, he'd wanted to rip it and all the others out of their locations.

She had pleaded with him to leave them in place and act like everything was normal. If Cave knew they were on to him, he'd suspect that they knew about the Collector and he might warn him to run.

Cave was already suspicious that Keri was the one who had stolen his files with dossiers on different abductors for hire. But he couldn't be sure of that. Even if he was, he didn't know how much Keri had discovered about his secret connections to this dark underworld or whether she had *him* under surveillance too. So he obviously didn't want to risk incriminating himself by contacting the Collector if he could possibly avoid it.

He believed they were in a surveillance stalemate. And considering that Jackson Cave had a lot more information than Keri did right now, she was pretty happy with that arrangement.

She had promised Ray that when allowing the bugs to stay in place became counterproductive, she'd get rid of them, even if it tipped Cave off. They even had a code phrase that meant it was time to dump them. It was "Bondi Beach," a reference to a beach in

Australia that Keri one day hoped to visit. If she said those words, Ray would know he could finally rip the device out of his visor.

"Satisfied?" he asked when she'd finished sweeping them both thoroughly.

"Yes, sorry. Listen, I got an email from our friend this morning," she said, choosing to be cryptic about the Collector even when she was sure they weren't being listened to. "He hinted that he'd be reaching out. I guess I'm just a little on edge. Every time my phone buzzes, I think it's him."

"Did he give you any kind of timetable?" Ray asked.

"No. He just said he'd be in touch soon; nothing beyond that."

"No wonder you're so agitated. I thought you were just overreacting to this case."

Keri felt the heat rise in her cheeks and stared silently at her partner, stunned at his comment. Ray seemed to know immediately that he'd gone too far and was about to try to clean it up when the security guard called out from the computer room.

"I've got something," he yelled.

"You are so lucky right now," Keri hissed angrily, storming ahead of Ray, who gave her a wide berth.

When they entered the computer room, the guard had the video footage cued up to 2:05 p.m. Sarah and Lanie were clearly visible sitting at a small table in the center of the dining area. They saw Lanie take a picture of her food with her phone, almost certainly part of the post Edgerton had found on Instagram.

After about two minutes, a tall, dark-haired guy covered in tattoos approached them. He gave Lanie a long kiss and after a few more minutes of chatting, they all got up and left.

The guard froze the image and turned to face Keri and Ray. Keri looked at the guard closely for the first time. He wore a nametag that read "Keith" and couldn't have been more than twenty-three, with greasy, pimply skin and a hunched-over back that made him look like a scrawny Quasimodo. She pretended not to notice it as he spoke.

"I got a few solid screen grabs of the guy's face. I put them on digital files and I can send them to your phones too if you like."

Ray gave Keri a look that said "maybe this guy isn't so incompetent after all" but shut it down when she glared back at him, still pissed about his "overreaction" remark.

"That would be great," he said, turning his attention back to the guard. "Were you able to track where they went?"

"I was," Keith said proudly and spun around to face the screen again. He switched to a different screen that showed the guy's movements throughout the mall, as well as those of Sarah and Lanie. They culminated with them all getting into a Trans Am and leaving the parking lot, headed in a general northbound direction.

"I tried to get the license plates on the car but all our cameras are mounted too high to see anything like that."

"That's okay," Keri said. "You did really well, Keith. I'm going to give you our cell numbers for those screen grabs. I'd also like you to send them to one of our colleagues at the station so he can run facial recognition."

"Of course," Keith said. "I'll do that right away. Also, I was wondering if I could ask a favor?"

Keri and Ray exchanged skeptical glances but she nodded anyway. Keith continued hesitantly.

"I've been planning to apply to the police academy. But I've held off because I don't think I'm ready for the physical requirements yet. I was wondering if, when all this settles down, I could pick your brains for some suggestions on how to improve my chances of getting in and actually graduating?"

"Is that all?" Keri asked, pulling out a business card out and handing it to him. "Call this pituitary case over here for the physical advice. You can call me when you need some help with the mental part of the job. And one more thing. If you have to wear a nametag for work, get one with your last name on it. It's more intimidating."

Then she walked out, leaving Ray to mop up. He deserved it.

Back out in the hall, she texted the screen grabs of the guy to both Joanie Hart and the Caldwells, asking if either recognized him. A moment later, Ray stepped out to join her. He looked sheepish.

"Listen, Keri. I shouldn't have said you were overreacting. Clearly there's something going on here."

"Is that an apology? Because I didn't hear the words 'I'm sorry' anywhere in there. And while we're at it, haven't there been enough cases that looked like nothing to everyone but me which turned out to be something for you to give me the benefit of the doubt?"

"Yeah, but what about all the cases…?" he started to say, then thought better of it and stopped himself mid-sentence. "I'm sorry."

"Thank you," Keri replied, choosing to ignore the first part of his comment and focus on the second.

Her phone buzzed and she looked down with anticipation. But instead of an email from the Collector, it was a text from Joanie Hart. It was brief and to the point: "never seen this guy."

She showed it to Ray, shaking her head at the depths of the woman's apparent ambivalence toward her daughter's well-being. Just then the phone rang. It was Mariela Caldwell.

"Hi, Mrs. Caldwell. This is Detective Locke."

"Yes, Detective. Ed and I have been looking at the photos you sent. We've never seen that young man. But Sarah mentioned to me that Lanie said her boyfriend looked like he should be in a rock band. I wonder if this might be him?"

"It's quite possible," Keri said. "Did Sarah ever mention a name of this boyfriend?"

"She did. I'm pretty sure it was Dean. I don't recall a last name. I don't think she knew it either."

"Okay, thanks very much, Mrs. Caldwell."

"Is that helpful?" the woman asked in a hopeful, almost pleading voice.

"It may very well be. I don't have any new information for you yet. But I promise you, we're focused hard on finding Sarah. I'll try to update you as much as I can."

"Thank you, Detective. You know, I only realized after you left that you're the same detective who found that missing surfer girl a few months ago. And I know that, well...with your daughter..." Her voice cracked and she stopped, clearly overcome with emotion.

"It's okay, Mrs. Caldwell," Keri said, steeling herself so that she wouldn't lose it.

"I'm just so sorry about your little girl..."

"Don't worry about that right now. My focus is on finding *your* daughter. And I promise I'm going to put every ounce of energy I have into that. You just try to stay calm. Watch a crappy TV show, take a nap, do anything you can to stay sane. Meanwhile, we're on this."

"Thank you, Detective," Mariela Caldwell whispered, her voice barely audible.

Keri hung up and looked at Ray, who wore a worried expression.

"Don't worry, partner," she assured him. "I'm not going to lose it just yet. Now let's find this girl."

"How do you propose we do that?"

"I think it's time we check in with Edgerton. He's had long enough to review the data from the girls' phones. And now we have a name for the guy in the food court—Dean. Maybe Lanie mentions him in one of her posts. Her mom may not know anything about him but I think that may be more due to lack of interest than Lanie hiding him."

As they walked through the mall toward the parking lot and Ray's car, Keri called Edgerton and put him on speaker so Ray could hear too. Edgerton picked up after one ring.

"Dean Chisolm," he said, dispensing with any greeting.

"What?"

"The guy in the screen grabs you had sent to me is named Dean Chisolm. I didn't even have to use facial recognition. He's tagged in a bunch of the Joseph girl's Facebook photos. He's always wearing a cap pulled down or sunglasses like he's trying to hide his identity. But he's not very good at it. He always wears the same kind of black shirt and the tattoos are pretty distinctive."

"Good job, Kevin," Keri said, once again impressed by their unit's resident tech savant. "So what do you have on him?"

"A decent amount. He's got several drug arrests. Some are for possession, a couple for distribution, and one for being a courier. He did four months for that one."

"Sounds like a real solid citizen," Ray muttered.

"That's not all. He's also suspected of being involved in operating a sex ring using underage girls. But no one's ever been able to pull him in on that."

Keri looked at Ray and saw something change in his expression. Until now, he'd clearly thought there was a more than solid chance that these girls were just out joyriding. But with the news about Dean, it was obvious that he had gone from mildly uneasy to full-on concerned.

"What do we know about this sex ring?" Keri asked.

"It's run by a charming-looking guy named Ernesto 'Chiqy' Ramirez."

"Chiqy?" Ray asked.

"I think it might be a nickname—short for *chiquito*. It means tiny. And since this guy looks to be well over three hundred pounds, I'm guessing it's a joke."

"Do you know where we can find Chiqy?" Keri asked, not amused.

"Unfortunately, no. He has no known address. He mostly seems to bounce around abandoned warehouses, where he sets up pop-up brothels until they get raided. But I do have some good news."

"We'll take anything we can get," Ray said as they got into his car.

"I have an address on Dean Chisolm. And it just so happens that it's the exact location where the GPS on both girls' phones shut off. I'm sending it to you now, along with a photo of Chiqy."

"Thanks, Kevin," Keri said. "By the way, we may have found a mini-Kevin working as a security guard at the mall; very tech-savvy. He wants to be a cop. I might put him in touch with you if that's cool."

"Sure. Like I always say, nerds of the world unite!"

"Is that what you always say?" Keri teased.

"I mostly think it," he admitted, then hung up before they could give him any more crap.

"You seem awfully centered for someone who just learned that the girls we're looking for may be caught up in a sex trafficking ring," Ray noted with surprise in his voice.

"I'm trying to keep it light as long as I can," Keri said. "I don't think I'm going to have the chance for much longer. But don't worry. When we find Chisolm, there's a decent chance I may do some amateur tattoo removal using my Swiss Army knife. It's nice and dull."

"Good to know you haven't lost your edge," Ray said.

"Never."

CHAPTER SIX

Keri tried to keep her heart from beating out of her chest as she crouched behind a bush on the side of Dean Chisolm's house. She forced herself to breathe slow and quiet, gripping her weapon in her hands as she waited for the uniformed officers to knock on the front door. Ray was in about the same spot as her on the other side of the house. There were two more officers in the back alley.

Despite the cool weather, Keri felt a trickle of sweat running down her spine, just under her bulletproof vest, and tried to ignore it. It was after 7 p.m. and the temperature was in the high forties now, but she'd left her jacket in the car so she'd have greater range of motion. She could only imagine how sticky she'd be if she'd left it on.

One of the officers rapped on the door, sending a jolt through her entire body. She bent a little lower to make sure no one peeking out a window could see her behind the bush. The movement caused a light twinge in her rib. She had broken several in an altercation with a child abductor two months ago. And while she was technically completely healed, certain positions still caused the rib to get grumpy.

Someone opened the door and she forced herself to shut out the street noise and listen closely.

"Are you Dean Chisolm?" she heard one of the officers ask. She could sense the nervousness in his voice and hoped whoever he was talking to couldn't as well.

"No. He's not here right now," a youngish but surprisingly confident-sounding voice answered.

"Who are you?"

"I'm his brother, Sammy."

"How old are you Sammy?" the officer asked.

"Sixteen."

"Are you armed, Sammy?"

"No."

"Is there anyone else in the house, Sammy? Your parents maybe?"

Sammy laughed at the question before getting control of himself.

"I haven't seen my parents in a long time," he said derisively. "This is Dean's house. He bought it with his own money."

Keri had put up with just about enough of this and stepped out from behind the bush. Sammy glanced in her direction just in time to see her holster her gun. She saw his eyes widen briefly despite his best efforts to act blasé.

Sammy looked like a carbon copy of his big brother, complete with pale skin and multiple tattoos. His hair was black also but too curly to make spiky. Still, he wore the required punk uniform—black T-shirt, skinny jeans with an unnecessary chain hanging from them, and black work boots.

"How did Dean manage to buy his own house at just twenty-four years old?" she asked without introducing herself.

Sammy stared at her, trying to decide whether he could blow her off or not.

"He's a good businessman," he answered with a tone that hinted at defiance without completely going there.

"Business been good lately, Sammy?" she asked, moving a step forward, staying aggressive, hoping to keep the kid off balance.

The two uniformed officers stepped down so there was no one between Keri and Sammy. She didn't know if it was a conscious decision on their parts or them just wanting to get the hell out of the middle of the confrontation. Either way, she was happy to have the floor all to herself.

"I wouldn't know. I'm just a lowly high school student, ma'am," he said, sounding more brazen.

"That's not true, Samuel," she charged, glad that she'd read the file on Chisolm that Edgerton had sent her while they drove to the house. She saw that using his given name startled him. "You dropped out last spring. You just told a lie to an LAPD detective. That's not a great start to our relationship. Do you want to repair it?"

"What do you want?" Sammy demanded, full of guarded petulance. He was off his game now, stepping out onto the stoop against his better judgment.

He was oblivious as Ray quietly came out from around the other side of the house and set up position a few steps behind the boy. Keri stepped toward him to keep his attention on her. They were now less than four feet away from each other.

"I want to know where Dean is," she said, dropping the playful pretense. "And I want to know where the girls he brought over this afternoon are."

"I don't know where he is. He left a few hours ago. And I don't know anything about any girls."

Despite being a juvenile delinquent in training, Keri she knew that Sammy had never been arrested, much less served time. She could use his fear of the prospect to her advantage. She decided to go in for the kill.

"You're not being straight with me, Samuel. And I'm losing patience with you. We both know what business your brother is in. We both know how he can afford this house. And we both know that you're not spending your free time working on getting your GED."

Sammy opened his mouth to protest but Keri held up her hand and barreled on without pausing.

"I'm looking for two missing teenage girls out there. They were brought here by your brother. It's my job to find them. If you help me do that, you can lead something close to a normal life. If you don't, it's going to go very badly for you. This is your one chance tonight to avoid getting put in the system. Cooperate or it's down the rabbit hole."

Sammy stared at her, trying to keep his face untroubled. But his eyes were unnaturally fixed and his breath was shallow and quick. He kept clenching and unclenching his fists. He was terrified.

What Sammy didn't know was that Keri didn't have a warrant. If he'd just stayed inside the house and refused to speak to them, they wouldn't have had much recourse other than to call for a warrant and wait outside until it was approved.

But by stepping outside to engage with her and leaving the door open, he'd made himself vulnerable. He didn't realize it yet but whether he agreed to help or not, they were getting in that house. His next decision really would determine his immediate future. Keri hoped he could tell she wasn't bluffing. She hoped he'd choose wisely. He did not.

"I don't know anything," he said, unaware that he was only sealing his own fate.

Keri sighed. She almost felt sorry for him.

"Did you hear that?" Ray asked.

Sammy, unaware that anyone was behind him, nearly jumped out of his boots.

"What the…?" he started to say. Ray interrupted him.

"Detective Locke, I think I heard some cries for help from inside. Can you hear them too?"

"I think I can, Detective Sands. Officers, can you hear that too?"

The two uniformed officers clearly couldn't but didn't want to be the weak links. They both nodded, and for good measure, the one who'd first knocked on the door added, "For sure."

Ray rolled his eyes at the clumsy effort but continued anyway.

"Officers, can you handcuff Mr. Chisolm and put him in the back of your car for now while Detective Locke and I check out that crying?"

"This is BS," Sammy shouted as one of the officers grabbed him by the shoulder and turned him around to cuff him. "You can't hear anything. This is an illegal search."

"I'm afraid not, Sammy," Ray said, unholstering his gun and preparing to enter the house. "Those cries we all hear create exigent circumstances. Maybe go to law school once you get that GED, buddy."

"You should have listened to me," Keri whispered in Sammy's ear before she walked up the steps and pulled out her gun. Ray nodded and they both entered with weapons raised.

The place was a sty. There were empty beer cans everywhere. Fast food wrappers littered the stain-dotted carpet. Music was coming from somewhere in the back.

Keri and Ray made their way through the house quickly. Neither of them expected to find much. The fact that it was devoid of people suggested that it had only been a staging area. Girls were likely brought here thinking they were attending a party only to be drugged and then moved en masse.

Keri found the back bedroom where the relentless techno music was coming from and turned it off. She stepped into the adjoining bathroom and saw a pair of panties balled up beside the toilet.

With a creeping anxiety, Keri returned to the bedroom and noticed something she'd missed before. There were three locks on the door. In addition to the standard one on the knob, there was both a deadbolt and a chain lock.

"Hey, Ray, come back here," she called out as she moved to get a closer look. The chain lock had lots of scuffs. It could have been her imagination, but Keri couldn't help thinking all the markings were a result of it repeatedly being locked in a rush, by someone trying to prevent people from getting out easily.

Ray stepped in the room and Keri pointed at the door.

"Lot of locks for a bedroom door," he noted, pointing out the obvious.

"I also found some panties in the bathroom," Keri said.

"There are a few other pairs strewn throughout the rest of the bedrooms too, as well as a few bras," Ray said. "I also found some coke and pot. I think we've got enough here to arrest Sammy if we want."

"Let's call in CSU to collect the drugs and see if they can find any prints. I want to take another run at Sammy. Now that he's facing real time, maybe he'll be a little more chatty, especially after sitting in the back of that squad car for a while."

"Sounds good," Ray said. "I'm going to turn on the TV to find a channel that sounds like girls screaming. You know, for the exigent circumstances and all. Got to make it look good, right?"

Keri nodded. While Ray fiddled with the remote control, she walked out to the squad car. One of the officers had turned on the flashing lights and a small crowd was developing down the street.

Keri was pleased at the effect. Everything was adding to the pressure on Sammy. She didn't want to put a sixteen-year-old kid in the system but she would if she had to, especially if the threat of doing so might rescue two abducted girls.

He was staring at her nervously through the car window as she approached him. She opened the door and knelt down to his eye level. She could go lots of ways with this kid but decided that at this point her strongest move was to just play it straight.

"We found the drugs, Sammy," she told him. "Pot, coke, who knows what else. The quantity suggests more than just possession. We're talking intent to distribute. And since you were the only one in the house, you're the only one we can pin this on. We also found female undergarments. We're bringing in our crime scene unit to check for DNA and dust for fingerprints. And I'm pretty confident we're going to find some for the girls I'm looking for, maybe others too."

Keri watched as Sammy gulped hard. She thought he might say something but he stayed silent, so she went on.

"I'm laying this all out for you so you know what you're facing. I'm not trying to trick you or play games. You're hosed, Sammy. I don't know what the sentence is for this off the top of my head. But if we can't get those girls back, I'm going to put all my energy into making sure you get the stiffest possible sentence. I'll testify against you. My partner will testify against you. I'll find a way to get the parents of these girls to testify against you, to tar you with these missing girls. Do you believe me Sammy?"

Sammy nodded.

"Good. So we're on the same page. With that, I'm going to give you one more chance to get yourself out of this. I'm not even going to ask you to implicate your brother. I just want to know the location of the warehouse where Chiqy took those girls. You give me that and it pans out, I'll go to bat for you with the DA. But this is a one-time-only offer. You're only good to me as long as I still have a shot at finding these girls. What do you say, Sammy? You want a second chance at saving your own life?"

Sammy lowered his head as if lost in thought. Keri waited patiently, knowing she had pushed as hard as she could and it was now out of her hands. After a moment he raised his head again and she knew she had him.

"The warehouse is in the Valley, in North Hollywood, on Vanowen," he nearly whispered. "I don't know the exact address. But I have it on my phone. If you give it to me, I'll find it for you. That guy has it."

Keri stood up and faced the uniformed officer he'd pointed at. It was the one who'd first knocked on the door. He was leaning on the hood of the car.

"Give me his phone," she ordered forcefully, then turned to face the house and yelled as loudly as she could. "Ray, get out here now!"

CHAPTER SEVEN

Keri wasn't in control and she hated it. She forced herself not to let her frustration show but it was hard. If she bit her tongue any harder, she feared it would bleed.

Because they were about to raid a warehouse that might be housing a prostitution ring run by a notoriously brutal pimp who maintained a small army, an LAPD SWAT team had been called in. They were running the show.

Keri and Ray stood with the team, who had set up a block away from the warehouse. They were listening to the team leader give final instructions. On his mark, half the team was to enter through the front and half through a door in the back. Keri and Ray would be allowed to join them once the place was secure.

Keri watched them approach the warehouse and, despite her resentment at being left out, couldn't help but admire their teamwork and efficiency as they quietly moved into place.

The team leader gave the go-ahead over the radio and she heard a series of bangs as the team members dispersed stun grenades before disappearing inside. She listened to the chatter as they secured the facility. There were no shouts, no gunfire, and little anxiety in their voices. Keri could tell within thirty seconds that there were no hostiles inside. After another two minutes, they were given permission to enter.

Once inside, Keri allowed herself a moment to take in her surroundings. The entire cavernous warehouse was comprised almost exclusively of mattresses scattered throughout. There had to be over two dozen. They were completely bare, without sheets or blankets. A few of the ones in the corners had curtains, which offered the barest semblance of privacy. A bitter thought entered Keri's head.

Maybe those are for the VIP clients.

It was immediately apparent why the SWAT team had sounded so casual. Other than the areas behind the curtains, which had clearly been checked, there was no place to hide. Despite the overhead lights being dimmed, the entire warehouse was visible and it was almost completely empty.

In fact, she only saw two people in the whole place who weren't law enforcement. One was a john who appeared to be passed out on the ground next to a mattress. The other was a young girl sitting on a mattress near the back of the facility. A SWAT officer stood over her, while a medic took her blood pressure.

Keri headed straight for her, followed closely by Ray. The girl looked to be about fourteen, with long stringy blonde hair. Her eyes were red and cloudy, as if she wasn't all there. She wore a tank top but didn't have any bottoms on. Instead, she was partially covered by a thermal blanket the medic had given her.

"Have you asked her anything yet?" Keri asked the officer.

"No ma'am. Not my area of expertise. Besides, I wouldn't want to step on any toes."

"Smart man," she said before kneeling next to the medic. He glanced at her briefly before returning his eyes to the girl.

"Blood pressure's low," he said quietly. "Makes sense considering she said she was drugged."

Keri nodded and looked closely at the girl. She seemed to be only partially aware of her surroundings. A puddle of vomit lay next to the mattress.

"What's your name, sweetie?" she asked softly.

The girl looked at her blankly, not seeming to register that she was being spoken to. Keri gently touched her arm and tried again.

"What's your name?"

The physical contact seemed to snap the girl slightly out of her stupor. Her gaze became more fixed on Keri.

"Lilah."

"How old are you, Lilah?"

"I'm fifteen."

"Okay, Lilah. My name's Keri. I'm a police officer. So is everyone else here. You're safe now. In a few minutes we're going to take you to the hospital and get in touch with your family. Does that sound good?"

Lilah nodded.

"But before we do that, I need to ask you a few very important questions. Is that okay?"

Lilah nodded again.

"Where is everyone else?"

"They're all gone," Lilah answered as if that explained everything. The medic leaned over to Keri.

"She's in shock," he whispered. Keri nodded and tried a different tack.

"Do you know what happened? It looks like they left in a hurry."

"They did. The big man ordered them to grab all the girls up and take them away. Then he left."

"Did the big man have a shaved head and long beard?"

44

"Yes," Lilah said, closing her eyes at the thought of him. "Once he left, the other men started grabbing all of us and pulling us outside. They started shoving us into a big van."

"Do you remember anything about the van?" Keri asked.

"It was brown. And even though it was big, they had trouble getting all the girls in. They were packed real tight."

"Why didn't they take you away too?"

"They were going to but I started throwing up. No one wanted to get close to me. Someone said to just lock me back inside so one of them shoved me on a mattress and closed the doors. I kept throwing up for a while after that and then I guess I fell asleep until you came."

"So all the other girls were put in the van?"

"I think so," Lilah said. Then she seemed to slump, as if the effort of answering the questions had used up all the energy she had. Ray tapped her on the shoulder. She looked up to see several female uniformed officers standing nearby.

"Lilah," she said, keeping her voice calm and comforting, "I can tell you're tired so I'm done asking you questions for now. These nice officers are going to help get you to the hospital. Once you've had a little break, they're going to ask you some more things."

"I don't want you to leave me," Lilah nearly shouted, showing true emotion for the first time. She clutched Keri's arm.

"I know, sweetie," Keri said, keeping her tone soothing despite Lilah's raw anguish. "But you need to go the hospital so the doctors can help you. And I need to look around here some more to see if there's anything here that will help us find all those other girls. We need to get them home safe too."

"Okay," Lilah said, seeming to lose her fire as quickly as it had come. Keri delicately pried her arm loose from the girl's grip and motioned for the uniformed officers to step in. They moved in quickly, whispering quietly to Lilah as the medic prepped the stretcher on the floor beside her.

Keri stood up and moved away before speaking to Ray.

"Not much to go on," she said. "I'm going to walk around and see what these guys might have left behind. Can you call in the brown van she mentioned to Edgerton so he can start looking for it?"

"Yeah," Ray said. "I know there are lots of cameras in these industrial areas. I'm sure he'll find it. A big brown van will stand out. The question is, how long will it take to track where it went?"

"Hopefully not too long," Keri said. "This Chiqy guy moves fast; first Dean's house and now here. We need to catch up before he moves again."

"Agreed," Ray said. "And what worries me is that he pulled up stakes from this place so fast. He obviously intended this to be the brothel location for the night. But it seems like he knew we were coming, like he got tipped off somehow."

They both stood quietly for a moment, wondering how that might be possible. Finally, Keri snapped out of it.

"We'll have to worry about that later. One thing at a time, right? Go ahead and call Edgerton and I'll start looking around here."

Ray nodded and went outside. Keri looked around the warehouse, wondering where to start her search. She decided to look at the curtained areas first. There had to be a reason they were separated from everything else.

She wandered over to the first one in the front left corner of the warehouse. Just as she started to pull out her flashlight someone turned the overhead lights up to maximum. After taking a second to adjust, Keri moved around the space, looking for anything out of the ordinary. But nothing seemed odd.

She moved on to the next curtained area in the back left corner of the warehouse. It also looked nondescript. She wasn't even sure what she was looking for. It seemed unlikely that she would find a wallet lying on the floor or a scrap of paper with the next address Chiqy had sent the girls to.

She was about to move on to the third curtained area when she noticed something out of the corner of her eye. There was a small piece of fabric poking out from underneath the far side of the mattress.

Keri stepped over to it and knelt down. It was teal.

Her heart skipping a beat, Keri pulled on her latex gloves and lifted the mattress up. Underneath was the rest of the fabric. It wasn't long—maybe four inches by two inches. And it was clearly ripped and not cut.

Keri lowered the mattress again, trying not to disturb anything as one overwhelming thought echoed through her brain.

This fabric looks as if someone tore it from their outfit and stuffed it under the edge of the mattress to be discovered later.

She yanked off her gloves and pulled out her phone, scrolling to a screenshot Keith the security guard had sent her. It was of Sarah and Lanie sitting at the food court table. Keri zoomed in on Sarah until she was sure. The girl's top was the same exact color as the one under the mattress.

"Ray!" she called out as she snapped several photos of the snippet of clothing.

She turned around to see her partner walking toward her. He was finishing up his conversation and held up a finger to let her know he was almost done.

He hung up. Before Keri could speak he launched into a description of what Edgerton told him.

"It's just like we thought. He says pulling up footage of the van leaving should be easy. But tracking it to its next destination is going to take a while. He recommended we come back to the station so could show us in person once he has something. You find anything?"

Keri smiled slightly and pointed to the piece of fabric.

"What is that?" Ray asked.

Keri showed him the screen shot from the food court.

"It's part of Sarah's top. She must have ripped it off and hidden it, hoping we'd find it."

"Are you sure?" Ray asked, uncertain.

"Raymond, this girl is smart. Despite everything that's happened to her, she's keeping her wits about her and fighting back the only way she can. She's leaving us clues!"

CHAPTER EIGHT

Keri felt like breaking something. As she stared at the tiny piece of equipment on Detective Manny Suarez's desk back at the Pacific Division station, she had the urge to pull out the butt of her gun and smash the small contraption into dust.

Instead, she took a long, slow deep breath, let her frustration pass, and asked her question as calmly as she could.

"And where did CSU find this again?"

"Right above the front door of Dean Chisolm's house," Suarez said. "It's a motion activated security camera and it's Internet-connected. That must be how this Chiqy guy knew you were coming to the warehouse. He would have seen you questioning Sammy Chisolm and assumed the kid would break at some point."

"Wow," Keri said, impressed despite herself. "We showed up at Chisolm's house just after seven p.m. and the SWAT team entered that warehouse before eight p.m. That means he completely cleared out the place in well under an hour."

"It also means Chiqy will be out to punish Sammy for betraying him," Ray noted. "We should get him in protective custody. Where is he now?"

Suarez punched up his location on his computer. Keri watched his fingers fly across the keyboard in amazement. Manny Suarez wasn't impressive looking, with his permanent eleven o'clock shadow, his spare tire, and his sleepy eyes. But Keri knew that under his schlubby persona was a whip-smart detective with great natural instincts. He was also a really fast typist.

"It looks like Castillo left about twenty minutes ago to take him for booking at the Twin Towers," he said.

The Twin Towers was the informal name for Los Angeles County's men's central jail. It was exactly the kind of place where Chiqy's minions would be waiting to get their hands on Sammy.

"Let's get Castillo on the line," Keri said. "I want to warn her about what she's dealing with. She's going to have to push hard to get him protection."

As Manny called Castillo, Ray turned to Keri.

"You don't think Castillo can handle this? I wouldn't tell her that. The chip on that girl's shoulder is almost as big as yours."

It was true. Officer Jamie Castillo was tough as nails and fearless to boot. Keri had learned that when she pulled the young cop into a last-minute, legally questionable attempt to catch the Collector. Castillo hadn't asked questions. She just showed up and had Keri's back. The trap hadn't worked but it wasn't Castillo's fault.

"Hello," came her voice over the speakerphone.

"Hey, Castillo. It's Keri here with Ray and Manny. You're transporting Chisolm to Twin Towers for booking, right?"

"Yup. We should be there in about a half hour. Why?"

"We're concerned that the guy his brother answers to knows he ratted him out and may try to get payback. We need you to make sure they put Chisolm in protective custody once he's booked."

"Okay," Castillo said as if it was no big deal.

"They might balk," Keri warned her. "If they give you a hard time or if you think they won't follow through, just bring him back. We'll keep him on ice here for a while if we have to. Can you handle that?"

She added the last line intentionally to piss the young officer off. If Castillo felt like someone was challenging her abilities, she was likely to go all out to prove her merit. That's part of why Keri liked her so much. The rookie cop reminded her of herself, just younger, more athletic, and Hispanic.

"Detective Locke," Castillo said, trying to stay respectful despite the edge in her voice, "I hope you're not doubting my competence."

"Not your competence, Jamie," Keri said, trying not to giggle at how easily she'd manipulated her. "I just doubt the competence of our friends down at county jail. They may need someone willing to be forceful. I think you're just the gal for the job."

"Any advice?"

Keri's phone rang and she looked down to see that it was Mariela Caldwell. She motioned for Ray to take over giving Castillo hints on how to navigate the bureaucratic maze that was the Twin Towers Correctional Facility as she stepped away to answer the call.

"Hi, Mrs. Caldwell. I'm sorry I haven't reached out to you yet," she said apologetically.

"I understand," the woman said, obviously trying to keep the anxiety out of her voice. "I just wanted to check in to see if you had any news."

"Of course. Things have been moving so quickly that I just haven't had much time."

She paused for a moment, not sure how to proceed with what she knew from personal experience would be devastating information.

"Detective?" came the worried voice on the other end of the line.

Keri decided there was no easy way to break the news and decided to just be straight with the woman.

"Mrs. Caldwell, I'm just going to be honest with you. The news isn't great. Your daughter was abducted. It looks like Lanie's boyfriend was working for a guy who operates a sex trafficking ring. He took them to a house where this guy and his crew were waiting."

Keri heard Mrs. Caldwell muffle a sob and then the voice of her husband softly comforting her. She ignored it and plowed through, not wanting to draw this out any longer than necessary.

"The girls were taken to a warehouse in the Valley where they were kept before being moved again. We know Sarah was there because we found a ripped piece of the top she was wearing. I believe she left it there as a clue for us."

Keri intentionally skipped over what had been happening at the warehouse and the fact that the piece of clothing was found partially hidden under a mattress.

Edward Caldwell's strained voice came on the line and Keri realized she had been on speakerphone.

"Do you know where she was moved to?" he asked quietly.

"Not yet. Our tech team is working on that now, using camera footage to track the vehicle the girls were transported in. But I have to warn you, it's a painstaking process and may take a while."

"You said it's a sex trafficking ring," Mariela Caldwell said. "Does that mean that she's already been...hurt?"

"There's no way to know that for sure, Mrs. Caldwell. But you should prepare yourself for that likelihood. I'm sorry to be so blunt. But you deserve to know."

"Thank you for being honest with us," Edward Caldwell said, his voice cracking slightly.

"I wanted to let you know where we are now in the investigation. But I don't want to call you with constant updates that don't really give you any meaningful new information. Please know that when I learn something substantial, I'll get in touch. But it may be several hours. I know it may be impossible, but you should both try to get a little sleep if you can."

"We'll try," he said and they all knew he was lying.

Keri felt her phone buzz. She had a new email.

"I've got to go now. I'll reach out when I have something," she said to the Caldwells, then hung up and clicked on the new message. She didn't recognize the sender. It took her a second to realize that it was the handle for the Collector.

She felt her legs start to give out and just managed to stumble over to an unoccupied nearby desk and half-sit on it. Her hands were

50

trembling as she tried to open the email. Her finger shook so much that it took three tries to hit the screen properly. When she finally did, the message she found was short and to the point.

l.a. live. go to lobby bar of marriott. Ask for package for jones. Follow instructions in package. 30 minutes. just you. no decoys. confirm.

Without a second thought, Keri replied, "Confirmed." Then she sat there on the edge of the desk, half-dazed with shock, unmoving despite her tight time deadline.

She looked over at Ray and Suarez talking Castillo through what she had to do at the Twin Towers. They were teasing her about whether she was up to the task and she was taking the bait. Ray glanced over at Keri with a broad smile on his face. She tried to return it but he immediately knew something was wrong.

"You got this?" he asked Suarez, and getting a nod of confirmation, he walked over to Keri. "What is it?"

She gulped hard before lifting her index finger to her lips, indicating he shouldn't say any more. She stood up, made sure her legs were working properly, then motioned for him to follow her outside.

"Just how many bugs do you think Jackson Cave has in that place?" Ray asked when they stepped out into the chilly night air.

"Enough to be extra careful," Keri said, pulling out her phone and showing him the email. Ray read it and looked up at her, concerned.

"A half hour from now? That's going to be tough."

"Why? I'll just use the siren," Keri said as they walked to her car.

"Yeah. But it's going to be crazy once you get down there. There's a big Lakers game against the Spurs tonight across the street at Staples Center. It'll probably end about ten p.m., right around the time you're supposed to meet him. Thousands of people will be coming out of the arena and heading to bars right near where you'll be."

"That must be his plan," Keri said. "The more crowded it is, the more control he has. And if things go sideways, he can just slip away amid that huge mass of people. I guess I better hurry then."

"I?" Ray asked. "Don't you mean 'we'?"

"No, Ray. This has got to just be me."

"Why?" he demanded as he reached for the passenger door handle of her car. She held up her hand to stop him and pointed silently at her steering wheel, where they'd discovered the listening

51

device weeks ago. Ray walked over to her and stood close as she spoke.

"The last time I tried this, he got skittish and bailed. He said it was because I sent a decoy but I don't know if that's true. Maybe he saw Castillo covering me from the rooftop. Maybe he's just a jumpy guy. But this is my last chance. You know if he gets spooked again, he'll dump that email address and I'll never find him again. And that means I'll never find Evie. I can't risk that. So I'm doing it his way."

"But what if he recognizes you? He knows who you are."

"That's why I always keep a disguise in my trunk," she said, popping it and pulling out her bag of supplies. "I've got a wig, glasses, a cap, even fake teeth. I'm just a client looking to have a co-worker eliminated. Remember? He'll buy it. And if he doesn't, I'll take him down and beat the answers out of him."

"I don't like this," Ray said. But his tone was full of resignation. He knew he'd already lost the argument.

"I know, partner. But this is the way it has to be. I've been waiting five years to meet this guy face to face. I'm not going to blow it. Besides, there's nothing we can do on the Caldwell front until Edgerton finds out where that brown van went. And now I've only got twenty-six minutes to get down there. I've got to go."

She started to open the door but before she could, Ray grabbed her and pulled her into a tight bear hug.

"Be careful, Tink," he whispered.

"I will, Snuffleupagus," she whispered back. Then she stood on tiptoes and gave him a quick kiss on the cheek before hopping in the car and pulling out of the parking lot, tires squealing.

CHAPTER NINE

With adrenaline pumping through her system, Keri finally pulled off the freeway. Her eyes darted back and forth between the road and the clock on her dashboard as she swerved in and out of the thick traffic on the exit ramp, eventually using the shoulder to get past the long line of unmoving cars.

Ray was right. Even with her siren blaring, it had been tough to get downtown to the massive L.A. Live entertainment complex by 10 p.m. By the time Keri pulled up in front of the JW Marriott on West Olympic Boulevard, it was already 9:58. She parked in a spot marked "loading/unloading only." As a valet walked over to chastise her, she flashed her badge and told him to make sure no one touched the car.

Then she hurried into the hotel, past the check-in desk to the large lobby bar in the central atrium area. As she arrived, she glanced at her watch: 10:01 p.m. Hopefully the Collector wasn't too much of a stickler for promptness.

She got the attention of the bartender, who walked over far too casually for Keri's taste.

"You just beat the rush," she said. "The Lakers game just ended. This place will be swarming in five minutes. What can I get you?"

"I'm picking up a package for Jones," Keri said, trying not to sound too desperate.

"Oh yeah, just hold on a second," the bartender said and walked over to the cash register to retrieve it.

While she waited, Keri glanced at herself in the huge mirror that ran the entire stretch of the bar. She was nearly unrecognizable, with a shoulder-length brunette wig, pink-framed glasses that covered half her face, fake teeth that gave her a serious overbite, and a weathered, black baseball cap that read "you should see the other guy." She hoped she was unrecognizable and that the cap would make the Collector let his guard down a bit.

The bartender returned with a paper Starbucks bag with the word "Jones" written on the front in black Sharpie. Keri looked inside and saw a note, along with a different baseball cap. She pulled both out.

The cap was a gaudy, rainbow-colored number with the words "University of Hawaii" plastered across it. It would definitely stick out among all the Lakers and Spurs caps everyone else was wearing.

She looked at the note, which was written in block letters. It read "put this on. go outside and sit on bench across from starbucks. wait."

Keri looked up at the bartender, who had a curious expression her face.

"I hope he's worth it," she said, "because that hat is ugly."

"What did the guy who dropped it off look like?" Keri asked excitedly.

"I don't know. It was left here before my shift started. The guy I replaced just said someone named Jones would come looking for it around now."

"Thanks," Keri said, switching out her own cap for the rainbow one. "Can I leave this bag with you for a few minutes?"

She held out the bag and the bartender shrugged and took it. Keri figured that if the Collector didn't show, maybe CSU could pull some DNA off the bag.

She looked at her watch: 10:03.

Time to go. Stay cool, Keri. This is it.

But as she walked out the rear exit of the hotel and made her way to the Starbucks across the courtyard, she felt her heart almost beating out of her chest. She was positive the Collector was watching her and allowed her nervousness to show. A regular person about to hire someone to abduct a co-worker would be nervous with all this cloak-and-dagger stuff. She played it up, shuffling her feet and awkwardly adjusting her glasses as she walked.

She saw an unoccupied bench across from the Starbucks and made her way to it, weaving her way in and out of the basketball fans in team jerseys. She noticed the people wearing the Spurs jerseys were hooting and hollering more than those wearing Lakers gear and assumed the visiting team must have won.

She sat down and, realizing there was nothing else to do, waited.

It was the first moment she'd really had to be still and breathe since she'd gotten the email. Involuntarily, thoughts of Evie flooded her brain. Memories of her as a young child unwrapping Christmas presents gave way to images of her as a baby in her crib, flailing her arms and legs happily at the mobile above her playing "Rock-a-bye Baby."

The thought that she might see her precious daughter again soon was almost too overwhelming to process and she forced the hope from her head.

Stay focused. This isn't the time to daydream. You've got a job to do. He could show up any moment.

And right then, he did.

Before she realized what had happened, a man dressed in a black sweater and blue jeans sat down beside her. She glanced over and realized it was him. He was wearing a wig too, one with thick black hair. He wore dark sunglasses that seemed ridiculous considering the hour.

But she knew it was him because of the tattoo. Other than his blond hair, her one enduring memory of the man who took her daughter was the long tattoo that snaked down the right side of his neck. She saw it now, peeking out from under the sweater as he sat to the left of her.

"Jones?" he asked under his breath.

She nodded, hesitant to speak right away. He didn't seem to recognize her but she'd been on the news recently after rescuing a girl and he might know her voice.

"You're looking for an independent contractor to deal with an infestation problem?" he asked.

"Uh-huh," she muttered in as low a vocal register as she could muster.

"Follow me," he said and stood up. Keri got up and tried to keep pace as he wended his way effortlessly through the crowd. He was clearly used to this.

Eventually, he got to a point where the throng thinned out, at the corner of Olympic and Francisco Street, near the entrance of one of the complex's underground parking lots. A sign indicated it was full and there were several roped stanchions blocking any cars from entering.

Leaning against the concrete barrier separating the walkway from the garage ramp, he turned to face her full on for the first time.

"I assume you are the client and not another substitute?" he asked, referring to their prior failed meeting in Santa Monica six weeks ago.

"I'm sorry about that," she said, "I was trying to be careful. I guess I overdid it."

"You're lucky. Most people only get one chance," he said in a neutral tone. His eyes, hidden behind the sunglasses, were impossible to read.

"Thank you," she said, not wanting to rock the boat.

"What are you looking for?" he asked.

"Oh, okay," she started, trying to sound hesitant. "Well, I work at—"

"No specifics yet—for both our protection. Just give me the big picture."

"Right. Okay. Well, I have a co-worker. He's a real asshole. Not only does he come to work drunk half the time. He steals my ideas. He's verbally abusive. And he's handsy."

"That sounds like half the offices in America," the Collector said. Apparently, in addition to being a child abductor, he was a social critic too. "Why do you want to take such drastic action?"

"We're both up for the same promotion. If he gets it, he'll be my direct supervisor. I can't have that. But I need this job. It pays decent. I'm divorced, a single mother, and I didn't finish college. There's no way I can go somewhere else and earn what I do there. But I can't be around this guy every day until I retire. I'll shoot myself."

He stared at her silently for a moment. With the sunglasses on, she couldn't tell if he was suspicious or buying her story. She'd worked hard on it and it sounded convincing to her. But maybe there was a flaw she hadn't considered. Or maybe her voice, despite her best efforts to mask it, was starting to sound familiar to him.

Suddenly the bulletproof vest she wore felt shockingly heavy. Her gun, sitting in the interior chest pocket of her jacket to hide the bulge, pressed uncomfortably against breastbone. She felt twitchy and it required all of her willpower not to let it show. Finally he responded.

"How are you going to pay for my services if your budget is so tight?"

She was ready for this one and allowed herself to relax slightly. She realized she'd been holding her breath until now.

"My father passed away a few months ago and left me a little money. It's not enough to retire on. But I figured that if… I invested it properly, it would be well worth it."

"How much was it?"

"Are we negotiating now?" she asked, and immediately realized it was a mistake. She sounded too confident, too sure of herself for a mousy office drone dealing with a jerk co-worker. She saw him stiffen slightly and knew he'd picked up on it too. She tried to fix it.

"Sorry if that's a weird question. It's just…it's not like buying a house. There aren't any articles on the Internet for how to negotiate…this kind of thing. You know what I mean?"

"I know," he said slowly.

"Good. I guess I just don't know the protocol yet."

"No. You misunderstand me. I know," he repeated.

"You know what?"

"I know it's you, Keri."

She froze. Time seemed to almost stand still as his lips curled into a cruel smile. All her years of training seemed to evaporate in a moment. She felt helpless.

No! You are not helpless. You became a cop for this moment. This is what you wanted. This is how you get your daughter back. So do it.

Despite the pit of bile rising in her throat, Keri forced herself to remain calm and respond.

"I think you're confused. I know we're not supposed to get into specifics. But my name is Emily."

"You really had me going," he said, ignoring her protestation. "The wig is cheap. But the glasses are a nice touch. And the teeth—fantastic."

Keri thought quickly as he spoke. Her jacket was only half-zipped but there was no way she'd be able to get her gun out before he made a move. One hand was already in his jeans pocket and she imagined that it might have a knife, maybe the same one he'd used to stab that teenager to death in the parking lot all those years ago.

She could tell he was itching to move and decided that her best bet was to give up the charade, anything that would change the dynamic and keep him from running or coming at her.

"Your wig isn't too great either," she said, allowing him to hear her real voice for the first time. "Not as memorable as those blond locks."

He smiled at the comment, clearly happy that everything was out in the open now.

"I'm impressed that you found me. But you know it's not going to help you find Evie. You know it all ends for you tonight. You do know that, right?"

Keri was almost relieved to hear him say it. Now at least she knew he wasn't going to try to escape. He was going to try to kill her. At least that was one variable gone.

She saw him take a deep breath and knew he was about to make his move. There was no way to avoid it. But maybe she could throw him off his game just a bit.

"How do you know it's not ending for you tonight?" she asked. "I think I may just have to make you my bitch."

"You can't do that," he said, still smiling. "Otherwise you'll never find your daughter agai—"

Before he could finish the sentence, she moved forward, punching him hard in the gut. He seemed startled but not badly hurt. Without any hesitation, he moved toward her, slamming his formidable frame into hers, pinning her against the concrete parking garage barrier.

Keri felt the breath escape her body and she gasped, desperately trying to regroup. She saw him pull something from his jeans pocket and realized it was a knife. It was smaller than the one she remembered, but it would still do what he wanted.

She saw it flash in the light of the streetlight as he brought it forward, keeping it low and aiming for her stomach. She knew she couldn't stop the momentum of the thrust, so she tried to shift her weight to the right as she grabbed his forearm and pulled it forward so he couldn't adjust the direction.

The blade narrowly missed her body and instead slammed hard into the concrete barrier behind her. She saw it pop from his hand. But rather than watch where it ended up as he was doing, she thrust herself forward, slamming her forehead into the bridge of his nose.

For briefest of instants, she felt his body, pressed hard against hers, relent. She used the moment to gather herself for what she knew would be the oncoming onslaught. It didn't take long.

He slammed up against her, trapping her lower body against the barrier and bending her upper body backward so that it was hanging out over the ramp leading down to the parking garage. As she pressed back against him, she glanced down and guessed it was at least a ten-foot drop to the hard concrete.

She looked at the Collector, whose face was only inches away from hers. Her head-butt had knocked off his sunglasses and she stared into his hazel eyes. She could tell he was thinking the same thing she was. If he simply stepped back and pushed, the weight of her upper body would send Keri crashing backward onto the ramp pavement below, likely on her head.

She saw the victorious glint in his eyes as he started to step back and push her at the same time. But at that exact moment, unable to think of any other option, Keri stopped pushing against him and instead wrapped her arms tightly around his midsection.

As she felt herself careening over the edge, with him on top of her, she kicked up her legs in front of her, hoping to generate as much momentum as possible. At the same time she squeezed him against her, refusing to allow him to break free.

And then they were falling, weightless and heavy at the same time. As they tumbled, both of them were completely inverted for a split second before their shared momentum propelled him down and her on top of him.

By the time they reached the asphalt, he was on the bottom and Keri was above him. She felt their bodies land with a massive thud and she heard a crack that sounded like his head hitting the ground.

Her knees, which were straddling him, hit the ground hard, sending waves of pain shooting through her. The side of her head slammed against his chest hard and bounced once before resting there. Once again, the air had been knocked out of her and she tried to gulp it back in.

She couldn't move. She could barely breathe. It felt like she'd broken both her legs. But she knew she was alive.

After what felt like forever, she placed her hands on the ground and pushed up slightly so she could more clearly see the Collector lying underneath her. His chest was heaving so she knew he wasn't dead.

She looked at his face. His eyes were open and he was blinking a lot. The wig had come loose and she could see his blond hair below it. A small pool of blood had collected below his head.

Keri looked around. No one else was in sight. Apparently their fight had been so sudden and quiet that no one else even seemed to have realized it had happened. Keri could still hear the loud shouts and cheers of people having a fun night on the town.

She pushed herself up so that she was now sitting almost upright, straddling the Collector as he lay on his back. He had made no effort to push her off. In fact, other than his blinking eyes, she realized he hadn't even twitched.

"Can you move?" she asked him. She realized she still had the fake teeth in her mouth and spit them out.

He stopped blinking and looked around as if trying to find the source of the voice. Finally his gaze rested on her.

"I think I broke my neck," he said, his voice audible but soft. "I can't feel anything."

Keri pinched his upper arm hard.

"Did you feel that?" she asked.

"Feel what?"

"I think you might be paralyzed."

"Wouldn't that be something?" he said vaguely. Keri noticed that the pool of blood below his head was getting larger.

"Tell me where my daughter is."

"What?"

"You're dying. Blood is pouring out of your head. You'll be dead before an ambulance can get here. No need to worry about prison. Just tell me where Evie is. Do one good thing before you die."

She was surprised at how calm she sounded. Her voice wasn't pleading. It was more like she was making a forceful suggestion.

"Why would I give you the satisfaction?" he asked. "This is your fault. If I'm dying, at least I'll know you'll suffer when I'm gone."

Keri felt her chest tighten as the rage welled up inside her. She tried to force it back down.

You don't know how much time he has left. Use it. Make it worth his while to tell you.

"Tell me where she is and I'll call for help," she said.

"You already said I'm going to die. You're just changing tactics, trying to take advantage of my diminished state," he said before hacking in what Keri suspected was an attempt to laugh.

"I'm no doctor. Maybe you can make it."

His eyes softened a bit, as if he couldn't fix his gaze on her anymore. He resumed blinking for several seconds and then seemed to regain control.

"Keri," he whispered and she leaned down close to him. "This is going to be so bad for you. Until now, you always had hope. But once I'm gone, you won't have any link to her. Imagine all the things that have been done to her. Those are on me. But the things that have yet to be done to her? They're on your head now. What kind of mother are you, to inflict such suffering on your own child?"

Suddenly he was gagging. Keri looked up and realized it was because she had wrapped her own hands around his neck. She was squeezing, harder than she had ever squeezed in her life. She looked at her knuckles turn white, and then turned her attention to the Collector, whose arrogant eyes were no longer blinking. Now they were wide, as if they might pop right out of his head.

And still she kept choking him. She squeezed until she no longer had feeling in her hands, until she felt his neck muscles stop straining against her fingers, until his chest stopped rising and falling below her.

And when she was sure he was done moving, Keri collapsed on top of him. Her own body began to heave with uncontrollable sobs. In the distance she could hear a voice.

"Hey, there are people down there!" a woman screamed. It sounded far away.

She didn't try to stop weeping. Rather, she let the heaving cries envelop her. She cried because she knew he was right. Once he died, whether due his shattered, bloodied skull or her hands around his throat, all hope of finding Evie was lost.

She couldn't tap his phone. She couldn't put a tail on him. She couldn't throw him in a cell and interrogate him. She couldn't do anything.

He was gone. And now, so was the only lead she had to find her precious daughter. As she lay there, listening to the voices getting closer, one thought consumed her.

I wish I was dead too.

CHAPTER TEN

Sarah felt panic creeping in at the edge of her mind and tried to shove it away. It was getting harder with each passing minute. She sat shivering on the floor of the cold, dingy motel room, wearing only her teal top, her panties, and her sneakers. She wasn't sure how long she'd been here.

The brown van had dropped them off and the men had yanked each of them out and dragged them to separate rooms of the two-story motel. She noticed the parking lot was mostly empty and wondered if this place even had customers. The man responsible for her had handcuffed her right wrist to the radiator, put duct tape over her mouth, warned her not to pull it off, and left, locking the door behind him.

The room was dark and there was no clock for her to orient herself. She tried to grab a blanket off the bed but it was too far to reach, no matter how much she stretched. She saw a phone on a nightstand on the far side of the bed but it might as well have been a mile away.

She tried to turn on the heat and despite everything, ended up laughing, because the radiator was broken. But after a moment, the laughs turned to tears as the memories returned in a rush: the man she'd kicked in the groin on top of her, forcing her back down every time she tried to pull away, seeming to enjoy her squirming and struggling.

It had only stopped when Chiqy started shouting, announcing that the police were on their way. The man climbed off her, pulling up his pants as he rushed to the exit.

Ignoring the pain she felt, she had rolled off the mattress and tried to crawl away. But Chiqy caught up to her, lifted her to her feet by her hair, dragged her to the van, and shoved her in.

Before she knew what was happening, twenty-two other girls were herded in after her. One girl was left behind because she couldn't stop vomiting. Sarah was pressed up against the cab of the van and worried that if she lost her balance she'd be trampled by the others.

She forced the memory from her head. It did her no good to obsess over what had happened to her. If she wanted to prevent it from happening again, she had to find some way out of this motel room.

She looked around the room for what felt like the hundredth time. But there was nothing she saw that could help her escape. She tugged on the radiator again but it didn't budge. Her wrist was bloody and swollen from the effort. She considered ripping the duct tape off her mouth but didn't see the point if no one who might care could hear her scream.

Suddenly she heard voices from down the walkway. She crouched into a ball, hoping to make herself small, as if that would do any good if they came in.

Please let them walk by this room. Please let them walk by this room.

But they didn't. She heard someone turn a lock and the door opened. Blue neon light streamed in, temporarily blinding her. When her eyes adjusted, she saw two men in the doorway. One was clearly Chiqy. She didn't recognize the other one.

Chiqy turned on the overhead light and closed the door behind them.

"Sarah," he said, "this is Mr. Holiday. You're his now."

Mr. Holiday proceeded to pull out a thick wad of hundred-dollar bills and count them out. As he did, Sarah studied him. He wasn't quite as big as Chiqy. But he was in much better shape. Wearing a track suit that was too tight for him and showed off his bulging muscles, he looked like one of those steroid-loving weightlifters. He had light, close-cropped brown hair and a square face with too-tanned skin.

He finished counting the bills, thirty of them in all, and handed them over to Chiqy, who took them and shoved them in his pocket.

"Nice doing business with you, little girl," he said to Sarah, before turning to Mr. Holiday. "Be careful with this one. She's feisty—likes to fight back."

When Chiqy left, Mr. Holiday locked the door and walked over to her. He stood directly above her, looking down at her like a butcher might look at a side of beef. Then he sat down on the bed.

"I know Chiqy had his rules," he said, speaking for the first time. His voice was surprisingly quiet, and almost warm. "But I do things a little differently. I'm going to explain what will happen to you so you don't have any questions. If I were in your position I'd be constantly worried about what was going to happen to me. I want to take away that uncertainty for you. Would you like that?"

Sarah nodded, not sure there was any other option.

"It's okay, you can speak," he said as he peeled off the duct tape, sounding like nothing so much as a comforting doctor. "Would you like me to walk you through the procedure?"

"Yes please," she said hoarsely. She hadn't had anything to eat or drink since the mall and her throat was dry. Mr. Holiday seemed to sense that. He got up, went into the bathroom to fill up a plastic cup with water, and handed it to her. As she sipped, he spoke.

"First of all, you no longer have a name. You are now Number Four." To reinforce that point, he pulled out a marking pen and wrote what she assumed was a "4" on her forehead. He looked at it, and apparently satisfied with his handiwork, he returned the marker to his pocket.

"You will answer to that name," he continued. "Now we're going to have to make a few changes. I want you to hold still so you don't get cut."

He pulled a pair of scissors from another pocket, then grabbed what remained of her teal top and cut it off. He did the same to her panties. Other than her sneakers and socks she was now completely naked. He then began to cut her hair. She saw huge chunks fall on the carpet beside her, and with each lock that fell, her heart broke.

It had taken her years to grow it that long.

As he cut, he went on.

"I understand that you are sixteen. But with a shorter cut, I think we can make you look closer to thirteen. Younger girls do better business so that's what you are now. If a client asks your age, you say thirteen, got it?"

Sarah nodded.

"So there's no confusion, I prefer 'yes, Mr. Holiday' or 'no, Mr. Holiday.' Try again."

"Yes, Mr. Holiday," she said, trying to keep her voice level, despite the fear rising in her throat.

"Good. As I was saying, clients like younger girls. I expect you'll be very popular. We're going to break you in here at the motel. But then we'll be moving you to your new, permanent home. When we get there, you should expect to service between twenty and thirty clients a day. You'll be worth more early on, when you're fresh. Most of them won't be using protection. They pay more for that thrill."

Despite her best efforts, Sarah started to cry. But Mr. Holiday seemed oblivious, continuing to chop off her hair and speak in that kindly, lilting tone.

"You should anticipate getting most sexually transmitted diseases—syphilis, gonorrhea, herpes, HIV. As the weeks go on and you're more used up, you'll cost less. That is, unless you can think of ways to keep it interesting for the clients. I recommend you do that. The more you can do to keep your price up, the more value you have to me. Do you understand that, Number Four?"

"Yes, Mr. Holiday," Sarah managed to whisper.

"Now, I prefer to avoid drugging my employees if at all possible. I've found that clients prefer their girls more alert. But if you become a problem, as Chiqy suggested you might, I may have to. You'll do the work either way. But if you're drugged, I'll just give you to my more…unsophisticated clients. Trust me, you don't want those. They tend to leave lots of bruises. Do you understand, Number Four?"

"Yes, Mr. Holiday."

"Excellent. I have high hopes for you. Now, because I can tell you are a smart girl from a good home, I'm going to tell you something I don't tell most of my employees. Obviously, after this your parents won't want anything to do with you—they'll be too ashamed. And you'll be too damaged and diseased to ever find a man to love you.

"But if you give me ninety days of solid work, and maybe even show a little enthusiasm, I will reward you at the end with a freedom of sorts. I will offer you the sweet release of death. Most girls don't get that offer. I have some who have worked for me for years, until they are dried up, strung out, and covered in open, festering wounds so bad that no one will pay to use them anymore. In the end, I put them down like dogs. I don't want that for you, Number Four. I want you to retain your dignity, at least as much as you can under the circumstances. So keep that in the back of your mind."

With that he stopped talking and stepped back to look at her. She didn't dare reach up to touch her head but she could tell he'd cut off the bulk of her hair. The back of her neck felt cold in the unheated room.

Mr. Holiday came close and she tried not to shiver. He unlocked her cuffed right hand and gently helped her to her feet. She'd been crouched on the floor so long that she couldn't feel her legs or support her own weight. He anticipated that and helped her over to the bed.

He maneuvered her so she was lying on her back and adjusted the pillow under her head. Then he took her unbruised left wrist, put the handcuff on it, and attached the other end to a bar of the bed's headboard. He stepped back to look at her.

"Perfect," he said, before pulling out his phone and making a quick call. "Send him up."

Sarah felt a new wave of fear course through her body. She didn't know how she still had the capacity for it. She thought she'd be desensitized to these horrors by now.

"Number Four, your first client as my employee is on his way up. I want you to be very nice to him. If he wants you to talk, you say the things he likes. Do as he says, no matter what it is. He may have some unusual requests. You are to do your best to meet them. This is the first test of our relationship, Number Four. Pass it and things will go better for you. Fail it and things will get much worse. You know that they can get worse, right, Number Four?"

"Yes, Mr. Holiday."

There was a knock on the door. He opened it and stepped aside to let in a wheezy, rotund man. Sarah guessed that he was in his sixties. He was balding but had a ridiculous comb-over that swept across the top of his head like a thatch of wet straw.

He wore a sport coat and a dress shirt that couldn't contain his stomach, which cascaded down over his slacks. His bushy mustache appeared to swallow his upper lip. Despite the weather, he was sweating profusely. He looked at Sarah, lying naked and handcuffed on the bed, and licked his hairy lip. She tried to stifle the urge to retch.

"Mr. Smith, this is Number Four," Mr. Holiday said as he started to leave the room. "She's delighted to make your acquaintance. Why don't I leave you two to get to know each other better?"

He closed the door, which Mr. Smith locked before returning to face her.

"You remind me of my favorite niece," he rasped before taking off his sport coat, making a show of draping it over a chair and lumbering toward her.

Sarah closed her eyes and tried to picture herself anywhere else. But as she felt the man's heavy carcass climb on top of her, her imagination failed her. She could think of nothing but the horror that was this moment.

CHAPTER ELEVEN

Keri sat in the back of the ambulance, numb to everything around her.

The EMT was asking her questions but she couldn't process his words. It was as if she was underwater and he was standing at the edge of the pool.

She watched a uniformed officer place crime scene tape around the Collector's body, which had yet to be moved. A long, thick trail of blood from his head wound had streamed down the parking lot ramp and started to drip into the rain grate at the bottom of the ramp. Her wig and glasses lay on the ground beside him.

Her knees both ached but she knew they weren't shattered as she'd been able, with assistance, to walk up the ramp to the ambulance. Her right jaw hurt from the impact of it slamming against the Collector's chest when he'd hit the ground. Other than those things, physically, she felt okay.

Psychologically, it was a different matter. Her head echoed with his words.

What kind of mother are you, to inflict such suffering on your own child?

It was true, Keri thought. Everything that happened to Evie from this point forward would be her fault. If she could have found some other way to handle this situation, her only link to her daughter might still be alive.

What if she had let Ray come, as he'd begged her to? What if she had managed to avoid making that suspicious remark and kept the charade going? What if she'd simply admitted who she was and offered him an obscene amount of money in exchange for Evie's whereabouts? Any of those would have been preferable to having her one lead lying dead on the hard cement of a parking ramp.

She felt someone gently shaking her shoulder and looked up. The EMT was speaking to her, a worried look on his face. She tried to focus on his words.

"...in shock. We're going to take you to the hospital. The police will ask you some questions there."

Keri glanced over at the crime scene. One officer was talking to some bystanders, apparently interviewing them. Even though she couldn't hear them clearly, from their expressions and the tone of their voices, she could tell they didn't have a clue what had happened. Nobody had seen the fight.

The officer who had put up the tape was kneeling near the Collector's body, marking off Keri's glasses and wig with numbered placards, making sure not to touch them. He was youngish looking, tall and gangly, with an unkempt shock of yellow hair shooting out from under his police cap. He seemed hesitant, as if this was new to him. He was nothing like Jamie Castillo.

She would have long since taken charge of the scene. She would have ordered the witnesses to be interviewed separately. She would have let experienced detectives mark all the evidence at the crime scene instead of doing it herself. She would have already interviewed Keri at this point. She would have the situation under control.

For the first time since the incident, Keri smiled. And as she did, she seemed to snap out of her daze. A thought began to circulate in her head.

This doesn't have to be over. You still have time to salvage this situation if you get off your ass and move.

"What's my status?" she asked the EMT, interrupting whatever he'd been saying.

"You're in shock. Your vital signs—"

"No. I mean physically. I hit my knees pretty hard when I landed. Any major damage?"

"Nothing seems to be broken," he told her, taken aback at the forceful tone of the woman who'd been nearly catatonic only moments earlier. "You're going to have some serious bruising and swelling for the next few days. But I don't see any long-term damage."

"And this area?" she asked, running her finger along the right side of her face, jaw, and neck. "It all made contact with his chest when we hit the ground. Do I have a concussion? Broken jaw?"

"The jaw's okay structurally. We'll do more testing on your head when we get to the hospital, put you in concussion protocol. But my early guess is that you don't have one. It looks like the lower half of your face took the brunt of the fall, not your skull. That's a good thing."

"Thanks," Keri said as she delicately slid down from the back of the ambulance and gingerly rested her feet on the ground. "That *is* a good thing."

"What are you doing, ma'am?" the EMT asked, his voice rising in alarm. "You shouldn't be standing up. We're about to transport you to the hospital."

"I don't think so. And it's not ma'am. It's Detective. Help me stand up, please."

The EMT, against his better judgment, did as he was told. The crime scene cop saw what was happening and hurried over, clearly irked.

"Ma'am, you need to stay in the ambulance," he said with a confidence she knew he didn't really feel.

"I don't think so, Officer...Dennehy," she said, peering at the nametag on his uniform as she pulled out her badge. "My name is Detective Keri Locke. I'm with the Pacific Division Missing Persons Unit. I was working undercover, trying to get that suspect to reveal the whereabouts of a missing teenage girl. Unfortunately, he attacked me and well, you see how that turned out. But the girl is still out there. And I need to find her."

Keri stopped to let Officer Dennehy process her words, all of which were technically true. She conveniently left out the fact that she wasn't authorized to conduct an undercover operation, that the missing girl was her daughter, and that she'd been gone for over five years.

"Detective," he said, clearly unsure how much he could push back, "I appreciate your situation. But you just survived a ten-foot fall onto concrete. And this is a crime scene. Once other detectives arrive, you can work out the logistics of your operation. But I need to keep this scene secure."

Keri admired his willingness to stand up to her. And usually, she didn't like to dress down uniformed cops, especially one who might very well be at his first-ever crime scene. But she didn't see how she had much choice here. Time was of the essence.

"Are you sure that's the line you want to stick with, Officer Dennehy? Because once the detectives arrive, I don't think they're going to be psyched that you were the one marking evidence. Usually they like to work with CSU to avoid contaminating the crime scene and stuff like that."

Officer Dennehy shifted uncomfortably from one foot to the other. Keri could tell he was thrown. But in order to do what she was about to try, she needed him more than uncomfortable. She needed him compliant. That meant pushing harder.

"And your partner over there," she continued, nodding at the officer interviewing witnesses. "Did it ever occur to him to separate those folks before questioning them? They're all hearing each other's versions of what happened. Inevitably, those versions are going to seep into each other's memories, influencing their take on what happened. You think your detectives are going to be happy about that?"

"Detective Locke, I didn't mean to—"

"Listen," she interrupted, realizing that she'd never have a stronger hand than right now, "I'm not trying to break your balls here. I'm not going to tell them. It's not the end of the world. I'm alive. The bad guy's dead. It's not like there's going to be a trial with a defense lawyer. These mistakes aren't case-killers this time. But they could have been, you understand?"

Officer Dennehy nodded. Now that he was in her debt, she made her move.

"But there is still a missing girl out there. And I'm worried that if this guy has a partner, he might get antsy if that dead guy over there doesn't come back soon. He might move the missing girl. So I don't have much time. That's why I'm going to search him."

And with that she headed for the Collector's body.

"What for?" Dennehy balked.

"Identification, maybe a cell phone. Who knows, maybe he's got a note in his pocket that says 'the missing girl is located here.' Help me out, please. This ramp is steep and I'm still a little shaky on my feet."

To her amazement, Dennehy complied, giving her his forearm to steady herself as she walked down the ramp to inappropriately search the body of the man she'd just killed.

This was suspension-level stuff, maybe even dismissal-worthy. But if it meant she could find a clue that would lead her to Evie, it would be worth it.

And she didn't have much time. Once those detectives arrived, her ability to control the scene would disappear. They wouldn't put up with these antics. They definitely wouldn't let her search the body.

I've got to find some kind of lead fast and get out of here before they arrive or I'm screwed. They'll take me down to their station, interview me. I'll be out of commission for hours.

Still, Keri walked slowly, trying to keep her balance. The incline was steep and the ramp acted like a tunnel, whipping the bitter night wind at her.

Once they reached the body, Keri took a moment to really look at the Collector for the first time without having to keep her guard up. His hazel eyes were open, blankly staring up at the night sky.

No longer a threat to her, he seemed smaller than she remembered. In her memory, he had been a brutal giant, galloping away with her daughter, tossing her into his van like a rag doll, swiftly and mercilessly killing a Good Samaritan.

Maybe it was that he could do her no harm in death. Maybe it was that in her years as a cop, she'd seen many more monsters. But

70

looking at him lying there on the ground, she realized he was just a normal-sized man, probably five-foot-ten, maybe 180 pounds, completely unremarkable.

And that was almost worse, that the source of all her pain was just some guy, like any other guy. The everyday nature of his evil was somehow harder to process than if he really had been a hulking, drooling giant.

Keri felt herself slipping into a raw, vulnerable place and realized that would do her no good right now. She shook it off, snapped into detective mode, and bent down to study him. He wasn't wearing a jacket, just that black sweater and jeans. That made him easier to search. She felt around in his two front pockets, ignoring her freezing hands, but found nothing.

"Help me out here, Dennehy. I need you to roll the side of his body up so I can check his back pockets. Try not to move him or disturb him too much—just enough so I can get my hand under him."

Despite it being a violation of protocol, Dennehy did as he was asked. He knew he was already in deep. There was no point in arguing about niceties at this point.

Keri didn't find anything in his right rear pocket and was starting to worry that after all of this, she was going to come up empty. But there was something in his left rear pocket. She pulled it out carefully. It was a valet parking stub.

Trying to keep her suddenly rapid breathing under control, she stood up, scanning the crowd. It only took a moment to see a parking attendant, sitting on a stool under a black umbrella next to a parking stand. He seemed to know she was looking for him and stood up.

"Take me over to that guy," Keri ordered Officer Dennehy.

Things moved fast after that. The parking attendant helped Keri find the Collector's car, a twenty-year-old Honda Accord. Part of her had been expecting a white van like the one he'd used to abduct Evie. But it would have been odd for him to drive around town for years in what was essentially a moving crime scene.

She found his registration in the glove box, as if he were a regular human being just doing what the rest of us would. It had his address, an apartment in Echo Park, less than fifteen minutes from here. And it had his name: Brian Wickwire.

She stared at it for a long moment, trying to process that some random guy named Brian was responsible for the complete collapse of everything that mattered in her life. He was dead now, at her hands, but it still didn't seem like a fair trade.

She took a photo of his address, ordered Dennehy to secure the vehicle, and left the parking garage, limping uncomfortably on bruised knees to her car just as the detectives were arriving. She glanced at her watch. It was 10:29 p.m.

She guessed that the fight and fall had occurred around 10:07. The uniformed officers had arrived on the scene less than five minutes after that. The EMTs were there a couple of minutes later. And now the assigned detectives were on scene barely twenty minutes after the incident.

Pretty good response time. But not quite good enough.

She got in her car and pulled out of the hotel just as Officer Dennehy, standing with a grizzled detective, looked around desperately, obviously wondering where she had gone.

*

A short time later, she stood in front of the door to Brian Wickwire's apartment on Allison Avenue, just off Sunset Boulevard. The building was less than a ten-minute walk from Dodger Stadium and Keri couldn't help but wonder if Wickwire was a regular attendee. What was the day-to-day life of a child abductor like? Did he keep a grocery list? How often did he go to the store? Did he like cottage cheese? Was he big on organic fruits and vegetables?

Even monsters have their personal preferences.

She used a credit card to open one lock. Finding the door also had a chain lock, she pulled out a small pair of bolt cutters and snapped through it. Stepping into the apartment, she was stunned at how normal it looked. She'd spent so much time imagining that this bogeyman lived in an underground dungeon or something similar that finding a copy of *Sports Illustrated* on a wooden coffee table next to a coaster threw her.

She wandered around, looking for anything out of the ordinary. She didn't expect to find a notebook labeled "My Ledger of Abducted Children." But it was hard not to think that somewhere in his home, the Collector kept some kind of record of his crimes.

Keri sat at the small desk in the corner of the living room and opened an unlocked knee-high filing cabinet beside it. She rifled through his files but there was nothing suspicious.

He had his last five years of taxes kept in one folder, along with his W-2s. Apparently he worked as a large-appliance repairman fixing mostly refrigerators and dishwashers. Maybe that explained his ability to travel and the white van. She'd have to interview his co-workers when time allowed.

His utility bills were well organized, as was his bundled phone, Internet, and cable bill. He had a box of postcards sent by friends when they were on vacation. In the same box were years of birthday cards from his parents, who apparently lived in Phoenix.

A laptop sat on his desk. She opened it but wasn't surprised to find it was password protected. That would take time. She'd need Edgerton's help to access its contents. She could take it with her, she thought. But she figured the best thing to do was to leave it here, let the local cops take it in as evidence, and deal with it then.

Other than that, the desk was immaculate. There was small notepad with a pen resting on top of it. It had several line items, including ground beef, cereal, milk, and popcorn. Apparently vicious child kidnappers did keep grocery lists.

This was no good. The detectives she'd eluded at L.A. Live would have found the same registration she had. Dennehy might even have mentioned that she'd taken a picture of the address. They'd be here soon. And they wouldn't be happy.

In addition to her other violations of protocol after the incident, she could add fleeing the scene of a crime and breaking into a private residence without a warrant. If these cops were anything like her, they wouldn't be interested in her excuses for why she'd done what she'd done. They'd arrest her first and ask questions later. She needed to find something useful and get out of here quick.

Keri shut the laptop, leaned back in the chair, and closed her eyes. She tried to picture the room around her without looking at it, scanning her memory for anything that seemed out of place.

It was all so was so average and unremarkable. Wickwire kept a clean house. He had a job. He stayed in touch with his parents. His friends sent him greetings from exotic locations.

His friends...

Something about that didn't sit right. Everything she knew about Wickwire screamed "loner." He may have stayed in touch with his parents but he lived in a different city from them. His apartment was clearly a bachelor pad, without any touches that suggested he was involved in a relationship.

His job allowed him to spend long stretches of time solo, traveling from assignment to assignment. He just didn't strike Keri as the kind of guy who had a circle of friends that would send him warm greetings from far-flung places.

She opened her eyes. Putting the box with the postcards on the table, she spread them out and studied each more closely. Almost immediately it became apparent that they weren't what they seemed.

Yes, they were all from faraway places: Hawaii, Thailand, Bali, Cancun, Puerto Rico. But the postal service stamps on each of them were from more local spots. One was marked Irvine, another Saugus, a third from Rancho Cucamonga. All of those were Southern California communities.

She didn't know how he'd gotten these postcards. Maybe he'd purchased them online. But it was clear that none of the cards had ever been anywhere other than California. And then she noticed the return addresses.

These were postcards, supposedly sent from some distant vacation spot. There was no reason to have return addresses. Even if they were real, the senders would have likely left their vacation spots by the time the postcard arrived. But they all had had them. And each return address was for somewhere in the Western states.

There were about forty in total. Two were from Utah; four were from Oregon. Three addresses were in Washington; a half dozen in Nevada; about the same from Arizona. The other half were California addresses. A few were from the northern and central parts of the state. But at least ten were from the greater Los Angeles area.

And the addresses themselves were odd, with strange notations and numbers that didn't seem traditional. They were clearly written in some kind of code. She settled in, preparing to study them for any connection she could make. As she pored over the first one, her cell phone rang. It was Ray.

She was tempted to let it go to voicemail. But something made her pick up.

"Hey, Ray. Any news on Sarah Caldwell?" As she asked she felt guilty. She hadn't thought about anything other than the Collector or Evie in the last hour, not even the other missing girl she was supposed to be searching for.

"I'll get to that in a minute," he said. "But first, I need to ask you, why is there an APB out on you?"

"What?"

"Downtown Division just put out an all-points bulletin for you. You're wanted for questioning in the death of a man found on a parking ramp at L.A. Live. What the hell is going on, Keri?"

"It's a long story, Ray."

"Well, you better explain it later because they're looking for you. A unit is headed to your apartment. And others are about to pull up at the dead man's place. So if you're at either of those locations and you don't want to spend the next few hours in a holding cell, I recommend you leave right now."

As he said it, Keri heard the sound of a siren in the distance, getting louder.

"Thanks for the heads-up. I'll fill you in later," she told him as she stood up and collected all the postcards.

"Okay, I'm going to text you an address. Meet me there ASAP."

"Will do. Where is it?"

"An abandoned motel in Inglewood. Edgerton traced the brown van there. It hasn't moved in a couple of hours."

Keri felt a new surge of adrenaline, one she didn't think was even possible after how much her body had produced in the last hour.

"I'll see you there," she said and hung up. She gathered up the postcards and hurried out of the apartment. With her swollen knees screaming at her, she limped down the stairs, leaving the building through a back entrance that led to the alley where she'd parked her car in case she needed just this kind of quick getaway.

She tossed the postcards in the glove compartment and pulled out of her spot with her lights off. As she drove quickly up the alleyway away from the apartment building, she saw multiple sets of flashing lights pull off Sunset and stop in front of the place. She could hear the shouts of several officers, including one who ordered a unit to drive around to the back alley.

But by the time they got there, she had left the alley and merged with traffic on Sunset, indistinguishable from all the other cars out late on a Friday night.

CHAPTER TWELVE

Sarah had stopped trying to push Mr. Smith off her. He was so heavy that even with all her strength, she couldn't budge his massive bulk.

When he first climbed on top of her, she'd been too frozen with terror to move. But as he squirmed on top of her, fussing with his belt, trying clumsily to undress, her fear had turned to anger.

She had tried to use it to her advantage and shove him off, but he was just too big. Eventually her arms gave out and she lay there, pretending to be somewhere else, letting the last few tears she could muster roll down her cheeks onto the pillow below.

He kept fumbling, and she kept praying that he wouldn't figure it out.

She focused on her right sneaker, which she could see despite the man's rotund, pasty flesh blocking out almost everything else. She remembered how she'd run to catch the bus in these shoes, how she'd worn them playing basketball in the driveway with her dad. How she and her mom had gone for ice cream after they bought them six months earlier, seemingly at eternity ago.

And then, like a flash of lightning, she remembered something else about that day. Fixing her eyes on the shoe, she tried to focus, despite the movement above her. And sure enough, she had the insight she was looking for.

With a renewed sense of purpose, she looked behind her at the wooden headboard. It was worn and splintered. She reached her hand back and found that it wasn't even really wood but some sort of cheap composite, one that could be easily scratched.

And that's exactly what she did. As the grotesque man on top of her finally undid his belt and struggled to lower his pants, oblivious to anything above her neck, she furiously scratched into the headboard with her fingernail, going over the same spots again and again until they created grooves in the composite that were clearly visible and hopefully legible.

It took her a moment to realize that his movement had stopped. She glanced back at Mr. Smith, terrified that he had seen what she'd been doing. But he hadn't. Instead, he was lying on top of her like an exhausted, beached whale, an embarrassed expression on his face. As he quickly pulled up his boxers, she realized: he'd been unable to get an erection.

For a moment she felt relief. Her prayers had come true. Despite her awful ordeal, she had yet to be sexually assaulted.

76

He was trying to gather the strength to roll off her. After much effort he finally succeeded, crushing her ribs as he did. Without a word, he got up and trudged to the bathroom. He left the door open as he sat on the toilet and relieved himself.

Sarah used the private moment to look at her handiwork. It was clear to her what it meant. But she wasn't sure it would make sense to the police if they found this place later. She considered scratching more but worried that if Mr. Holiday returned and saw it, he'd realize it was more than just random letters. She'd have to hope that they could figure it out.

Then she noticed something else. The receiver to the phone on the bedside table had fallen out of its cradle. In all the banging, Mr. Smith must have slammed the mattress into the table and knocked the receiver loose. It had been too far for her to reach earlier. But now she stretched and was able to get her fingertips on it and then grasp it in her hand.

She picked it up, listening, hopeful she could dial.

But to her dismay, it was dead.

Sarah heard the toilet flush and used the noise to mask the sound of her pulling the base of the phone closer to the bed. She returned the receiver to its proper place and put her arm back by her side just as Mr. Smith reentered the room. She noticed, without surprise, that he hadn't washed his hands.

He sneered at her, clearly humiliated.

"It's going to take me a while to be ready," he said. "But I brought a few tools that will be good substitutes until I'm ready."

He rifled through his duffel bag and pulled out some kind of large sex toy. Sarah stifled her gasp of panic and forced herself to respond in a level voice.

"Mr. Holiday said he doesn't want me damaged. I'm brand new. You don't want to make him angry."

Mr. Smith laughed heartily at her comment, his guffaws turning into short-breathed wheezes.

"Good try, girlie. But we negotiated this ahead of time. He knows my preferences. Besides, I'm good at breaking in the newbies. Most girls don't talk back after I'm done with them. You'll understand better in a few minutes."

He climbed back on top of her and smacked his lips as he held the toy up close to his face, admiring it. Then he looked down at her lower body and she knew he was about to use it.

She waited until the last possible second, until she was absolutely sure his attention wasn't on her hands. Then as he lowered his hand to violate her, she grasped the base of the phone and yanked hard, smashing it into the side of his head.

Mr. Smith looked up, more stunned than anything, trying to figure out what had just happened to him. Blood ran down his left temple. Before he knew what was going on, she hit him with the phone again, this time square in the face. A gush of blood spurted from somewhere in the middle of it.

He squealed in pain, reaching up to protect himself. But the sudden movement sent him careening sideways. He lost his balance and his massive weight sent him toppling off the bed. He landed with a thud.

Sarah shimmied to her left to see what had happened. Mr. Smith was on his knees and elbows, clearly dazed, shaking his head repeatedly as if he was being annoyed by a pesky fly near his face.

She tried to hit him again but the cord attaching the phone to the wall prevented it. She pulled hard and it popped loose. Turning her attention back to the man on the ground, she saw that he had moved from his elbows to his hands and was starting to push himself up.

That gave her a better angle as she slammed the base of the phone down on the top of his skull. His arms gave out and he slumped to the floor. He was still conscious but clearly stunned. He moaned softly as his fingers balled up into fists, clutching at the worn carpeting like a newborn baby ripping an adult's finger.

Sarah knew she didn't have long. Someone might have heard his moans and be on their way to the room right now. Even if they hadn't, she needed to find a way out of here fast. Mr. Smith would regain his senses soon. And unless she was willing to beat him to death, she had to be gone before that happened.

She looked at the bar of the headboard the handcuff on her wrist was attached to.

If the composite was fragile enough for me to scratch a message into it, maybe it's weak enough to crack if I give it a good whack.

She gathered what strength she had left in her arm and slammed the base of the phone at a spot just above the handcuff. Sure enough, the material cracked loose. She disentangled the cuff and, finally able to move, tried to stand up.

Her legs buckled and she slumped back down. She realized that she had spent most of the last few hours either crouching or lying down, being sexually assaulted. No wonder her body wasn't jumping into action.

Too bad. You don't have a choice. If you want to live through the night, make your body move!

She did just that, grabbing the headboard for support as she pulled herself back to a standing position. Gingerly, she made her way past the still moaning pile of corpulence and grabbed his sport coat off the back of the chair where he'd left it. She buttoned it up, fully aware that other than that and her sneakers, she was naked.

Mr. Smith seemed to be regaining his senses so Sarah grabbed the phone and gave him one more good whack on the back of his head. He collapsed again. This time he wasn't moaning, only rasping through his puckered, bloody lips.

It took everything Sarah had not to try to beat the brains out of his skull. Part of it was that she didn't want to let them turn her into a person capable of something like that. Another part of her had a much more practical reservation.

It would take too long.

She dropped the phone on the bed and hurried to the bathroom, where she saw a small window above the shower. She was able to open it but it was too high to pull herself up and climb out.

She returned to the main room, looked at the door, and briefly considered leaving that way. But she was sure she'd be spotted within seconds. The window was the only real option so she grabbed the chair and set it up in the shower directly below the window. Stepping up, she peered out.

She was on the second floor, about fifteen feet up. She couldn't drop straight down. But about six feet to the left was a closed dumpster just below the window of the room next door. She figured that if she dangled out the window facing the motel wall and got up enough momentum, she could swing over and land on top of the dumpster. That would only be a drop of about eight feet—far more manageable.

She clambered out as quickly as she could without making noise and began to swing. Her arm strength, never much to begin with, was seriously diminished by the time being handcuffed, as well as by her attempts to push Mr. Smith off her and her use of the phone as a bludgeon.

Sarah could feel her forearms fading fast and her fingers starting to lose their grip on the windowsill. Unsure if she had built up enough energy to make it but certain that she couldn't hold on any longer, she leapt.

She landed safely on the top of the dumpster, tucking into a roll to lessen the impact. But she hadn't accounted for the momentum of the swing and could do nothing to stop herself from rolling off the dumpster and toppling to the asphalt below.

She felt the gravel dig into her palms, elbows, knees, and thighs. For a moment she just lay there on the ground, trying to catch her breath and assess if any further damage had been done.

It didn't seem so. Slowly, she got to her feet, brushed the gravel out of her skin, and started to walk. A high chain-link fence ran the length of the rear of the property, making it impossible for her to escape that way.

So she ran along the back of the motel. When she reached the edge of the building, she peeked around the corner. The fence continued all the way to the street, about a hundred yards away. It was clearly a major one as it had at least six lanes and cars were zipping by at a good speed. If she could get to it, there would be lots of vehicles to wave down.

Unfortunately, the space between her location and the street was comprised of a large parking lot. Many of the overhead lights were burned out but there were still enough that she doubted she could cross the distance without being noticed.

"There she is!"

Sarah looked up to see a man's head poking out of the window she'd jumped through and felt her heart sink even as a jolt of adrenaline shot through her.

"She's at the corner of the building!" he shouted loud enough for anyone nearby to hear.

I guess I'm making a run for it.

She broke into a jog, testing out her legs. When they didn't crumble beneath her, she moved into a full-on sprint, ignoring the pain in her body, keeping her focus on the street now only fifty yards away.

Sarah sensed movement out of the corner of her eye and glanced that way. It was Mr. Holiday, tearing toward her, his arms pumping violently at his sides. Despite that, his expression was blank, as if he was patiently waiting in line at the store.

She turned her attention back to the road. She was only twenty-five yards from it now, with just a bit of asphalt, a green belt, and a sidewalk separating her from freedom. She dug in, pounding her feet against the ground, pushing herself as hard as she could.

She had just reached the green belt when Mr. Holiday leapt in the air and slammed into her like a linebacker tackling an undersized halfback. She felt her feet leave the ground as his shoulder slammed into her ribs, ripping the breath from her chest.

She landed hard, his body weight smashing her into the grass below. She lay there face down in the grass, her left side in agony, unable to breathe. Glancing up, she saw that all the cars on this side

80

of the road were still a few hundred yards away, idling at a red light. There was no way any drivers would be able to see her from that distance in the dark.

She barely had time to process that before she felt herself being jerked to her feet by her hair. She would have screamed but she still hadn't caught her breath.

Mr. Holiday had a chunk of her now-short hair in his fist and was pulling her roughly along, back to the motel. She stumbled a few times but he didn't seem to care and simply dragged her along, her shins scraping the asphalt until she regained her footing.

He didn't release his grip until they were all the way back to the building. Sarah was hesitant to look him in the face but decided that at this point, after what she'd done, there was no point in trying to win his favor by pretending to be meek or pliant.

Slowly, since her neck was sore, she looked up to meet his gaze. Amazingly, he still had that same bland expression, as if nothing unusual had just happened. But when he finally spoke, she noticed that his voice was even quieter than before and there was a new edge to it.

"I warned you, Number Four. I told you that this was a test and that if you failed it, things would go far worse for you. You've failed the test. You do understand that, don't you, Number Four?"

Sarah glared at him, refusing to play his game. He seemed unperturbed and continued.

"I was going to keep you at our fancy location. But now I have no choice but to take you to what other girls call 'the Bad Place.' I think you'll find the name is accurate. That's where you'll die. But not before every last ounce of you has been used up. And I can assure you that there will be no escape, not even from death, not until I say. You'll be chained up so that you can't harm yourself. Only my clients will be allowed to do that. And you won't even receive the drugs that would otherwise allow you to numb yourself to your situation. I want you to feel everything, every last bit of pain, right up until the end. You shouldn't have crossed me, Number Four. Do you regret it?"

Sarah forced herself to straighten her back and stand upright. She looked him square in the eye and in a hoarse but defiant voice, answered him.

"Go fuck yourself, Mr. Holiday."

And with that, she spit in his face.

For a moment, he looked stunned.

He didn't even bother to wipe her spit as it ran slowly down his cheek.

For the first time since she'd seen him, the man gave a truly genuine smile. It was an ugly one. His lips twisted, almost forming a grimace, but not quite.

"Prep her for departure," he said to one of his men and turned to return to the motel office. Sarah watched him go and made sure to wait until he had stepped inside and closed the door before she gave in and allowed her body to collapse into a heap on the ground.

CHAPTER THIRTEEN

Keri's breathing had finally returned to normal. She had passed two black-and-whites going the other way on Sunset and gritted her teeth each time, expecting to see either of them make a U-turn with sirens blaring and lights flashing. But neither did.

She waited until she was safely headed south to Inglewood on the 110 freeway before calling Ray. He picked up after one ring.

"You on the way?" he asked.

"Yeah. I should be there in about fifteen minutes. You?"

"About the same."

"Do we have backup?" she asked.

"Yep. Inglewood Police are setting up behind a church three blocks away. That's the address I gave you. Make sure to keep a low profile. Castillo's en route too. She secured protective custody for Sammy Chisolm at Twin Towers and decided she hadn't had enough drama for the night. Now do you want to tell me what the hell is going on?"

Keri thought for a moment, debating whether she really wanted to do what was percolating in her mind. Ultimately she decided she didn't have much choice. She'd just have to deal with the consequences later.

"I do. But first, I've got to tell you, Ray, when this is all over, I want to take a real vacation, maybe a week on Bondi Beach or something."

Ray was silent for a long second. She could picture him processing exactly what those words meant. She was pretty sure he wouldn't have forgotten.

Then she heard a muffled sound that was almost certainly him ripping the bug out of his sun visor and tossing it out the window.

"I'm ready to go right now," he finally said.

"Well, we've got to take care of a few things first," she replied as she dug her hand into the hollow spot in the steering wheel where she knew her own listening device had been planted.

"Like what?" he asked. Clearly he could tell what she was doing and was stalling for her benefit.

"Like get Downtown Division to shut down their APB on me. Maybe you can ask Hillman to have a word?"

"Maybe I could if I knew what was going on," Ray prompted her. "Can you tell me?"

She managed to get her fingers on the bug, rip it from its hiding spot, and toss it out her own window.

"He's dead, Ray. The Collector's dead."

"What? What happened?" her partner asked, shocked.

"I'll explain more later. But the short version is that he figured out who I was and attacked me. We struggled and toppled over a barrier onto a concrete parking ramp. He was on the bottom."

Keri wondered why she didn't mention the part about choking the man to death.

Is that because some part of me is worried Jackson Cave might have another bug in the car and catch me admitting to a felony? Or is it because I'd be ashamed if Ray knew the whole truth?

"Were you able to find out where Evie is before he died?" Ray asked.

"No," she answered, feeling a sudden cascade of emotion rise in her throat.

She tried not to choke up but Ray must have heard the catch in her voice.

"I'm sorry," he said quietly.

"He said that anything that happens to her from now on is my fault. And he was right."

"No, Keri, he wasn't. You didn't choose for your daughter to be kidnapped. And you've spent almost every minute since then trying to get her back. He was just trying to torture you one last time before he died. Don't let him."

"Yeah," she replied as she blinked the tears out of her eyes, trying to shake it off. "He was pretty unrepentant, taunting me even as the life was bleeding out of him. He wanted me to suffer after he was gone."

"Well, it sounds to me like he let something slip when he tried to do that."

"What?"

"If he said that anything else that happens to her is on you, that means she's still alive. You may have believed it before. But now you know it."

She felt a sudden jolt of hope. He was right.

"I hadn't thought of that," Keri admitted. "I guess I just never considered the possibility that she wasn't. So it never registered that he was confirming it."

"See?" he said, trying to buck her up. "This evening may be turning into a net positive, despite, you know, falling onto a parking ramp and being on the lam from the cops."

Keri laughed despite herself. Changing lanes swiftly, she took the ramp from the 110 freeway south to the 105 freeway west.

Traffic was surprisingly light and she guessed she'd be at the address in just a few minutes.

"So why were you in an apartment off Sunset?" he continued. She knew he was trying to keep her focused on the now and help her avoid falling into the emotional hole she'd been circling. She didn't mind.

"It was his place. I knew Downtown Division would be swarming it soon so I needed to get there first to see if I could find anything."

"And did you?" he asked.

"Maybe. There were these postcards. But something about them wasn't right. I need to look at them more closely when I get a second. So I took them."

"You took potential evidence?"

"I did. After everything else I've done tonight, it didn't seem like that big a deal. So can you get Hillman to have the APB dropped?"

"I'll call him. He's going to be pissed and with good reason. But I think that under the circumstances, he might cut you a little slack. Let me reach out to him now. I'll know more when we meet up."

"Thanks, Ray," she said, "for...everything."

"Of course..." he answered. He sounded like he wanted to say more and Keri waited for it. But in the end he simply said, "See you soon," and hung up.

CHAPTER FOURTEEN

By the time Keri pulled into the church parking lot on Hawthorne Boulevard at 101st Street less than ten minutes later, she felt like a balloon about to pop.

The combination of her narrow escape from Wickwire's apartment, her technical status as being on the run from authorities, and potentially being on the verge of finding Sarah had her on edge. She had to repeatedly remind herself to take her foot off the gas so as to not be pulled over for speeding.

She actually passed the motel on her way to the church but a glance in that direction didn't reveal anything overtly suspicious. Like half of the buildings on the street, it looked to be in disrepair.

It was a great place to set up shop if you wanted to avoid foot traffic or the unwanted attention of nearby business owners. Seemingly every other storefront was boarded up or papered over.

Ray wasn't there yet but it looked like half of the Inglewood Police Department was. Technically they had jurisdiction. But unlike the SWAT unit in North Hollywood, the sergeant on the scene deferred to Keri's knowledge of the case and didn't seem to mind if she took point. Sergeant Henriksen was a tall bald white guy in his forties with a bushy mustache and a laconic demeanor that suggested he was used to being steamrolled by LAPD.

"You let us know where you want us and we'll move accordingly," he said after they introduced themselves.

"You know the area better than me," Keri said. "Any recommendations?"

She saw the look of pleasant surprise in his eyes and knew she'd made the right call. Keri wasn't normally one to collaborate well with others. That was Ray's thing. But she figured these officers would be more willing to put themselves on the line if they were invested in the operation. And she needed them invested, for Sarah's and Lanie's sakes.

"Okay," Henriksen said and pulled out a map of the area. He laid it out on the hood of one of the cars. "The motel is surrounded on three sides by chain-link fence, which offers protection from prying eyes. But the surrounding lots are all abandoned and we could easily send teams of officers on foot with bolt cutters to enter at the back and the sides of the property."

"That's a solid idea, Sergeant," Keri agreed. "Meanwhile, a small insertion team can approach quietly from the front. We can see where their people are and report back to you. When the guys in back are in place, we could have them create a diversion. With Chiqy's crew focused on the back of the motel, you send in backup and we'll swarm the place, hitting every door simultaneously. And we create a perimeter at the edge of the parking lot so no one can slip through. What do you think?"

"I like it," a voice said from behind them, "as long I can be part of that insertion team."

Keri turned around to see Officer Jamie Castillo walking toward her. It was nice to see a familiar face and not just because Castillo had her back when she'd gone after the Collector/Wickwire a few months ago.

Castillo was also just a badass. She was only about two inches taller than Keri but she was far more imposing. Her uniform clung to her muscled, athletic frame and her black hair was tied back in a businesslike ponytail. Her dark eyes glittered with intense focus. For an officer out of the Academy for less than six months, she had the bearing of a seasoned veteran.

"Officer Castillo," Keri said, forcing herself not to smile, "nice to have you along."

"I wouldn't miss it, Detective."

Just then, Ray pulled into the lot. He hopped out of his car and joined the huddle of officers around the map. They reviewed the plan for him.

"It sounds good," he said when they were done. "I just checked with our tech guy back at the station. Based on what he could glean from cameras in the area, he thinks there are between five to seven men there."

"How sure is he of that?" Sergeant Henriksen asked.

"He warned that the footage is grainy and downloads in chunks every fifteen to thirty minutes. The last update was fifteen minutes ago, so it's possible that more men might have arrived in the interim. Also, we think there are well over twenty girls spread out among the rooms."

"Thank you, Detective Sands," Henriksen said before turning to his own officers. "I want the bolt-cutting teams to head out now. Let me know when you're in position. I want to breach ASAP."

As the Inglewood officers scurried into position, Ray pulled Keri aside. From his furrowed brow, she suspected something was wrong.

"You're not pissed I took the lead, are you?" she asked.

"Not at all," he answered, surprised that she even had doubts. "You seem to know the lay of the land on this one and Henriksen likes you. Keep it up."

"What is it then?"

"I talked to Hillman," he whispered.

"And…?"

"He was pissed at first. But not as much as I expected. I think you've just worn him down so much that he's used to you ignoring his orders."

"I knew that being unprofessional would pay off eventually," Keri said.

"Yes, that's the lesson to draw from this experience," Ray said sarcastically. "Can I continue?"

"Please," Keri said, biting her tongue.

"He understood. He wasn't happy that you hid all this from him *or* that you fled the scene without being interviewed by the Downtown detectives *or* that you broke into the guy's apartment without a warrant. I mean, can you blame him? But he gets it. It's your daughter and you thought this could help you get her back."

"So what happens now?" Keri asked.

"He's tight with the captain of Downtown Division so he thinks he can smooth things over. Plus, he doesn't want to pull you off this case while we're in the middle of it. He was pretty sure they'd drop the APB if you agree that the second this case is done, you'll come in for questioning."

"Seems fair," Keri said, hiding her relief.

"Yeah, I'd say it's more than fair. Most detectives in your situation would either be on leave or in cuffs right now. You should really get that guy a fruitcake."

"So does this mean I don't have to take you in?" someone behind Keri asked. She turned around to see Castillo.

"How long have you been standing there listening?" she asked the younger officer.

"Let's see. Fled the scene of a crime, must come in for questioning, fruitcake. I guess for pretty much all of it," Castillo said, a smile playing at her lips. "Don't worry. I wasn't going to drag you in, even if Hillman ordered it."

"That's very reassuring, Officer Castillo," Keri said snarkily.

"And I'll keep your offer of insubordination under wraps," Ray added.

"I'm glad you got him, Detective," Castillo said, dropping the tough gal act. "I was worried that you'd never get another chance after it didn't work out in Santa Monica last time."

"Thanks, Jamie," Keri said.

All three members of West Los Angeles Pacific Division stood there awkwardly, uncomfortable with the rare moment of genuine emotion, unsure what to say next.

They were rescued by Sergeant Henriksen, who called them over.

"My units are in position. They've cut through the fencing and are waiting for the instructions."

"Great," Keri said, shaking off the sentiment of the prior moment and shifting focus to the task at hand. "Detective Sands, Officer Castillo and I will approach from the front. Henriksen, maybe a couple of your officers can join us?"

"Of course. I'll assign two men to flank you. Is that enough?"

"Initially, yes," Keri said. "We'll scout the motel and try to get as close as possible without detection. Then we'll have your men in back create that distraction. When they confirm they've got the attention of these guys, you can follow us in and strike in force. Sound okay?"

"Sounds okay," Henriksen agreed. "Let me get my men for you."

As he picked them out, Keri looked at Castillo.

"You got a coat you can throw over that LAPD uniform? It's a little conspicuous."

Castillo ran to her car and grabbed a windbreaker. The two officers Henriksen had assigned to join them were also wearing jackets that covered their uniforms.

"Hopefully with this weather, no one will be suspicious of the heavy coats," Henriksen noted, "which should effectively hide your firearms."

"Agreed," Keri said as everyone assembled. "Okay, let's get moving. We'll walk along the sidewalk in front of the motel about thirty yards apart from each other. Ray, you and Jamie walk together like you're a couple and take the southern end. I'll follow behind and stop near the center of the property. You two linger at the northern end of the property," she said to the Inglewood officers.

They started out along the sidewalk. Keri waited until Ray and Castillo were well ahead of her before she began walking. After she reached 102nd Street, she motioned for the Inglewood officers to follow.

She glanced at her watch. It was 11:32 p.m., kind of late for a gal to take a casual stroll by herself in a tough neighborhood. She hoped the oddity of it didn't draw too much attention. As she continued to walk, she zipped up her coat to protect against the buffeting late night wind. The temperature was now in the mid-forties but it felt colder than that.

As Keri crossed two more intersections, getting closer to the motel, she couldn't help but notice how dark it was. At least half the streetlights were out and even the businesses that didn't seem to be shut down were completely dark, without any exterior lighting to ward off interlopers. She suspected they'd been knocked out so often that the owners had given up replacing them.

As she crossed the intersection at 104th Street, the motel finally came into view on her left. She tried not to turn in that direction. After all, she wanted to project the image of a person just trying to get home after a late shift at work. There would be no reason for her to look anywhere other than forward.

Ahead of her, at the corner of Hawthorne and 105th Street, Ray and Castillo came to stop. She wrapped her arms around his waist as if to both embrace him and protect herself from the wind. It was convincing and, despite her best efforts, Keri felt a pang of jealousy.

She took a few more steps until she reached a waist-high bush on the greenbelt. When she got to it, she bent down, as if to tie her already laced shoe. Confident that the view of anyone looking out from the motel would be obscured, she glanced back at the Inglewood officers. They were huddled close together, neither of them looking at the motel, both smoking or at least pretending to.

Keri spoke into the small speaker attached to the earpiece in her right ear.

"Everyone in position?"

She saw Castillo rise on her tiptoes as if to whisper in Ray's ear.

"In position," she said.

"In position," said one of the officers as he exhaled on a drag from his cigarette.

"Your guys ready, Sergeant?" Keri asked.

"Just waiting for your word to go," came his voice over the radio.

"All right, everyone hold position," Keri said. "I'm going to approach the motel to get a better view. Hopefully even if I'm seen, one civilian female won't be suspicious looking."

"Proceed with caution," she heard Ray say in her ear. It sounded completely professional but Keri knew that it was more than just an admonition from a colleague.

"Will do."

She stood up and ambled casually onto the greenbelt, making sure to stay behind bushes and out of the glow of the few working streetlights. In the distance she could see a brown van parked in front of what looked to be the motel office. There were three other cars in the lot, parked at a sizable distance from each other, almost as if to give the impression that the place was still in business.

But the closer she looked, the more obvious it was that this wasn't a normal motel operation. There were a total of four vehicles in the entire parking lot. But she counted twenty-four motel rooms, twelve on both the first and second floor. And the lights in all but one of them were on.

She wanted to move closer but that would mean stepping into the actual parking lot where there was no cover. Anyone watching her would likely quickly shift from curious to leery.

"I think there might be girls in every room. I'm not sure how many johns there are though. There are hardly any cars in the lot."

"They must have been told to park on the street," Ray said. Keri glanced at the long row of cars parked one after the other along Hawthorne and realized he was right. That meant that each of these girls was likely being assaulted right now.

Keri felt her blood quicken and forced herself not to react. She was leading this operation and she needed to keep a clear head. She took a few deep breaths to regroup.

Just then, the door to the motel office opened and a man walked out. Before the door closed, Keri saw two men inside. One of them appeared to be Chiqy.

The man who'd left the office walked up the stairs to the second floor and stepped mostly out of view behind an exterior wall. Keri could still see part of his lower leg. She waited a moment before realizing that he had taken up a guard position.

"Hold a moment," she told everyone. "I see an exterior guard."

She looked across the walkway to the same spot at the other end of the motel. In the shadows she saw another man positioned in the opposite location. And then she saw a third, barely visible just below him on the first floor.

She moved slightly to the left and sure enough, a fourth man was positioned next to the wall behind the office, unmoving, hidden to anyone not looking directly at him. They had all four corners of the motel covered.

Suddenly that fourth man made a motion with his arm. It took a second for Keri to realize he was speaking into a radio. After a second, the man walked to one of the rooms, unlocked it, and stepped inside.

"Be advised," she whispered to everyone on the line, "I count six men: four guards positioned at the corners of the building on the first and second floors; and at least two more in the office, including one who appears to be Chiqy."

A moment later, another man, dressed in khakis, a sweater and jacket, stepped outside. He looked to be in his early thirties with thin strawberry blond hair and a pale complexion. The guard poked his head out the door and the two of them spoke briefly. Then the guard shut the door and the blond man walked away. He was headed in her direction.

"Sergeant," Keri said. "I think we're going to have to move a bit earlier than expected. "I've got a john headed in my direction. If he sees me, he may warn the others."

There was a long pause.

"Sergeant, did you hear me?"

At that point, an unfamiliar voice came on the line.

"Detective Locke, this is Captain Roy Granger of Inglewood PD. I've been monitoring the line from the station. Did you just say this case involves Ernesto 'Chiqy' Ramirez?"

"Yes, Captain. We believe these girls were taken as part of a sex-trafficking ring he runs."

"I'm well aware of who he is, Detective," Captain Granger replied curtly, "But I wasn't aware that this operation involved him. Had I known that, I wouldn't have authorized my men to take a front-line role."

"What are you talking about?" Keri asked, shifting position behind the bush as the blond john got closer. The pain in her knees from hitting the parking ramp concrete was really bothering her. The guy was less than fifty yards away now.

"We believe that Ramirez was responsible for the death of two of our undercover officers last year. I've expressly forbidden direct engagement with him without a SWAT unit involved."

Keri wanted to scream into the speaker for this guy to get with the program. But she knew that wouldn't do any good, especially with the john getting closer. He was less than thirty yards away from her now.

He pulled out his key and hit a button on it. A car beeped nearby and Keri turned to see it was a Black Lexus only fifteen feet to her left. The john would surely see her as he walked by.

"I'm terribly sorry for the loss of your men, Captain. But please," she pleaded quietly, "we are in the middle of this thing. There are as many as two dozen girls in danger right now. We can't take these guys out without your help. Your men are in position. Let's do this thing."

There was another long pause. The john was less than ten yards from her now.

"Hold, Captain," she heard Ray whisper. "The john is approaching Detective Locke's location. He'll hear your response. Radio silence for now."

The john was almost on her now. Keri knew the bush wouldn't hide her any longer. She had to act. As he stepped next her hiding spot, he glanced to the left just as she leapt up and smashed the left side of his jaw shut with the padding of her open right palm.

His knees buckled and he stumbled backward, sinking to his knees. Just as he was gathering his senses and opening his mouth to shout, Keri dove at him, slamming her left forearm into his temple as she rolled over him.

Keri turned back to face him, ready to clock him again if needed. But it wasn't. He was lying spread-eagle on the grass, unconscious. She quickly grabbed him by the ankles and dragged him behind the bush, where she resumed her pained crouching position.

"You still there, Captain?" she panted.

"Yes Detective. Is everything okay? Did you secure that john?"

"He's secure," she answered, as she rolled him onto his stomach and cuffed his right wrist behind his body to his left ankle. "But everything is not okay. We need to breach that motel now. And we need your help to do it."

"I'm sorry, Detective Locke. I just can't authorize that. If you wait twenty to thirty minutes, I can have a SWAT team on scene. We can proceed at that point."

"How many of these girls are going to be brutalized in the next twenty to thirty minutes, Captain? Besides, these guys move fast. They could decide to up and leave any minute. Then what do we do, try to take them out when they're holding the girls? And this john beside me could wake up again soon. What am I going to do, keep knocking him out every five minutes until your team gets here? We've got the advantage now. Let's use it!"

She waited, hoping he'd been persuaded.

"Sergeant Henriksen," she heard the captain say, "pull your men out. Retreat to a safe distance until SWAT arrives. I'll give you an ETA as soon as I have one. I'm sorry, Detective."

Keri looked at the two Inglewood officers standing on the corner. They seemed at a loss as to what to do. Then Henriksen came on the line.

"All officers return to mobile headquarters immediately. We're on standby until further notice."

93

Keri saw one of the officers on the corner shake his head in disgust as he dropped his cigarette to the sidewalk and angrily stubbed it out with his shoe. He and his partner turned and headed back to the church.

Keri thought she heard a noise from the motel and turned her head. Sure enough, it was coming from one of the rooms. And the sound was distinct. It was a girl crying out in pain.

"Jesus," she heard Ray mutter under his breath.

"What are we going to do?" Castillo asked, clearly horrified.

Keri felt rage flash through her veins. She knew it was the wrong answer, but she couldn't stop herself from giving it.

"We're going in."

CHAPTER FIFTEEN

Keri stood up from her hiding spot behind the bush and headed toward the motel, unzipping her jacket as she walked. She noticed that the soreness in her battered knees had subsided a bit, overwhelmed by the endorphin rush she felt as the motel got closer. The cries of agony she'd heard earlier from one of the rooms were intermittent now but clearly not over.

"Can you guys hear me?" she asked Ray and Castillo as she weaved back and forth, making sure to stay out of the glare of the few working lights in the parking lot.

"Yep," Ray assured her. "We're coming. "

She glanced to her right and saw both of them scurrying quickly along the fence in the same direction as her.

"How are we handling this?" Castillo asked quietly.

"Detective Locke," came the urgent voice of Sergeant Henriksen over the radio, "please stand down. My men are no longer onsite. You do not have the tactical advantage. Wait for our SWAT unit to arrive and provide support."

"Thanks for the input, Sergeant. I don't know what your policy is in Inglewood. But we generally don't ignore the screams of teenage girls being raped. So unless you plan to help out, I'd appreciate it if you maintained radio silence so the rest of us can do our jobs without distraction."

She knew it was harsh. Henriksen obviously didn't want to stand down and had only done so on orders. But at this moment, she didn't really care. He didn't respond.

"Castillo, here's your answer. Let's stick with Tasers for as long as possible. The new models we were issued last month give the same jolt up close as they do with the electrode darts and they don't require an immediate recharge. Just hit skin and your subject should be incapacitated. We don't know what these guys will do if they hear gunfire. And we don't know if any of those johns in the rooms are armed. Let's try to take them down quietly if possible."

"Roger that," Ray said. "We have a sightline on the guard outside the motel office. If Castillo distracts him, I should be able to tase him from behind. Stay close to the guard at the opposite end of the ground floor, Keri. If he sees what's happening, he'll react. So be ready to take him down. We can deal with the upstairs guys after that."

"Sounds good," Keri said. "But be careful. I don't know how thin those office walls are. You don't want to tip off Chiqy."

"Understood," Ray said. "We're almost to the guard. I'm going quiet now."

Keri wanted to move closer but worried that the guard Ray and Castillo were about to take down would see her from his vantage point. The guard on her end couldn't see her from his angle but she was still at least fifteen feet from him. It would be hard to get close enough to disable him in time if he saw anything across the way.

She glanced up at the guards on the second level. Neither was looking out at the parking lot. In fact, one of them was peeking through a window at the events transpiring in the room closest to him. The other guy was watching the first, clearly annoyed that his cohort was violating sex-trafficking guard protocol.

Ray and Castillo disappeared from sight. Keri stood in her spot, her Taser in hand. She watched the corner near the office closely for any movement.

And then it happened. She heard a slight electrical surge, like a mosquito flying into a zapper on a hot summer night. A moment later the guard near the office appeared briefly as he slumped forward. Keri thought he might fall, ruining everything. But Ray managed to catch him before he hit the ground. That was Keri's cue.

She sprinted to the corner where she knew her guard stood, even if she could only see his shadow against the wall. As she got close, she saw his arm come into view. He was raising a radio to his mouth. He must have seen what had happened and was about to warn the others.

His thumb was about to press down the "speak" button when she reached him, jabbing the Taser hard against his right forearm. He dropped the radio, which Keri managed to snag just before it dropped on the floor.

He let out a low moan as he slumped back against the wall. Keri zapped him again and he slid to the ground, unmoving. She turned and quickly scanned the second floor, unsure if the noise her guard made had been loud enough to alert the others.

She didn't hear or see anything unusual, which she took as a good sign. Looking across the way, she saw Ray and Castillo giving her the thumbs-up. They whispered something to each other and Ray shook his head no. Castillo patted him on shoulder and smiled. Keri knew that body language. The young officer was ignoring him.

Sure enough, a second later, Castillo had grabbed onto the metal railing of the stairwell and started climbing up with a speed and agility that shocked Keri.

Was this girl a gymnast in an earlier life?

It occurred to Keri that she'd never really spent enough time with the rookie to find out. Hopefully she'd have the chance to remedy that.

She peeked out from her position and saw that the second-floor guard Castillo was headed for still had his eyes on the guard above Keri, who must still have been peeping. She decided to carefully make her way up the stairs to offer support.

She glanced at Ray, who was glaring at her and mouthing "no." Like Castillo, she ignored him. She was halfway up the stairwell when all hell broke loose at once.

First, a voice, almost certainly Chiqy's came over the guards' radios.

"Report."

That made the guard above Keri look guiltily across the way at his second-floor partner. Unfortunately, he did so just as Castillo was climbing over the top rung of the stairwell railing. His eyes widened and he lifted his arm to point.

The other guard saw something was wrong and turned around just in time to get tased in the chest by Castillo, who was now on the second floor.

"Report, I said!" the voice shouted again as Castillo's guard flopped back heavily on the walkway.

Keri saw the indecisive look on the peeping Tom guard's face. He was deciding whether to answer the radio or deal with Castillo. A moment later, he made his choice and so did Keri. He reached into his back pocket for his gun. As he did, Keri went for hers as well.

"Jamie, take cover," Keri hissed into her microphone, even though she knew there was nowhere for Castillo to go.

The guard was raising his weapon to fire when Keri shot him in the right side. The force spun his body to the right. Keri fired again for good measure, nailing him square in the chest. He crumpled to the ground.

"Shots fired! Shots fired!" she heard Sergeant Henriksen yell over the radio. "All teams converge."

A second later someone burst out of the office below. It wasn't Chiqy but another man. He was holding a machine gun. The first thing he saw was Keri, standing halfway up the stairwell at the opposite end of the motel. He raised his gun to fire.

Keri turned to make a mad dash for the upper floor, where she hoped to use the walkway for protection. But she knew even before the first step that she'd never make it. It was too far.

And then she heard a single shot. Looking down, she saw that Ray had fired at the man from his position behind the office.

The man was still holding the gun but was leaning against the office wall. It looked like he'd been hit in the leg.

"Get upstairs, Keri!" Ray yelled.

She realized that the man with the gun below was pointing it in her direction again. She immediately turned and darted up the stairs, diving onto the walkway as she heard the sound of an automatic weapon firing below here. She could feel thudding as the bullets slammed into the bottom of the walkway only inches below her body. In the distance she began to hear sirens.

"All teams close in now!" she heard Henriksen shout.

Suddenly a door behind her opened. Keri turned, about to pull the trigger when she realized it was a john, wearing only boxers and socks.

"Get back inside and lie flat on the ground!" she screamed at him. His eyes wide with terror, he slammed the door shut.

She spun around on the floor to prepare to return fire at the machine gun guard when she noticed the guard Castillo had tased was getting up. Because she'd zapped him over the clothes, the stun must not have been as effective. Castillo was oblivious, her eyes focused on the action below. From her angle, she couldn't see the guard with the machine gun at all and was leaning out carefully to try to get a better view.

"Jamie!" Keri shouted just as the guard reached her. Castillo didn't have time to raise her weapon as he pushed her over the railing. Keri saw her drop her gun so she would have both hands free as she flipped over the railing. She tried to grip the top bar but her fingers slipped and she fell to the second, where she held on by her fingertips.

As she tried to get a better grip, the guard who'd pushed her picked up her gun. Keri didn't wait to see what he would do next and fired twice into his back. He stumbled forward and toppled over the very railing Castillo was clinging to. Keri didn't see him land but she heard the thud.

Castillo managed to hook her left arm over the bar and lock it there while she tried to pull herself up with her right hand. Keri started to crawl toward her when a new fusillade of bullets sprayed in her direction.

She realized that if she moved any further, the guard below would have a clean shot at her. She could see flashing lights now, streaming in from all directions. They were almost to the parking lot entrance.

"I'm okay," Jamie shouted. "Stay where you are."

Keri didn't really have a choice. She looked down to see that they were in a stalemate. She couldn't go anywhere, much less to help Castillo, who was dangling by her arm. The guard with the machine gun was stuck where he was due to his leg injury. But he was also protected from both her and Ray by the office wall.

Then it hit her. There was one person who wasn't accounted for.

"Ray?" she shouted.

"I'm here," came his voice from somewhere below. He sounded desperately worried. "Are you okay?"

"I'm fine. But Ray—there's one more guy. Remember, Chiqy's still in the offi—"

At that moment, she heard what sounded like a massive smashing sound followed by grunting.

"Ray!" she screamed. Unable to see anything, she shimmied backward until she had a sightline on the hallway below. It took her a second to process what she was seeing. It looked like Chiqy had somehow jumped through the interior hall-facing office window and landed on Ray. They were rolling around on the ground, each trying to get the upper hand. Neither man seemed to have a weapon in his hands.

It wasn't going well for Ray. He was one of the most physically imposing men Keri had ever met. But Chiqy had a good seventy pounds on him and he'd clearly learned how to use it to his benefit. He had somehow managed to get on top of Ray, straddling him, with his arms around her partner's throat, squeezing.

She scurried forward to try to take a shot when the machine gun guard fired on her again, forcing her backward. She couldn't get any closer without risking getting hit and she couldn't get an angle to fire on Chiqy from where she was. Then she heard Ray start to gasp.

"Henriksen," she shouted, "where the hell are your people? I'm pinned down and Ray is in trouble."

"That guard with the machine gun is firing at my men," he shouted back over the gunfire and sirens. "We had to hold at the parking lot entrance."

"Chiqy is choking Ray!"

"We're trying, Detective!"

Not good enough.

Without even thinking about what she was doing, Keri got to her feet and started to scamper down the stairwell.

"No!" Castillo shouted at her before focusing her words on Henriksen. "Sergeant, Detective Locke is going down the stairs. Have your men draw that guard's fire!"

She was halfway down the stairwell when the machine gun guard realized what she was doing and trained his weapon on her again. As he raised it to shoot, she leapt away from the stairwell into the air.

It all seemed to play out in slow motion. He turned to follow her body, trying to aim at a moving target. As she hurtled toward the ground, Keri kept her gun steady, waiting until she had a clear target of her own. She got off one shot before she hit the ground.

The wind was immediately knocked out of her as her stomach, chest, and elbows all slammed into the pavement. Unable to breathe, she realized her eyes were clenched shut and forced herself to open them.

Somewhere in the back of her brain, she could hear Castillo's voice.

"The guard is down! The guard is down! All units converge. Detective Sands is under attack."

Keri's eyes searched the area in front of her, moving past the body of the man she'd shot, who was lying face down on the ground, until she found what she was looking for.

There in the hallway, Chiqy was still on top of Ray, choking him. She could hear her partner's gasps and see his hands on Chiqy's forearms, trying futilely to knock them off. Chiqy was smiling.

She looked back across the parking lot to see officers running in their direction. But they were so far away, they'd never make it time. She looked for her gun and saw it, resting about four feet in front of her.

She tried to move toward it but her body wouldn't respond. Her lungs were still desperately trying to suck in air and simply wouldn't allow her to do anything but that.

She looked back over at Ray and watched helplessly as the person she was closest to in the world had the life squeezed from his body.

His fingers seemed to loosen their grip on Chiqy's arms. His left arm slumped to the ground. His right hand lingered a little longer. It appeared about to sag as well when he suddenly released it entirely and stretched it out, as if he were reaching out for air with his arm instead of his lungs.

Then she saw his hand ball up into a fist. And almost quicker than her eyes could follow, he smashed that fist into Chiqy's left elbow, snapping it inward at a grotesque angle it was never intended to go.

Chiqy collapsed onto Ray, his screams of agony audible over the police sirens. After several seconds, Ray shimmied his body a little until Chiqy slid off him. He rolled over onto his side and propped himself up onto his knees to look down at the man who tried to kill him.

Keri's view was briefly blocked as the Inglewood officers ran past her in the direction of the screaming. But she was able to see as Ray reached up his fist and brought it down onto Chiqy's face, fast and with enormous force.

And then again.

And again.

By the time the officers dragged him away, he'd gotten in at least a half dozen punches.

The last thing Keri noticed before she lost consciousness was that Chiqy was no longer screaming. Or moving.

CHAPTER SIXTEEN

When Keri came to, she found herself in the back of an ambulance for the second time in less than two hours. This time she was lying on a stretcher. Everything from her sternum to her belly button ached. A female EMT was hovering over her, studying her vitals on the monitor nearby.

"How long have I been out?" Keri asked hoarsely, startling the woman, who didn't realize her patient was now conscious.

"Less than five minutes, at least based on the timing your colleague gave me," she said, nodding at the back door of the ambulance.

Keri glanced up to see Castillo standing just outside the ambulance's back door. She was talking to someone Keri couldn't see and her left arm was in a sling.

"Jamie," she called out as loud as her voice would allow. The younger officer turned and, seeing Keri awake, moved quickly to her.

"How are you feeling, Detective?" she asked, unable to hide her concern.

"I'm not sure yet. You?"

"Sprained shoulder; other than that, mostly bumps and bruises."

"What about Ray?" Keri asked, terrified of the answer.

"I think he's going to be okay. They're treating him where he is. They don't want to move him until they're sure his neck is all right. But he's responsive and surly. That's a good sign, right?"

"Surly is good. Can you give me an update on the overall status?"

"I just asked that myself," Castillo said. "Henriksen's coming over now. I'm sure he can fill us in."

"How did you get clear of that railing?" Keri asked.

"Once I didn't have to worry about people shooting at me, I was able to pull myself up most of the way. Then a few Inglewood officers arrived and helped me the last little bit."

"Did you used to be a gymnast or something? The way you scaled those bars was pretty impressive."

"Nah. But I was really into parkour as a teenager. I was kind of crazy back then."

"You're still kind of crazy."

"You should talk, Detective. Taking a flying leap six feet in the air off a stairwell to shoot at a guy aiming a machine gun at you? That's not exactly sane."

"My partner was in trouble. I didn't have a choice."

Castillo looked at her hard, as if she wanted to say something else but wasn't sure how. But at that moment, Sergeant Henriksen arrived.

"How are you doing, Detective?" he asked.

Keri stifled the urge to ream him out and replied with a simple "Okay."

"I'm glad to hear that," he said. "And I'm sorry about what happened back there. It wasn't my call and it wasn't my preference. But I had orders."

"I understand," Keri said, despite her residual anger. It wasn't his fault after all. And she still needed his help. "Can you fill me in on the scene status?"

"I'll tell you what I know. We're still piecing a lot of it together. But it appears that you three took out every bad guy who was here at the time. We're rounding up all the johns from the rooms. That reminds me, I believe these are yours." He handed her back her handcuffs.

"I assume that guy's taken care of?" Keri asked.

"He's crying in the back of a squad car as we speak," Henriksen answered. "We're questioning all of them. But it looks like most of them only communicated with the pimps via text. So far no one has been able to ID anyone we don't already have in custody."

"And the girls?"

"We've accounted for twenty-one. They're still in the motel rooms. We don't want to move any of them yet, not until the EMTs can check them out more thoroughly. They were all tied up to the beds. Some of them were out cold, either drugged or beaten into unconsciousness. And there's another thing. It looks like these guys literally tagged the girls. They all have numbers written on their foreheads."

Keri and Castillo exchanged a glance, both briefly shocked into horrified silence.

"You said you accounted for twenty-one," Keri said, regrouping. "Does that mean you think there were more?"

"Well, there are twenty-four rooms. And the three that were empty had unmade beds. It certainly looks like they were used. But it's possible girls might have been moved from room to room. We just don't know yet."

"What about the numbers written on them?" Castillo asked. "Maybe that will help. How many do they come to total?"

"We don't know for sure. Some of these girls are too shaken up for anyone to get close enough to look. But it seems a bit random.

One girl has 'twenty-seven' and another has 'forty-three.' We know there weren't that many here."

"Have the guards told you anything?" Keri asked, refusing to ask specifically about Sarah. She didn't want to be callous to the other girls and she doubted any of them had been identified yet anyway.

"You mean the ones that are still alive?" Henriksen asked, his eyebrows raised. "There are only three of those, including Chiqy. The other two are still woozy from being tased but we'll question them more once they're coherent."

"No luck with Chiqy?" Keri asked.

"He wasn't talking much. They had to sedate him so he'd stop screaming. They're stabilizing him in another ambulance right now so they can take him to the hospital. Frankly, I'd have been screaming too. His arm was bent in a direction I didn't think was possible. I'm probably going to have nightmares about it for a while."

"When he's conscious, he needs to be questioned immediately," Keri insisted, ignoring the sergeant's comment about the arm. She had zero sympathy. "If anyone knows about the big picture, it's Chiqy."

"Don't worry," a familiar voice just out of sight said. "I'll take care of that."

Ray stepped into view. He was wearing a neck brace and several of the capillaries in his eyes had busted, giving them a weird reddish hue. But he was standing upright and smiling.

"Hey, Raymond," Keri said, managing to keep the wave of relief she felt out of her voice. "You really disappointed me back there. I thought that chubby fella had you for a minute."

"Me too," he admitted genuinely, refusing to play along with her attempt at emotional distance. "How are you feeling, Keri?"

"I'm very sore. But I think with a little assistance, I could get up and actually help with this investigation."

Ray looked at the EMT, who shrugged.

"Her vitals are steady. If she can handle the pain, there's no reason she can't move around. I mean, I'd like to take you back to the hospital to have a full work-up done, Detective. But I'm assuming that's not going to happen."

"Your assumption is correct," Keri answered as she tried to prop herself up on her elbows. The action made her wince and she looked down to see they were both heavily bandaged.

"Yeah," the EMT said. "Your elbows were pretty torn up. I found bits of skin embedded in the concrete where you landed.

There's nothing more to be done about it and it's going to hurt worse once your adrenaline subsides."

"You have one hell of a bedside manner," Keri said.

"I figure it would be wasted on you. I can give you some pretty solid pain meds that should keep things manageable."

"Yes, please."

The EMT gave her two pills, which she swallowed immediately, and another six to be taken at intervals over the next twenty-four hours. Then the whole group helped her out of the ambulance. She leaned on Ray until she was sure she could support herself.

As she started to walk away, the EMT called out.

"I think you'll be needing this," she said, holding out Keri's gun. "Someone found it lying on the ground next to you earlier."

"Thanks," she said, forcing a grim smile to her lips before turning to the others. "Shall we take a look around?"

"Sure," Ray said as they started toward the motel, before turning back to Sergeant Henriksen. "Let me know when they're ready to take Chiqy to the hospital. I want to be in the ambulance with him."

"You got it," Henriksen said. "I'll let them know now. And it goes without saying that when you have some time, our detectives will need to question all of you about how things went down."

"Get in line," Keri muttered quietly so that only Ray and Castillo could hear her.

The three of them nodded their assent and then walked to the last room on the first floor, farthest from the office. Peeking in, they saw an officer sitting with a girl who was curled up on the bed. Someone had thrown a sheet over her bare body.

"I'm hesitant to question any of these girls in their current state," Keri said. "Let's just see if Sarah or Lanie is here. If any of the girls look like they're in shape to talk, we can see what they know. Sound good?"

Ray and Castillo agreed. But it became quickly apparent that none of the girls would be much help. They were all unconscious, catatonic, or crying uncontrollably. The sight was staggering, and broke Keri's heart. She had never seen so much suffering of innocent people in one place.

Yet none of them was Sarah or Lanie.

She sighed heavily. By the time they reached the room closest to the office, they were exchanging hopeless looks.

"Detective Sands," Henriksen called out from nearby, "they're about to take Chiqy in. And he's regained consciousness."

Ray walked quickly to the ambulance with Castillo right next to him. Keri limped along a few paces behind them. Ray opened the door and Keri could see Chiqy on the stretcher, propped up at a forty-five-degree angle, his left arm in a giant splint.

"How you feeling, Ernesto?" Ray asked.

Chiqy smiled back at him. His eyes were cloudy and Keri realized immediately that he was seriously drugged up.

"I'm good, Mr. Clean," he said lazily.

"You do know you're bald too," Ray pointed out.

"Whatever."

"Is this all the girls, Chiqy?"

The pimp gave him a him nasty smile before responding.

"No, man. These are only the leftovers. I sold off the best cuts of she-meat already."

Keri felt the fury rising in her and briefly considered punching Chiqy in his destroyed elbow.

"Who did you sell them to, Chiqy?" Ray asked insistently, refusing to be baited.

"Oh, I can't tell you that, man. Confidentiality and all that, ya know?" He smiled again before a short cough turned his face into a tight grimace.

"We've got to get him to the hospital now," one of the EMTs, a twenty-something African-American man, said insistently. "I'm concerned that one of his arteries may have ruptured. If he doesn't get into surgery soon, he could lose the arm entirely."

"And wouldn't that be a shame?" Ray asked sarcastically, smiling. "Well then, he better start answering my questions before you take him anywhere."

"He's going to the hospital right now," the EMT said, holding his ground despite the obvious fear in his eyes. "I know you have a job to do, Detective. But so do I. Come if you want. But this ambulance is leaving immediately."

"Yeah, man. Come with us," Chiqy piped in sluggishly. "You looking for a holiday? Sounds like you need...holiday."

Keri tapped Ray on the shoulder.

"Just go with him. He's too loopy to be much good right now anyway. After his surgery, you can question him some more. Plus you can get your neck checked out while you're there. We'll keep looking around here."

"Yeah, you keep looking, Blondie," Chiqy said to her. "But you ain't gonna find what you're looking for. I know who you're after—the prime she-meat. But that's long gone. Taking a holiday..."

He giggled briefly as his words faded out and he slipped into unconsciousness again. Ray climbed into the back and took a seat.

"Keep me posted," he said, just before the door shut.

"You too," Keri shouted back, but her voice was drowned out by the ambulance's siren as it tore out of the parking lot.

Once the siren had faded into the distance, Keri turned back to face Castillo.

"You okay?" the younger officer asked.

"I don't have a choice. Let's get back to work."

*

Sarah tried to open her eyes. Everything felt so thick and slow. Thinking was nearly impossible. After an enormous effort, she finally managed to open them a fraction.

Everything was cloudy. She could tell she was in some kind of moving vehicle but wasn't sure what it was. She looked down and saw that in addition to a seatbelt, her arms were strapped down to the seat by bungee cords.

She tilted her head slightly to the left and saw a man beside her. He had on a cap and sported a long, unkempt beard. After a few seconds, it registered. He was a trucker and she was in the passenger seat of his cab.

She tilted her head a bit more to the left and saw two girls lying in the bed of the cab. She recognized them from the warehouse, the van, and the motel. They were strapped down too. But both were unconscious and slid back and forth a bit when the truck hit bumps.

She turned back to the trucker and saw that he was looking at her with a wolfish stare.

"Mr. Holiday says that if I help get you to the Bad Place safe and sound, I can have a go at you. So you can start dreaming about that, girlie."

Sarah tried to respond. She wanted to ask where they were going, where the Bad Place was.

She opened her mouth to speak but the effort was too much and she slipped back into her drugged slumber.

CHAPTER SEVENTEEN

Keri was getting desperate. She hadn't found Sarah or Lanie yet and there were only two rooms left to check on the second floor. Worse, three of the rooms had been empty, which seemed to confirm that some girls had already been transported elsewhere as "she-meat."

When she got to the second to last room, she saw a female officer trying to comfort a girl with her back to them. In between sobs, the girl kept muttering the same phrase over and over.

"My fault. My fault."

Keri stepped inside the room to get a better look at her. Castillo lingered in the doorway, hesitant to enter a place so full of pain. Despite the girl's condition, it was quickly apparent to Keri that this was Lanie.

Her hair had been cropped short, but the distinctive blonde mixed with blue and pink Keri remembered from the mall security footage was still evident. And with nothing but a blanket to cover her, the multiple tattoos on the girl's porcelain skin served as further proof. A big black "11" was written across her forehead.

"Lanie?" Keri said softly.

The girl looked over at her. Her terrified eyes were puffy and red and her cheeks were streaked with a river of mascara.

"Who are you?" she asked suspiciously between sobs.

"My name's Keri. I'm a detective. I've been looking for you."

"You have?" Lanie asked, sounding more like six than sixteen.

"Yep, for hours now. I know you've been through something awful. But you're safe now."

"What about Sarah? Is she okay?" Lanie asked.

"We're still looking for her. Was she brought here too?"

Lanie nodded.

"We all were. But I don't know which room she was taken to."

"That's okay. We'll find her," Keri assured her. "Do you remember anything else that might help? Were there other men here?"

"I don't know where Dean went after the house. There was this fat guy named Chiqy and all his guards. And Mr. Holiday."

Keri felt her pulse quicken but tried not to let it show.

"Who's Mr. Holiday," she asked quietly.

"He was the one in charge. He cut my hair to look like this. Chiqy wanted to sell me to him but Mr. Holiday said I didn't have the right look. He said I was too used up."

"What did Mr. Holiday look like?" Keri asked, pushing past everything else Lanie said for fear that acknowledging it would make the girl fall apart again.

"He's really muscular and tan, brown hair. He wore a track suit."

"Do you remember anything else about him?" Keri asked.

"He had a soft voice but he said awful things."

The memory seemed to set her off and she started to break down again before suddenly regrouping. She grabbed Keri's hand and stared hard at her, willing her to understand.

"It's all my fault this happened," she said. "My boyfriend worked for these guys. He tricked me. I thought he loved me. But he was just using me to turn us into…he used us."

"It's going to be okay, Lanie."

"No! It's my fault this happened to Sarah. She's the only decent person I know. And now, because of me, she's—"

She broke down into tears, unable to continue. Keri looked at the female officer sitting beside her and motioned for her to hug Lanie.

"When she's able, get her to give a full description of Holiday to an artist," she whispered in the officer's ear.

Then she quickly left the room, waving for Castillo to follow her. They stepped out onto the walkway.

"This Mr. Holiday sounds like a piece of work," Castillo muttered.

"Agreed. I think Chiqy was referencing him before too. All that talk about taking a holiday while he was drugged up—too clever by half. And it sounds like Sarah was exactly the kind of 'not used up' girl this Mr. Holiday would be willing to buy from Chiqy. She's almost certainly gone."

She looked in the one room they hadn't checked, just to be sure. The girl in there, sprawled out and unconscious on the bed, was African-American. That made it official. Sarah was nowhere to be found.

"What now?" Castillo asked.

Keri stood there silently, going over everything in her head. After a good ten seconds, she finally spoke.

"We know she was here. If we can determine which room she was in, we might be able to find a clue. She left us one at the warehouse. I bet she'd try to do it again."

"How do we know which room she was in?" Castillo wondered.

"I think we can assume she was in one of the ones we found empty. We didn't really look at them closely once we saw they weren't occupied."

"Okay, which one first?"

"When we were staking the place out, I noticed that one room didn't have its light on. That makes me think whoever was in there got moved a while ago. Let's start with that one. It's here on the second floor."

She led the way down the hall to a room they'd only peeked in before. Keri stepped in and turned on the light. It was immediately obvious something had happened in here.

There was a pool of blood on the carpeting next to the bed. A phone lay on the floor beside it. It had been ripped from the wall. Keri knelt down to get a closer look. One corner of the base of the phone was covered in dried blood.

Keri stood up again and looked at the bed. She noticed that a bar was missing from the headboard in the same spot where the other girls had been handcuffed.

Maybe this one got free and tried to escape.

She wandered into the bathroom. A chair was lying on its side in the tub and the small window was open. She stood the chair upright and climbed up to peek out the window. It was a long way down with only a nearby dumpster to break a fall.

"What do you think?" Castillo asked from behind her.

"I think the girl in this room got the upper hand on her john and tried to escape."

"Maybe she got away," Castillo said hopefully.

"I doubt it. If she had, we'd know about it by now. A naked, handcuffed girl would have gotten some kind of mention on the radio by this point."

Keri returned to the bedroom and slowly walked around. She was sure that if Sarah had been the girl in this room, she'd have left some kind of clue.

She stared at the bed where the girl had been handcuffed while she was assaulted. It made sense that if her left hand was handcuffed to the headboard, she had somehow managed to use her right hand to grab the phone and hit her rapist with it.

Moving closer to the right side of the bed, she imagined the girl lying there, a man forcing himself on her for who knows how long, unable to do much more than squirm.

And scratch.

Keri looked at the right side of the headboard and saw multiple scratches where the girl must have struggled. They looked fresh.

Little bits of splintered wood still clung to the edges of the scratch marks. Keri looked closer and then, despite herself, she gasped.

"What is it?" Castillo asked from across the room.

"Look."

"What? All I see are a bunch of scratch marks."

"They're not just random marks, Jamie. They're letters."

It was Castillo's turn to gasp.

Keri leaned in, and without actually touching the headboard, she traced her finger over them.

"It says 'sc xile.' Is that how you read it too?" she asked.

"That's what it looks like," Castillo agreed. "So 'sc' is Sarah Caldwell. But what is 'xile'? Is that short for 'exile' or something?"

"I don't know. But it's from her. I'm sure of it."

She took out her phone, snapped a photo of it, and stepped out onto the walkway.

"Sergeant Henriksen. We need you," she called out before turning to Castillo. "We need CSU to check this room thoroughly— the bed, the bloodstains on the floor, the phone, and especially the area near those scratches. They should be able to find fingerprints and DNA to confirm that Sarah was in this room. Can you honcho that?"

"Of course. Are you going somewhere?"

"Yeah. First I'm going to send this photo to Edgerton to see if he can put 'xile' into his databases to determine what it means. And then I have to take care of something."

"Is everything okay?" Castillo asked, clearly confused.

"Listen. Tech is checking the cameras from the area for vehicles that might have left before we arrived. Ray is waiting to interrogate Chiqy when he's out of surgery. We'll see if Edgerton gets a hit on this 'xile' thing. But other than that, there's not much we can do right now. So I'm going to take care of some personal business. Call me if anything comes up, okay?"

"Okay," Castillo said, still perplexed.

Keri left her that way. She didn't have much choice.

What am I going to do? Tell her that I'm going to study some stolen postcards from the apartment of a guy I killed for clues about my missing daughter?

She might not have been able to tell Castillo that but it was exactly what she planned to do.

111

CHAPTER EIGHTEEN

It was all Keri could do not to toss her hot coffee on the innocent doughnut shop employee who filled it up for her.

Her frustration was near boiling over and she was tempted to take it out the nearest person. In this case it just so happened to be the sleepy-eyed guy who refilled her cup without asking, messing up the delicate balance of cream and sugar.

Of course, that wasn't what she was really upset about. It was 12:45 in the morning and she'd been sitting under the fluorescent lights of the doughnut shop for fifteen minutes, her knees, elbows, and everything in between aching, poring over the postcards laid out on the table in front of her. And still she hadn't figured out what they meant.

Keri had been studying the return addresses, which she sensed were the key to everything. She suspected that these might even be the locations of the abducted children, if she could ever find a way to crack the code.

She knew she could take the postcards to Edgerton and he would eventually figure it out. But he and the entire tech team were using all their resources to find Sarah and the other two missing girls. Besides, she'd obtained the postcards illegally and didn't want to implicate anyone else in what she'd done.

More pressing, she worried that Jackson Cave had found out about the death of the Collector, or Brian Wickwire, as she now knew him. If, as she suspected, he'd been helping Wickwire facilitate the sales of these abducted children, he would almost certainly warn their "clients." And if he knew that Wickwire had died in an altercation with her, the first people he'd warn would be the ones holding Evie.

It wasn't an unreasonable leap to make. Until recently, Downtown Division had an APB out on her. Cave would have easy access to that information. And when he learned the bugs he'd had put in her and Ray's cars were no longer working, he'd put two and two together. If he was awake at this hour, he might be coordinating it all right now.

I have to figure this out fast.

Forcing all other thoughts from her head, Keri returned her full attention to the postcards.

All the addresses were from States west of the Rockies. But nothing else about them made sense. Each address began with what looked to be initials, followed by a street address in a real city.

But when she punched those addresses in her phone's map, nothing came up.

Beyond that, most of the addresses didn't even make alphabetical sense. Some had multiple consonants in a row, so that they were essentially gibberish. She looked at one in suburban Salt Lake City for the third time, completely bewildered:

vb
243 gzqodq lane
taylorsville, ut
84123

She knew Wickwire had written it down. His telltale refusal to use capital letters was everywhere. Taylorsville was a real place. But there was no Gzqodq Lane or street or avenue. It was just a jumble of letters as far as she could tell.

She rifled through the postcards some more until she came to one that was short enough that she was willing to give it another go. It read:

jn
33 dkj road
salem, or
97302

Again, Salem was real but there was no road called Dkj. Keri tried to move the letters around to see if they were an anagram but since they were all consonants, nothing worked. She looked at every street in the 97302 zip code, hoping for anything that might jump out at her. There was a Decker Jones Street and Dokij Lane. Both were kind of close to dkj. But she knew they weren't right. And there was an Elk Road.

She stared at that last one and felt a tingling sensation in the back of her brain. Something about it seemed possible. It was the right number of letters, even if they didn't all fit. She looked at them again and noticed something that hadn't occurred to her before.

If you inserted the next letter in the alphabet for each letter in "dkj"- "e" for "d," then "l" for "k," and finally "k" for "j," it spelled the word "elk."

She typed "33 Elk Road" into the map. Nothing came up. It was a rural road and there didn't seem to be more than a dozen houses on it.

What if he played with the house numbers too?

There was no 44 Elk Road, which wasn't a shock. If there was no 33, there wouldn't be a 44.

What if, for the numbers, he substituted backwards?

She tried typing "22 Elk Road" and sure enough, an address popped up on the map. Feeling the excitement build in her, Keri flipped back to the Utah address. Using the same method, 243 gzqodq lane became 132 Harper Lane. She punched that in and got a real address as well.

She did it with several others. They all worked. But none of them told her which abducted child was at the address. She'd have to go into property records to find the owner, then see how many children they had and if there were photos. It would take forever.

Maybe not.

Keri looked at the letters above the address. If they were initials and he'd used the same trick as with the street same, she could find out where Evie was.

"More coffee, ma'am?"

Keri looked up blankly. The guy with the coffee pot was standing over her, a bland smile on his face.

"What? No. Go away," she told him and returned her attention to the postcards. She flipped through them quickly, looking for "dk," the letter combination that preceded "el"- Evelyn Locke.

And then she found it. For a second Keri stared at the address, frozen. If it was legitimate, then her daughter was being held at a home on Carson Drive in Lomita. That was a twenty-minute drive from her current location. Was it possible that Evie had been only miles from her all these years?

She punched the address in her phone and ran out of the doughnut shop. The air was bitterly cold but she barely noticed. And the pain she'd felt only moments earlier was gone.

*

As she tore through Lomita on the way to the address on the postcard, Keri hung up her phone. She'd just called the station and learned that Wickwire's death, her involvement, and the subsequent APB were all over the police scanner. If Jackson Cave was awake, he knew about it.

Keri pulled up to the intersection near the address on the postcard, got out of her car, and walked half a block to the actual address. She could feel herself starting to hyperventilate and forced her breathing to slow down.

It took a second to realize that the address was actually a business, not a home. The sign on the front said Alliance Imports/Exports. Something about that stirred a connection in her brain but she couldn't place why.

Before she could ponder it further her attention was caught by a man walking out the side entrance of the building. He was tall and skinny with thinning gray hair. Keri guessed that he was in his early fifties.

He was moving quickly to an unmarked gray van in the parking lot. He unlocked it and opened the sliding side door, then returned to the building at a quick jog.

Keri moved closer along the sidewalk across the street, more than a little suspicious. She tried to stay in a crouch, hiding behind one car, then another. As she was about to move to a third, the man stepped into view. Only this time he wasn't alone.

He was pulling the arm of a waifish young girl, about thirteen years old, with short blonde hair and skin so pale that it must not have been exposed to the sun in years. Even at this distance, she could see the flash of green in those eyes.

It was Evie.

CHAPTER NINETEEN

Keri felt a combination of emotions she didn't know could all co-exist at once: hope, joy, fury, fear, and determination. She stood up from her hiding place behind the car and began to run toward her daughter, pulling her gun from her holster as she did.

She was still a good forty yards away when the man saw her. Without a word, he yanked Evie's arm and pulled her toward the van. The girl looked to see what had him so agitated and saw her mother sprinting toward them.

"Evie!" Keri shouted.

Her daughter's eyes went wide with shock.

"Mommy?" she said, her expression so familiar and so alien at the same time.

Before she could say another word, the man had shoved her into the van and closed the door. He was opening the driver's door when Keri raised her weapon. She considered shooting but worried she'd accidentally get Evie. He slammed his door shut and started the ignition.

"Mommy! Mommy!" Evie screamed from somewhere inside the van.

Suddenly, through the windshield, Keri saw the man pull out a gun of his own.

"Back off or I'll shoot her!" he yelled.

For one brief moment, Keri considered firing anyway. She was a good shot and she didn't know if she'd ever get another chance like this again.

But what if I hit Evie? I can't risk it.

Keri held her gun above her head, pointing it to the sky. Slowly, she took a step back.

"It's okay. We can work this out," she said, trying to keep her voice calm.

"Drop your gun right now," he screamed.

This isn't working. He feels cornered. He could do anything right now.

"Okay. I'm putting it down."

She placed the weapon gently on the ground and took another step back.

"Mommy! Help me! I love you!" her daughter yelled.

"Shut up or I'll shoot your mother to death," the man growled. Evie went silent.

The man put the van in drive and hit the accelerator, aiming right for Keri. She dived out of the way, barely avoiding getting clipped.

As he peeled out, she looked at his license plate, committing it to memory. Then she picked up her gun and ran back to her car, ready to give chase and radio every law enforcement agency in Southern California his plates.

She put on her seatbelt and started the car. Somehow, despite the chaos and desperation of the situation, she still felt composed. All her training had kicked in and she was able to set aside the emotion of the moment and focus on the task at hand. It was the best way to save Evie.

As she clicked her seat belt into the buckle, she heard a screech and looked up. The van had turned around and was coming back. Maybe the guy had realized that he was sure to be caught unless he took Keri out. She couldn't think of any other reason why he would return. She aimed her gun out the window at him.

He was about forty feet away when she realized that he was going to ram into her head-on and there was nothing she could do about it. He was going at least thirty miles per hour. She didn't have time to get out of the car. And even if she fired at him, he'd still slam into her. All she could do was brace herself.

The impact of the collision shot her back against the seat and then forward again into the airbag. The crunching sound of the hoods smashing into each other was deafening. And then, for several long seconds, there was no noise but the soft hiss of steam from her engine.

She took a moment to see if anything was broken. Her neck ached but other than that, the only pain she felt was what she'd already been dealing with all night.

Suddenly there was another scraping metallic sound. With the airbag blocking her view, Keri couldn't see it but she knew the guy was backing up. She didn't know whether he was about to leave or preparing to pull up next to her and shoot.

Glancing down, she saw she still had her gun in her right hand. She lifted it up, pressed it against the airbag, and fired. The loud popping sounded like a bomb going off in front of her. As the thing deflated, she tried to move it aside so she could get a better view of what was going on.

She saw red lights and aimed in that direction. It took her a moment to process that they were the van's brake lights as it slowed and turned left at the end of the street. Apparently the man had decided that he would make a run for it after all. She thought she could hear Evie's voice in the distance, calling out for her.

Keri put her foot on the brake, shifted into drive, and then pressed the accelerator. Nothing happened. She pressed harder. The engine sputtered and died.

With a growing sense of dread that she wouldn't be able to pursue the man, Keri reached for her police radio to call in his license plate number. But she was having trouble grabbing the receiver. Her vision was blurry and her hand felt heavy.

I think I have a concussion or something.

That was her last thought before she lost consciousness.

CHAPTER TWENTY

Keri sat in the back of the squad car, mostly numb, as it drove her back to her to her apartment. Everything that had happened since she regained consciousness seemed to be part of a dream that she was half participating in, half observing.

She had been shaken awake by another driver who'd come across her smashed, smoking car. Within minutes, a black-and-white arrived and took down everything she could remember: the description of the man and his van, his license plate number, and of course, every minute detail of Evie's appearance.

When she'd described it all to the officers, she felt like she was underwater. They looked shimmery and indistinct and their voices sounded far away. She knew she should be overwhelmed by desperation at her daughter being ripped away from her a second time. But she couldn't seem to locate any emotion inside at all, much less something as intense as desperation.

Someone had reached out to Lieutenant Hillman, who filled them in on the back story of this missing girl. Even in her diminished state, Keri noticed that the cops around her seemed to move faster and with greater purpose once they knew the full situation.

It was Hillman who had ordered that Keri be given a ride to the station and said that he'd call Keri back momentarily with an update. Only when the officers left the scene with her in the back did she insist that they take her home instead of to Pacific Division. She thought they might argue but something in her tone must have warned them off and they agreed without question.

Keri tried to rev up her brain, to make it work faster and more effectively. She knew this was a critical time and that being a walking zombie was counterproductive. But she couldn't seem to do anything about it.

Her hands were shaking so she shoved them in her coat pockets. Her right hand bumped up against something and she pulled it out. It was one of the postcards from Wickwire's apartment. She glanced at the return address. It said Tucson, Arizona.

Something about that bounced around in her skull. It was important somehow.

Tucson is the return address. But it's not real. Tucson is where the girl is. The girl is hiding there. No, not hiding—being kept.

Her thoughts were still jumbled but one of them rose above the others and nearly screamed itself at her.

These postcards say where the girls are being kept. But Cave knows I know. He's going to have them moved. I have to save them.

But she wasn't sure how to do that other than by simply willing it to happen. She stared at the address, hoping that somehow the answer would pop into her head.

That's when her phone rang. She looked at the screen and saw it was Hillman.

"Lieutenant?" she said.

"Hi, Locke, how are you holding up?" He didn't sound like his normal self. He was being nice. She ignored that and rushed to tell him her thought before she lost it.

"Lieutenant, the Collector wrote the addresses where he took the girls he abducted on postcards. I found them in his apartment. But they're in a code. I figured it out. That's how I found Evie. But the lawyer who was working with the Collector knows I figured it out. He's calling the houses where these girls are and warning them to move the girls. They're all over the western states. You have to call the police departments in every city and get them to go to those houses now."

She had said it all in rush so she wouldn't forget anything. Both of the officers in the front looked back at her oddly but she couldn't understand why. Hillman waited a long time before responding.

"Detective, are you all right? You don't sound like yourself."

"I'm okay. I've just been knocked around a lot tonight. If I give you the key, can you reach out to those jurisdictions?"

"Of course," he answered, his voice still weird.

Keri proceeded to walk him through the letter and number substitution pattern. She found that as long as she stayed focused on the task, her head was pretty clear. But the second she took a break to regroup, things got woozy. So she stopped taking breaks.

After ten minutes, Hillman had all the addresses and handed them off to the team to start making calls. Keri looked out the window. It took her a moment to orient herself, but once she did, she realized they were only a few minutes from her place.

"Keri," Hillman aid hesitantly, "would you like an update on our search for Evie?"

"That would be good," she told him, wondering why he didn't just launch into it as he usually did.

"Okay. We located the van she was taken in about twelve miles from where you found her, in a Walmart parking lot. Unfortunately, she was no longer in it. But the driver was. He fits the description you gave, fifties, tall, skinny, gray hair. He was dead—shot in the head."

"Wow. Who did that?" Keri asked.

The brief silence before Hillman responded suggested he thought her reply was unusual.

"We managed to get in footage from the store a little while ago. It looked like the guy in the van was waiting to meet someone. But a man in a ski mask snuck beside the driver's door and shot him. Then he took Evie and carried her to a black Lincoln Continental. He put her in the trunk and drove off. The car didn't have any plates or other distinguishing characteristics. We managed to track it with cameras to a parking garage a few blocks away. But when our people searched the garage, the car wasn't there. We don't know what happened to it. I'm sorry."

"How do you know it was a man?" Keri asked.

"What?"

"How do you know the person in the ski mask was a man?"

"I don't know for certain. It just looked that way based on size and frame. Did you hear what I said before, Keri?"

"I did. You said a masked man killed the guy who had my daughter, took her, and now they've both disappeared. Do I have that right?"

"Yes."

"Okay, Lieutenant. I understand. It sounds like you all did everything you could. There are no leads to follow on Evie or on the Sarah Caldwell case. There's nothing left to do. And I'm really sore and tired from everything that's happened today. I'm not coming into the station. I'm just going to go home and rest for a bit."

"But Locke, I'm worried that—"

Keri hung up on him and sat in silence for the rest of the ride home, ignoring the occasional troubled glances from the two officers in the front seat.

When they dropped her off a few minutes later, she walked around to the alley and took the short flight of stairs to the second floor. Her apartment, above a Chinese restaurant, came cheap because Ray was friends with the guy who owned the building.

She'd only lived there six weeks but she'd already hit it off with the restaurant's friendly kitchen staff, who often gave her free meals. The situation was much better than her last place, a dilapidated houseboat in the marina without a shower.

Keri went inside, removed the hidden camera from her bedroom and the listening device from her living room, tossed them both in the bathtub, and turned on the water. When she was sure they were ruined, she returned to the living room and plopped down on the loveseat in front of the blank TV screen. The clock read 2:12 a.m.

She was tempted to just lie down and sleep, but worried that she wouldn't able to face her nightmares.

She considered calling Ray, but after the motel attack and his neck injury, she figured he needed his rest so he could be at full strength when he interrogated Chiqy after his surgery.

As she sat still in the quiet, dark apartment, alone and unmoving for the first time in hours, her head started to clear a bit. It also hurt. She knew she probably had a concussion, which was partly causing her mental hiccups and emotional detachment.

But she suspected the latter was also because if she allowed herself to fully comprehend what Hillman had said, she might break into a million pieces. And after everything that had happened, she doubted she'd be able to put herself back together again. If she let herself give in to the grief she felt circling at the edges of her heart, she'd be lost forever.

She stood up and went to get a glass of water. As she poured it, she glanced at the notepad on the counter. It reminded her that she was supposed to meet Mags for lunch tomorrow. That was definitely off.

Margaret "Mags" Merrywether was Keri's only real female friend outside of work. And even that friendship was new. They'd met when Keri was investigating the disappearance of a wealthy society wife named Kendra Burlingame. Kendra and Mags had been close and Mags had helped a bit with the investigation.

After Keri had discovered who had murdered Kendra, the one thing that had survived that case was the connection Keri had made with Mags.

Margaret Merrywether was a walking contradiction. A tall, striking, sophisticated Southern belle divorcee with flaming red hair, she was also a crusading columnist for a local alternative weekly newspaper, writing under the pseudonym "Mary Brady." For reasons she couldn't quite understand, Keri had a sudden urge to call her.

Without thinking about it, she picked up the phone and dialed. She regretted it almost immediately when she heard Mags' sleepy voice.

"Keri?" she said hazily.

"Oh, I'm sorry, Mags. I forgot what time it is. Go back to sleep."

"No, wait. I'm awake now. What's going on, darling?"

"It's just, you know, I've had a really awful day. I've been trying to find this missing girl and it hasn't gone well. And then I got a lead on Evie, my daughter, who was abducted a few years—"

"I know all about that, sweetie," Mags said soothingly.

"Well, I found her. But before I could get her back, the man who had her crashed into my car and got away and now he's dead, shot by someone in a mask, and she's gone again and my boss says they don't know where…"

Suddenly she was sobbing uncontrollably. Everything she had been trying to hold in came pouring out of her at once. Tears rolled down her cheeks. Her nose was running and she felt strands of saliva dripping from her lips. She didn't care about any of it.

"You're going to be okay," she heard Mags whisper softly on the other end of the line. "You'll be okay, dear."

"But I won't, Mags. That's the thing. All that's kept me going these last few years has been the certainty that one day I would find Evie; that I would bring her back home and be the mother she deserves. But that's over. She's gone. There are no clues. Whoever did this was a professional and left no trace. I don't have a thing to go on. I've failed her, Mags. I failed my daughter *again*!"

"Why don't I come over, sweetie? I can make you some tea and we can talk."

"Mags," Keri said, ignoring the offer, "maybe you could write something."

"What do you mean?"

"You could write some kind of column that draws the masked man out and we could set up some sort of sting…I don't know exactly how but we could come up with something."

"Keri, apart from the ethical considerations, I wouldn't even know where to begin. I want to help but I don't see how anything I might write would have any impact at all."

"What are you talking about?" Keri demanded. "One of your columns brought down the deputy mayor. You can make a big difference."

"But I knew what I was dealing with then. I don't have the first clue here. Anyway, darling, let's not get into a disagreement over this. Please let me—"

"What did you mean by 'ethical considerations'?" Keri interrupted. "What considerations?"

"I just meant that a journalist doesn't typically use their work as bait to catch a criminal."

Keri paused long enough to swallow, long enough to fume.

"This is my daughter we're talking about, Mags!"

"I know, Keri. I didn't mean anything by it. It's just…you took me by surprise, dear."

"I'm sorry I bothered you," Keri said.

"Now don't say that. I'm sorry, Keri. Please, let's keep talki—"

Keri hung up on her. A call came in from Mags only seconds later but she rejected it. A text followed but Keri didn't even look at it, tossing her phone on the coffee table.

She chugged what was left of her water and walked over to the cabinet where half a bottle of Glenlivet rested, staring back at her. She hadn't touched the stuff in over a month and could feel the difference. She slept better. She felt better. She even looked better.

But right now she didn't care about any of that. She opened the bottle and poured it in her water glass until it was almost overflowing. She put it to her lips and took a sip. Then another. And as she heard the buzz of another text from Mags, she began to chug.

*

When Keri awoke to the sound of Ray's ringtone on her phone, it took a second to determine where she was. Faint rays of light streamed in through cracks in the curtains. Her head pounded. Eventually she realized she was lying on the floor in front of the living room loveseat, where she must have drifted off last night.

She reached for her phone. The time on it said 6:08 a.m. She'd started drinking around 2:15 and passed out soon after that. So she was working on about three and half hours of sleep. That felt about right.

"Hello," she said quietly into the phone, a little afraid of her own voice.

"Are you dressed?" Ray asked, his voice booming, rattling her teeth.

"Why?"

"Because I'll be at your place in ten minutes," he said. "We've got a new lead in the Sarah Caldwell case."

"How?"

"I got Chiqy to talk."

CHAPTER TWENTY ONE

Sitting in the passenger seat of Ray's car fifteen minutes later, Keri kept her attention on the stripes of the road in front of her, breathing in the cold morning air through the open window, hoping the combination would keep her from throwing up.

"Are we going to talk about it?" Ray asked from the driver's seat.

"About what?"

"About Evie. Hillman filled me in."

"I can't, Ray," Keri said, looking out the passenger window at the buildings whizzing by. "Not yet."

"Okay. Can we talk about something else?"

"What's that?"

"Hillman said you sounded really out of it last night. He was worried about you."

Keri sighed and turned to look at him. He was no longer wearing the neck brace from the previous night and his eyes weren't as red as they had been. Physically he looked to be in decent condition.

But his brow was furrowed and his lips were pursed. She almost felt bad for him. He was trying so desperately to find out what was going on with her but he was terrified to say the wrong thing.

"I'm pretty sure I got a concussion in the crash. And I kind of shut down after...they got away. So I wasn't in tip-top chatting shape."

"And you're better now?" Ray asked skeptically.

"Comparatively. Why?"

"Because you kind of smell like a distillery," he said bluntly.

She gave him a withering look but didn't respond. He went on.

"I just want to make sure you're up for this."

"I don't even know what *this* is," she reminded him.

"I told you—I got a lead from Chiqy."

"And how exactly did you get him to be so forthcoming?" Keri asked, her eyebrows raised.

"I'm not at liberty to say."

"Really? You're not going to tell me?"

"You're better off not knowing, Keri. Then you can tell the truth when Internal Affairs questions you."

"Jeez, Ray—Internal Affairs? What the hell did you do, break his other elbow?"

He didn't answer and they sat without speaking for a good two minutes. Neither minded it. They weren't angry. In fact, the silence was comfortable. Eventually, Ray spoke.

"We're quite a pair, aren't we?"

"We are that," Keri agreed.

Ray got on the 405 freeway at Culver Boulevard and headed south.

"Care to tell me where we're headed?"

"A truck stop in Tustin. Chiqy mentioned a trucker who was supposed to transport Sarah and two other girls to a meet there. He was supposed to hand them off to a guy in a red big rig, who was going to take them to something called the Bad Place."

"What's the Bad Place?" Keri asked.

"He didn't know much about it, just that it's where the 'problem' girls are taken. I tried to get a location out of him but he didn't know."

"You're sure?"

"I was pretty…forceful in my interrogation. He gave up everything else. If he knew where this place was, he'd have told me."

"So what are we looking for exactly?" Keri asked, her mood if not her stomach slightly better as a result of having a lead.

"The trucker's name is Curt Stoller. Edgerton sent me his DMV photo and info on his vehicle. Unfortunately, he's almost certainly handed off the girls to whoever was driving the red truck by now. Patterson's looking through video footage from the truck stop right now, trying to tag any red eighteen-wheelers."

Detective Garrett Patterson was Edgerton's right-hand man. Nicknamed "Grunt Work," Patterson was a short, bookish guy in his thirties who loved poring over minutiae that bored just about everyone else. He was definitely the right man for this job.

"That's a start," Keri said with more enthusiasm than she'd felt in hours. "Maybe he'll have something for us by the time we get there. What I'm wondering is if there's any information on this Mr. Holiday."

"I wondered the same thing," Ray said. "Suarez put the name and physical description that Lanie gave us through the system and came up completely empty. I can't believe that someone who runs such a huge sex trafficking operation has never been picked up or even ID'd. It's like he's a ghost."

"That is weird," Keri agreed. "He's either really lucky or really good. Speaking of Lanie, I was thinking of calling the Caldwells to check in and see if those scratched letters I found in the headboard mean anything to them. You think it's too early?"

Ray looked at the car's clock.

"It's not even six thirty. I'm hoping they managed to fall asleep for a few hours. If you call, it'll get them all riled up when we don't have anything worth sharing. Maybe text them when we're closer to Tustin?"

"Yeah, that sounds good. It's a fine line, you know—trying to keep parents informed but not drive them crazy."

As she said it, she realized she wasn't just talking about the Caldwells. Ray knew it too and tried to delicately broach the subject again.

"Listen, Keri, I know you don't want to get into it. But if you change your mind, I'm here, okay? I'm always here for you. You know that, right?"

"I know and I appreciate it. But she's gone, Ray. I was so close. I saw her. She called out to me. And now there are no leads and there's nothing I can do about it. And I just can't let myself process that right now. If I do, I think it might break me. I've just got to put it away in a box and focus on what's in front of me. It's the only way I can survive this."

"I'm sorry," Ray said quietly.

"Yeah, me too. But accepting that has helped me make a decision."

"What's that?"

"I may not be able to save Evie," she told him. "But I've still got a chance to save Sarah Caldwell, to bring her back to her parents. And if I have to go to hell itself and drag her back out, that's what I'm going to do."

CHAPTER TWENTY TWO

Keri was getting anxious. They were only a few minutes from the truck stop and Patterson still hadn't pinpointed which red truck Curt Stoller might have transferred the girls to. After sending the text to Mariela Caldwell's phone, she called Patterson for the third time in less than an hour. Ray looked at her dubiously.

"Keri, don't you think he'd call *us* if he had something?"

"That guy gets so into the details he might just forget. I'm going to give him a little jumpstart."

"You're going to give him an ulcer," Ray countered. But it was too late. Detective Patterson had already picked up.

"I'm working on it," he said before she could speak.

"Yeah, well I'm going to help you work on it, Garrett, because we're almost there. You found Stoller's truck, right?"

"Yes," he said. "I saw it on a surveillance camera driving past the main building before it went into the huge lot in the back."

"That's great. What time was that?"

"About four a.m." he replied. "But there are over fifty trucks back there and all the cameras are mounted on buildings hundreds of yards away. There's no way to see vehicle colors, much less license plates."

"Okay, let's try it another way, then," she suggested. "I bet there are more than just three girls being transported in that red truck and I doubt the driver is going to want to hang out in a crowded, public place like that any longer than he has to. So check for red trucks that arrived less than an hour before Stoller got there and left within an hour after he arrived."

"Checking," Patterson said, obviously glad to have another course of action.

Keri looked over at Ray while they waited and gave him her best "I told you so" look. He stuck out his tongue at her.

"How's it coming, Garrett?" she asked after waiting in silence for two minutes. "We're pulling off the freeway now."

"Okay, I've got three red big rigs that fit your criteria. Kevin is cross-checking the plates to see if any of the drivers have records."

"Edgerton?" Keri asked eagerly.

"Patience please," he said irritably over the speakerphone. "Even geniuses need a moment or two."

"Cut them some slack," Ray whispered to her. "They've been up all night."

"Got it!" Kevin shouted. "Of the three drivers, only one has a record. He's been busted three times, all drug trafficking convictions. His name is Reginald Jones. I'm sending you his info now."

Ray had reached the truck stop but pulled over on the side of the road, waiting for instructions.

"Good," Keri said. "Edgerton, we need to know which way that truck went."

"Checking cameras now. It went north on the 5 Freeway. Then it took the 55 north to the 91 east. That's the last we have of it. As of ten minutes ago, it was approaching the 241, headed toward Corona."

"That seems odd," Keri noted. "Why would one guy take them south, only to have the next one take them northeast?"

"Maybe this Mr. Holiday ordered it," Ray suggested, as he pulled back onto the road and made a U-turn back to the freeway. "He seems big on compartmentalizing information."

"Regardless," Edgerton butted in, "if you take the 241 and really book it, you might be able to cut him off near the 71."

"Already on it," Ray said as he turned on the siren and hit the accelerator.

*

Less than twenty minutes later, Ray and Keri, along with a half dozen squad cars from the Orange County Sheriff's Department, had the truck in their sights. Unfortunately, the driver was well aware of them and didn't seem interested in pulling over.

In fact, he picked up speed so that at one point he was pushing ninety miles per hour.

"Pull back," Keri shouted into the radio. "If there are girls in that truck and it crashes, none of them will make it."

The cars did as she asked and at first, it looked like the truck was easing up to match them. But it quickly became apparent that he was slowing down for another reason.

"He's getting off at Green River Road," one of the sheriff's deputies announced.

Sure enough, the truck veered onto the exit ramp and went barreling along, ignoring any potential traffic.

"Where does this road go?" Keri asked anyone willing to answer. They were well out of her neck of the woods. A random deputy answered.

"It skirts along the eastern edge of the Cleveland National Forest before heading east and reconnecting with the 15 freeway. Luckily, there's not much traffic around here at this time of day."

"Do we want to get ahead of him and place a spike strip?" another deputy asked.

"No, it's too dangerous," Ray insisted. "We may just have to wait him out."

Keri turned to him with a worried look on her face.

"I don't think we can just wait. Who knows what he might do? Pull up next to him and I'll try to talk some sense into the guy."

"What if he's armed?" Ray asked, clearly not convinced.

"We'll have another unit pull up on the passenger side. If he pulls a weapon, they can take him out. Hopefully I can get him to slow down enough that the truck will be okay if he's incapacitated."

"I don't know, Keri."

"Just keep an eye out. If things go south, you can always hit the brakes. I'm going to pass the word."

She explained the plan to the deputies as Ray prepared to pull up on the driver's side of the truck. As he did, Keri lowered her window and took off her seatbelt. When they were right beside the truck, she waved at the driver, an African-American man in his forties who looked at her incredulously.

But amazingly, when she motioned for him lower his window, he did so.

"Reginald," she shouted, "we don't want this to end badly."

"Don't see how it can't," he yelled back. She noticed he had slowed down a bit from about sixty to fifty. Ray reduced speed to match him.

"Whatever cargo you have isn't worth dying for. Pull over. You're obviously just a courier. Roll over on your boss and you might not even do much time. Let me help you out."

"There's no way I'm not going down for a long time if I give up," he yelled, slowing even more so that he could be heard.

"That depends on who your boss is. If he's a big enough fish, you never know. It's better than the alternative."

"What's the alternative?" he asked.

She could tell from his voice that he wanted this to end well, that he didn't have some kind of death wish. She decided to play to that.

"If you don't stop, it probably ends with you crashed in a ditch or with a bullet in your head."

"What? Over some bricks of coke?"

Keri looked over at Ray, who was as shocked as she was. Then she turned back to Reginald, who was now going barely over thirty miles per hour.

"Reginald, are you telling me that you are only transporting drugs?" she asked.

"What else would I have?"

"Girls—underage girls."

"I don't got no girls in here!"

"Prove it," Keri demanded. "Pull over. We're looking for kidnapped girls. If you don't have them, your day might not end so badly."

Just then, Keri glanced at the road ahead and saw that she was wrong. It was going to end very badly for Reginald Jones. He was looking at her and clearly hadn't noticed the sharp leftward bend of the road coming up. Even at his reduced speed, he was too close. There was no way he would make it."

"Reginald, look out!" she shouted. "Hit the brakes!"

He looked up and immediately saw the danger. The road veered sharply left and he wouldn't be able to make the curve without toppling over to the right. He slammed on the brakes.

The road, on the edge of the forest, was dusted with morning dew and his wheels didn't grip as he hoped. The truck skidded off the road and slammed into a rocky mountain embankment before careening left and tipping over.

Ray pulled over. Keri got out even before he was completely stopped and ran to the vehicle. If he was lying and there were girls in that truck, it was hard to imagine they'd fared well.

As she got close, two arms appeared at the passenger side window, which now faced the sky. Reginald pulled himself up and sat on the exterior of the door with his hands up.

"You better not be lying to me about not having girls in there, Reginald, or I will shoot you a lot."

"I don't ship girls, lady," Reginald insisted. "I'm a drugs man."

Ray had caught up to her. As he caught his breath, she spoke.

"I think he's telling the truth."

"If that's true, look on the bright side. If those girls were in there, they'd be in bad shape right now."

"Yeah," Keri said. "But if Sarah's not in that truck, where the hell is she?"

*

131

Sarah reminded herself to stay calm. She'd already screamed enough. She screamed when she awoke an hour ago to discover that she was lying in the undercarriage of a big rig, speeding along a freeway. She screamed again when she realized she was packed in with over fifty other girls.

By the time she figured out that the vehicle was actually a cattle truck and that the cows were right above her, her screams were more rasps than anything else. She didn't even react when the animal waste from above drained down and dripped onto her and the other girls.

Even though it was daylight, everything was dark under the truck and it was impossible to identify anyone among the mass of bodies. She had no idea if Lanie was there with her. And she was too tired and cold and sore to call out anyway.

She managed to reposition herself so that she was close to the side of the undercarriage. If she adjusted her body just right, she could see out of the metal slats to the side of the road. She grabbed hold of two slats and leaned back so that she had a better angle.

It worked. She was now able to see the signage on the side of the freeway. It said that she was on the 5 south. That rang a bell for her. But with her exhaustion, dehydration, and physical pain, along with the overwhelming smell of cow waste, she couldn't quite comprehend what it meant.

Then she saw another sign and everything became clear. It read: Mexican Border – 79 miles. That's when Sarah realized where the Bad Place was. She and about fifty other girls were being shipped across the border, like human cattle, to be abused in some off-the-grid whorehouse in another country.

And that's when another realization hit her. If she crossed that border, she'd never see her parents again. She'd never go back to school. She'd never be heard from again, unless it was by someone who stumbled across the shallow grave Mr. Holiday was certain to eventually dump her in.

And knowing that, despite having no voice and no strength, Sarah began to scream again.

CHAPTER TWENTY THREE

Keri felt like slamming her cell phone against the dashboard. It took her last ounce of self-control to grip it tight and continue to speak in a professional voice.

"Patterson, I don't understand how you could pinpoint almost the exact location of Reginald Jones's truck but you've completely lost the other two red big rigs that left the truck stop around the same time."

"We haven't lost them," Patterson said in a tone that suggested he was trying to keep it together as well. "We know they both got on the 5 freeway headed south. There just aren't as many cameras along that stretch of highway so it's taking longer to pin them down."

Keri bit her tongue. She knew everyone was exhausted and on edge. Pushing them further wouldn't help. It was a waiting game now.

"I'm almost out of gas," Ray said. "Let's pull over at that gas station. I'll fill up. We can take bathroom breaks and load up on coffee. Maybe they'll have something new by then."

Keri nodded. As he got off the freeway, she reviewed the status of the case. Assuming Chiqy had been telling the truth, the girls were in one of two red big rigs headed south on the 5 freeway. But at a certain point the 5 connected with Interstate 8. That meant they could be headed to Arizona, San Diego, or possibly even Mexico. But without that camera footage there was no way to know for sure.

When they pulled into the station, Ray pumped the gas while Keri went to the restroom. She did her best to freshen up, splashing cold water on her face.

Looking in the mirror for the first time since she'd been woken from her slumber on the floor of her apartment, she was shocked at how much she'd aged in just sixteen hours. Yesterday afternoon, she'd been a well-rested, sober-for-a-month, thirty-five-year-old turning heads and solving cases.

Now she looked about a decade older. Her whole body hurt. She'd fallen off the wagon again. She'd soon have to go in for questioning for leaving the scene of a crime at which she'd killed the man who'd abducted her daughter. She had almost saved Evie, only to have her ripped away, possibly forever this time. And she had no leads in the kidnapping of a girl she'd promised to return to her parents.

Not a great stretch.

133

She chuckled slightly to herself at the magnitude of how badly things had gone off the rails, then stopped herself short, consumed by guilt.

She headed into the convenience store to get a big coffee and a pastry she could wolf down before taking some more of the pain pills the EMT had given her last night.

Glancing at her phone, she saw that it was 8:15 a.m., over an hour since she'd sent the Caldwells the text and photo of the headboard scratches. She was surprised she hadn't heard back and hoped that it meant they were deep in sleep. In the days after Evie was taken, that was often the only time she could get a break from the pain of losing her. And sometimes not even then.

She returned to the car and waited for Ray to come back. Just as she was finishing her apple fritter, Mags called. She thought about sending it to voicemail again but decided against it and picked up.

"Hello," she said.

"Hi, Keri," Mags replied, her normally composed voice strangled with emotion. "I'm so sorry. I handled things badly last night. Please forgive me."

Keri was used to hedged apologies, full of phrases like "if I offended you." This had none of that and it took her by surprise. To be petulant in the face of such remorse seemed small.

"Of course I forgive you."

"Thank you so much. I haven't slept a wink since we spoke. My insides have been bubbling like a crawfish boil."

"Same here," Keri admitted, although she didn't totally get the reference.

"Well," Mags continued, "I couldn't just leave it like that. I had to do something. So I came up with a notion. And I think it might have done some good."

"What do you mean?" Keri asked, confused.

"All right, hear me out, darling. This will all make sense in a moment. Two years ago, I was working on a piece about sex trafficking in the city. I was never able to publish, partly because I couldn't nail some details down solidly enough. And partly because my editor was worried that I might face retribution."

"What kind of retribution?" Keri asked.

"The permanent kind. You might remember that Lawrence Kenneally over at the *Times* did a similar story about six years ago. About a week later, his car blew up in the driveway when he started it."

"Your editors thought you were at risk even though you write under a pseudonym?"

"Yes," Mags said. "That only offers so much protection. And since I didn't have enough hard evidence to name names, it didn't seem worth the risk."

"Okay. So how does this affect me?"

"Part of your description of what happened last night—a guy being shot by a man in a mask—fit the M.O. for someone I'd heard about in my research. He was known as the Black Widower. Supposedly bigwigs use him to clean up messes for them. And his standard method was a gunshot to the head. Any chance he left the scene in a black Lincoln Continental without plates?"

"Yes!" Keri nearly shouted.

"I suspected as much. That's part of his custom as well. He's been doing this for years. But because he's a hired gun, no one can establish a pattern to his crimes. The only similarity is that they always seem to occur when a major mess needs cleaning up."

"Okay. I feel like there's more you're not telling me, Mags."

"There is," Mags said. "During the course of my investigation, I was given a way to reach out to him if I ever needed a job done. Obviously, I never did. But I always held on to it, just in case. This morning, I reached out."

"How?"

"Craigslist, if you can believe it. I was told to post in LA's "strictly platonic" section, using a few specific keywords."

"Have you heard back?" Keri asked anxiously.

"Not yet. But it's only been a few hours. I heard sometimes he replies the same day. Sometimes it takes weeks or even months. Sometimes he never responds. But I've baited the hook at least."

"Thank you, Mags."

"Of course, sweetie. I almost didn't do it. I don't want to give you false hope. But it sounded so similar that I had to try."

Keri saw Ray coming out of the store. He had a coffee in one hand and a breakfast burrito in the other. She didn't want him to know she'd confided in Mags and not him so she started to end the call when she had a thought.

"Hey, Mags—when you were investigating this story, did you ever come across the name 'Mr. Holiday' or something called 'the Bad Place'?"

Mags was quiet for a moment, clearly thinking, before she finally responded.

"Not specifically. But I remember interviewing several teen prostitutes who talked about not wanting a holiday. I'd ask them if they had tried to get out of the life and they all used the same phrase—'I don't want a holiday.' It struck me as odd but I never

135

knew what to make of it. But if it was a reference to a person, it might make more sense. I could try to reach back out to them but it might take a while. As you know, these girls aren't exactly easy to find."

"That's okay," Keri said, rushing to wrap things as Ray reached the car. "I actually know a girl who might be able to help. And I know exactly where to find her. I've got to run, Mags."

"Of course. But we're good?"

"We're good, Margaret. I'll be in touch," she said, hanging up as Ray sat down.

"Who was that?" he asked.

"Just Mags Merrywether checking in. She gave me an idea."

"What's that?

"Remember Susan Granger, the teen prostitute I found in Venice earlier this year?"

He gave her a disbelieving look.

"You mean the fourteen-year-old girl with a pimp named Crabby who you beat to a pulp? The girl you've been visiting every week since then at that girls' group home in Redondo Beach? Yeah, I remember her, Keri."

"Just checking," she said, unable to hide her smile at how well he knew her. "Mags mentioned that a lot of prostitutes she interviewed for a story kept referencing the word 'holiday.' Maybe Susan knows what that's about."

"It's worth a shot," he said. "Especially since we still have nothing else to go on. Suarez just called me and said they found that trucker who drove the girls to the truck stop, Curt Stoller. He gave the same description of Mr. Holiday but he was almost useless otherwise. He said this was his third time transporting girls and he always follows the same routine. He leaves the cab of his truck unlocked when he gets to the truck stop, then goes into the rest area for twenty minutes before returning to the truck. He said that when he left this time, the girls were all drugged and unconscious. When he got back, they were gone. He never saw who took them."

"That's all they got out of him?"

"He did mention that Holiday promised him that if he kept doing a good job, he'd get to spend some private time with the girls somewhere called the Bad Place. But he didn't know where that was and he didn't want to press Holiday. Apparently, he's pretty scared of the guy."

"Great," Keri said, frustrated. "Just so we're clear: all our law enforcement resources are coming up empty and we're hoping a former teen prostitute might give us a bread crumb we can follow?"

"Pretty much," Ray conceded.

Keri scowled as she dialed the number of the group home. The phone was picked up by Rita Skraeling, the woman who ran the place. Keri would have recognized her raspy, cigarette-bruised voice anywhere.

"Hey, Rita, it's Keri," she said. "I need to talk to Susan. Is she available?"

"Usually, I'd say no. But for you, any time. Give me a minute to get her. She's on mop duty."

Rita put down the phone and Keri imagined the little, wrinkled force of nature shuffling down the hall in her thick glasses. A few seconds later Susan picked up.

"Hi, Detective Locke," she said, her voice full of enthusiasm.

Susan had come a long way in the months since Keri had found her hooking on a Venice street in the middle of the night, her grotesque pimp only steps away.

It had taken her a while to believe that she was actually free of that life. But with support from Ms. Skraeling, her therapist, and the other girls at the home, along with regular visits from Keri, she'd finally come out of her shell.

"Hi, Susan," Keri said, knowing the girl would be disappointed that this wasn't a social call. "How are you?"

"Pretty good," Susan said. "I finished that Nancy Drew book. We could talk about it when you come over next. Is that why you're calling—to set up a visit?"

"I do hope to visit soon. But not this weekend. I'm out of town on a case. I'm actually hoping you might be able to help me out."

"Me help you?" Susan said excitedly.

"Yeah. But it means telling me something about your time on the streets. And I don't want to ask you about that if you're not okay with it."

"What's it for?" Susan asked, her voice turning guarded.

"I'm searching for a girl that was kidnapped yesterday—she's sixteen," Keri told her, starting to regret that she'd called at all. "We think some bad people are trying to turn her into a prostitute and we're trying to find her before it's too late."

"What can I do about that?"

"Well, we keep hearing references to someone named Mr. Holiday who may be involved in taking her. Does that name mean anything to you?"

"No, sorry."

Keri looked over at Ray, but he wasn't looking back. He was staring at his phone. Obviously some new information had come in.

137

He held up the phone for her to see. It was a text from Kevin Edgerton that read "Found trucks. One still headed south toward San Diego on the 5 freeway. Other going east to Arizona on the 8 freeway. Advise."

"Are you mad at me?" Susan asked.

Keri realized that she hadn't responded to the girl and that she must have interpreted the silence as anger.

"No, Susan, of course not," she said. "It was a long shot. Thanks for trying."

"Was there anything else they said?"

Keri thought for a moment.

"Some people mentioned something called the Bad Place. Does that ring a bell?"

"I've heard of it. Crabby used to say it was where troublemaking whores were sent when they'd stepped out of line one time too many. I don't know if it's even real."

"Did Crabby happen to mention where it was?" Keri asked.

"Sure. He said it was in Mexico."

Keri and Ray looked at each other. This time she made sure not to leave Susan hanging.

"Are you sure about that?" she asked.

"Yeah. He said it all the time. 'If you act up I'll have to send you to the Bad Place down Mexico way.' After a while I assumed it was just a story he was making up. Does that help at all?"

"It might," Keri told her.

"Does this mean you can get that girl back?"

"We're sure going to try, Susan. And if we do, you'll be part of the reason why. I've got to go now but we'll talk again soon, okay?"

Okay," Susan said and Keri could actually hear her smiling through the phone.

She hung up and turned to Ray, who had started up the car and was pulling out of the gas station.

"South, I assume?" he said.

"Yep, south. All the way to Mexico."

CHAPTER TWENTY FOUR

Keri could feel time slipping away from them. Even though Ray had the siren on and was pushing 100 miles an hour as they tore down the freeway, a creeping sense of dread was overtaking her. If that truck crossed into Mexico, she doubted they'd never find Sarah or the other girls again.

They had everyone on speakerphone at the station and, after explaining what they'd learned, the entire team took on assignments. Lieutenant Hillman was calling the San Diego Sector of the Border Patrol to request they hold the truck if found and warn them about the nature of the situation.

Detective Manny Suarez was doing the same thing with San Diego County Sheriff's Department and the San Diego Police Department. Of course, it was hard to get assistance when all they knew definitively from the video footage was that the truck had a red cab and a white trailer that said "Maersk" on the side.

Using freeway cameras, Detectives Edgerton and Patterson had only managed to intermittently track the truck so far because, until recently, it had been on a quiet stretch of freeway in the very early morning traveling at a constant speed. But now it was after 9 a.m. and they were deep into rush hour in a major city. The highways were choked with traffic and there were likely dozens of Maersk trucks with red cabs close to crossing the border into Mexico.

That's why Patterson was trying to clean up freeway sign camera screenshots to get a decent image of the license plate. They knew it was from California and suspected that the first letter was "V" but they couldn't be certain. The process was slow and painstaking.

Patterson was having the same issue as he looked at images taken through the front windshield of the truck from overpass cameras. If the computer could clean up the picture of the driver, then he could employ facial recognition technology to attempt to identify him. But right now, it was just a blur.

Jamie Castillo was poring over surveillance footage from the truck stop, hoping to find a clean image of someone in a red Maersk truck filling up to see if it matched the license info Edgerton had gleaned so far.

Even the old-timers were helping out. Detectives Jerry Cantwell and Ed Sterling were reviewing receipts from the truck stop for anything useful. And Frank Brody, only months from retirement and not known for his tireless work ethic, was trying to get Maersk on the phone to review their driver information.

Keri tapped her feet nervously on the floor of the car as she watched vehicles move right so that Ray could have a clear path along the carpool lane. But even then, it was slow going. According to the last sign she'd seen, they were still eleven miles from the San Ysidro border crossing, the most likely spot for the truck to pass into Mexico. Even if there was a massive backup at the border, she doubted they could catch up.

"I've got it," someone shouted over the phone. It took Keri a second to realize that it was Edgerton.

"What?" she heard Hillman bark from nearby.

"I've got four digits of the license plate. That's enough to ID the truck and driver. I'm pulling up his license now. It belongs to a…Roberto Alarcon. Garrett, can you see if his photo matches what you have so far from facial recognition?"

There was silence on the line and Keri and Ray knew everyone back at the station was probably hovering over one computer monitor. After a few seconds, they heard a collective cheer.

"Hey, guys," Patterson said, letting them know what they couldn't see, "we've got an eighty-eight-percent match, pretty darn good, considering how fuzzy this image still is."

"All right," Hillman barked. "I'm going to pass this info along to Border Patrol. Suarez, you do the same with County and SDPD. Castillo, put out a general APB for all of Southern California on this guy and the truck. Roberto Alarcon isn't going anywhere. Edgerton, patch Sands and Locke into my office. I want to talk to them privately."

Keri and Ray exchanged worried looks. They recognized the tone in Hillman's voice. It was the one he used when he had to deliver bad news. And the fact that he wanted to talk to them privately only reinforced their concerns. A few seconds later he came back on the line and they could tell he was no longer on speakerphone.

"Great work, you two," he said. "We'd be nowhere without your efforts on this."

"With all due respect, sir," Ray replied, "we're still nowhere. Until that truck is stopped and we find Sarah Caldwell in it, we're not out of the woods. We've thought we found her too many times to get overconfident now."

"No one's getting overconfident, Ray. I'm just saying you did well."

"But…" Keri said, knowing he was holding something back.

"But I need you two to come back. There's nothing left for you to do down there now. Three law enforcement agencies have been notified. They're not going to want a couple of LA detectives trying to horn in on the case, especially the Border Patrol. You know how proprietary the feds get."

"Horn in?" Keri demanded. "This is *our* case. We're primary on it. Besides, Sarah's going to need someone there who knows what she's been through. That's us."

"Keri," Ray said sounding defeated. "Don't you get it? That's not the real reason he's calling us in. Is it, Lieutenant?"

There was silence on the other end of the line. It lasted so long Keri thought the call had dropped.

"It's *a* reason. But no, it's not the only reason," Hillman finally said in a softer voice than Keri was used to from him. "Detective Locke. You've been through a lot in the last day and frankly, I'm worried about you. You were in a shootout that could have killed you. Your car was hit by a man who escaped with your missing daughter. And you were in an altercation with the man who originally abducted her, an altercation that left him dead and you on the run. It would be irresponsible of me to leave you in the field after all of that."

"It's that last one that's got your boxers in a wad, isn't it?" she said sharply, the hairs rising on the back of her neck as her voice got louder. "You're tired of holding off Downtown Division on their interrogation of me. Why don't you just admit it?"

"That's not it," he said, his tone still much more restrained than she would have expected. "I've told them you'll need at least twenty-four hours' recovery time before any interview. I'm more concerned about your state of mind. You sounded really out of it last night. Do you even remember that you gave me information which led to the rescue of almost thirty children?"

"Vaguely," Keri admitted.

"Listen, I know that losing Evie a second time has to be affecting you. You haven't had any real break, Keri. I'm worried about you."

She opened her mouth to respond but Ray put his hand gently on her knee and shook his head.

"We understand, Lieutenant," he said. "We're coming back. Please keep us posted on any other developments."

He hung up without waiting for a reply and began moving the car right across lanes to get to the next exit.

"What the hell was that?" she yelled.

"Listen. I know you didn't want to hear that. But he was actually taking it easy on you."

"What do you mean?"

"Do you realize the favors he had to call in to get that APB on you pulled down? And to delay your interrogation? You left a crime scene where someone died, Keri. I know it was the frickin' Collector. But there are rules. You broke them and he's trying to pick up the pieces for you. Cut him some slack."

"But why now? What difference does another few hours make?"

"I don't know. But I'm sure he has a good reason. I wouldn't be surprised if the chief herself gave him an ultimatum. Your job could be on the line here. And getting into a pissing contest with the Border Patrol will guarantee you lose it."

They sat quietly for a minute as Ray finally got all the way right and managed to exit the freeway.

"Okay," she said quietly.

"What was that?" he asked, dumbfounded.

"I said 'okay.' I get it. He's putting himself on the line for me. We'll go back."

"I never thought I'd live to see the day when Keri Locke conceded an argument to me," he said playfully. "You really must have gotten a concussion last night."

"Shut up," she said. "And pull over at that gas station. I need another coffee."

As he eased into the parking lot, Keri's phone rang. It was Ed Caldwell. She picked up immediately.

"Mr. Caldwell, are you okay? I was starting to worry when I didn't hear back from you."

"Detective Locke," Mariela Caldwell replied breathlessly, "it's actually Mariela. I'm so sorry. I fell asleep last night scrolling through photos of Sarah. Ed let me sleep late this morning and I only realized my phone battery had died when I tried to call you after I woke up. It's charging now. That's why I'm calling from Ed's phone."

"That's okay. I'm just glad you got some sleep."

"Thank you," she said. "Do you have any information for us? I'm putting you on speaker so Ed can hear too."

Keri did the same so Ray could chime in if he wanted.

"We're still on the hunt," she said. "We think we've narrowed down her location to a big rig truck traveling south toward Mexico on the 5 freeway. We've alerted the Border Patrol and San Diego law enforcement. They've taken over the case and are attempting to intercept the vehicle."

"So you're not looking for her anymore?" Mariela asked, obviously perturbed by the development. Keri looked over at Ray, not sure how to respond.

"We've been instructed to stand down for now," he answered. "But we're monitoring the situation closely."

"Mrs. Caldwell," Keri interjected, "if your phone is up and running, can you take a look at it? I sent you a photo this morning and I wanted to see if you could make any sense of it."

She heard rustling and a moment later Mariela came back on the line.

"It's still charging but I can turn it on. Give me a second to open your message," she said, and then a few seconds later asked, "What is this?"

"We think it's a message that Sarah scratched into a bedpost at a motel where she was being kept. I have a feeling she intended for us to find it. But I don't understand it. Clearly the "SC" is Sarah Caldwell. But I don't understand what she means by "xile." Is that short for "exile" or is it some kind of code?"

There was silence on the other end of the line and Keri knew both parents were churning through their memory for any relevant connection. Suddenly she heard a gasp.

"Oh my god!" Mariela shouted. "I think I know what this is. That first letter isn't an 'x.' It's meant to be a 't.' She was writing 'tile.'"

"What does that mean?" Ray asked.

"I had completely forgotten. She's wearing her sneakers, right?"

"I believe so," Keri said.

"Last year, someone stole her favorite pair of sneakers from the locker room at school. It had happened again six months ago. So when we bought her next pair we cut a tiny slit in the tongue of one shoe and put a small Tile Bluetooth device inside it, so we could find them if they were ever taken again."

"Are you saying we can track her location?" Keri asked, trying to keep her excitement in check.

"Kind of. If anyone else near her Tile is running the app, it should ping her location. We put the app on both our phones. Let me pull it up."

After a few seconds, they heard her sigh in dismay and start to cry.

"What is it?" Keri asked anxiously.

"I thought you said she was headed south to Mexico," Ed said.

"I did."

"According to this map, she's already *in* Mexico."

CHAPTER TWENTY FIVE

Sarah clung to the metal slats of the big rig undercarriage for dear life. The truck was speeding down a pothole-strewn road at high speed. She could hear sirens behind them.

The last ten minutes had been so disorienting that she didn't know what to make of them.

After screaming herself hoarse earlier in the morning, she had eventually stopped and simply lay on the floor of the undercarriage, resigned to her fate.

After a while, she was able to tell they reached the border itself because the truck had slowed to a near standstill. Moments later, she heard a loud grinding sound and a series of metal grates closed over the slats, shutting her and all the other girls into complete darkness. Some began to whimper but not as many as Sarah expected.

Maybe they're like me—too exhausted to do anything.

A thickly accented Mexican voice came over some kind of speaker system.

"We are at the border. The compartment has been closed. It is soundproof. No one outside can hear you. But if you scream, the air will go away faster. If we get through in normal time, you will have enough air. If we have problems or you scream and yell, there is probably not enough air to make it. Your best chance to live is to stay quiet and still."

If she'd had the energy, Sarah would have laughed at the notion of a bunch of them screaming and yelling in their condition. After all, she didn't even have the energy to laugh.

Even though she couldn't see anything, she could tell the truck had picked up some speed. She thought that was odd considering that the border was notorious for sometimes taking hours to cross.

After a minute, the truck came to a complete stop. Sarah started to notice that it was getting harder to breathe. The oxygen must be depleting fast.

The truck was only stopped for about thirty seconds but it felt like an eternity. When it started up again, she suspected that meant they were now in Mexico. They were going far too fast to still be in any line of vehicles.

The brief standstill was almost certainly the inspection point. And judging by how little time they'd been stopped, she was pretty sure the inspector had been bought off to let them through. She doubted Mr. Holiday would have taken the risk of transporting dozens of girls across the border in the hidden compartment of a truck without assurances that they would get through.

Her suspicions were confirmed when, just as she was beginning to feel light-headed, the grates opened. Obviously the driver felt he was out of danger. A rush of freezing air poured into the undercarriage and she gulped at it greedily.

As her head cleared, she realized that the border crossing had been her last chance at rescue.

Whatever future I have left, it's going to happen in the Bad Place.

But just as that thought passed through her brain, she heard the sirens, far away at first but then much closer. Using the slats she was gripping for support, she pulled herself right up to the side, trying to catch a glimpse of who was chasing them.

She thought she saw the words "*Policia Tijuana*" on the side of one car as it pulled up near the truck. The truck was hitting bumps on the road at such enormous speed that she could hear some of the cows above her slamming into each other and toppling over. A sudden whooshing sound made her turn her head to the middle of the undercarriage.

To her horror, she saw that a panel of the floor had suddenly slid back, leaving a coffin-sized gap. The girl who must have lying on the panel had dropped through. She was clutching the edge of truck floor with her fingertips, screaming as the lower half of her body dragged on the road below.

Two girls nearby desperately reached for her, trying to grab her forearms and pull her up. But the truck hit another bump and in an instant, the girl had disappeared from sight, leaving the others grasping at empty air.

A second later they heard screeching tires behind them, followed by a sickening thump. And then, as if on cue, the police car beside them pulled back, completely gone from view. The sirens shut off. The truck began to slow to a less bruise-inducing speed. Moments later the panel slid shut again, returning them to darkness. No one said a word.

They were all alone on the road as it sped away from the only home Sarah had ever known. She loosened her grip on the grates, lay back down on her stomach, and rested her head on her forearms. She ignored the smell of cow waste all around her and tried to sleep, to at least temporarily shut out the nightmare her life had become.

*

As Ray pulled back onto the freeway in the direction of the border, Keri checked to make sure the Tile app was working on her phone. Mariela had given her access to the account. Sure enough, there was an image on the map. Sarah's sneaker was headed south on Mexico 1 in the direction of Rosarito, a beach town only a few miles from the Pacific Ocean.

She dialed the station back and got on the line with Hillman. When he picked up she didn't even wait for him to speak.

"Lieutenant, we've changed our minds," she said firmly. "We're going after her."

"What?"

"Lieutenant," Ray piped in, "she's crossed over into Mexico. I don't know if Border Patrol and the San Diego force got the message too late or if someone at the border was paid off. But our resources down there failed and now Sarah Caldwell is in Mexico."

"How do you know that?"

"Her parents remembered they put one of those Tile devices in her sneaker months ago," Keri told him. "They checked it and it gave her location. She's in Mexico, headed southwest away from Tijuana. They gave me access so we're tracking her in real time."

"Okay then. I'll inform the Tijuana police and they'll pursue the truck."

"Are you kidding me?" Keri demanded. "Who knows how many of those guys are corrupt? For all we know, they're in on it."

"Detective Locke, you can't just go barreling into another country like a loose cannon. You don't have any law enforcement authority down there."

"Then we'll go in as very well-armed civilians," she replied. "Listen, Lieutenant, I get that you're worried about me. But I made a promise to Sarah's parents that I would bring her back. I've lost enough innocent girls for one day. I'm not losing any more."

There was silence on the other end of the line for a long moment before Hillman spoke.

"You won't have any backup."

"I'm okay with that."

"We both are," Ray said. He looked over at her and his eyes spoke volumes.

"Keep me apprised," Hillman said curtly. "And good luck."

Less than a minute after they'd hung up, Keri got another call. It was from Jamie Castillo.

"What's up, Jamie?" Keri asked.

"I couldn't help but overhear your conversation with the Lieutenant. The whole station did. And I thought I might be able to help."

"How's that?" Keri asked.

"Well, you're right about the Tijuana police. Many of them are decent officers trying to do the right thing. But the force is riddled with corruption and I'd be willing to bet a bunch of them are on Holiday's payroll."

"So you're confirming that we're on our own?" Ray asked, a little annoyed at being told the obvious.

"Not necessarily, Detective," Castillo replied, ignoring his tone. "My uncle is the chief of police in a small town not too far from Rosarito called Ejido Morelos. And I can guarantee you, he's not corrupt. In fact, he's kind of an asshole about it."

"Are you saying he can provide backup for us?" Keri asked.

"I'm not sure about that. The town only has about two thousand people. I think their entire department in under ten officers. But he might have heard something about this Bad Place if it's in the area. Or maybe they know about Mr. Holiday. I can reach out and see what he's heard."

"Thanks, Jamie," Ray said. "We'll take any help we can get. And I'm sorry about the attitude before."

"That's okay, Detective. You kind of remind me of my uncle, at least the asshole part."

Keri saw Ray bite his tongue, in part because he deserved it and partly because they had reached the border. He found the law enforcement lane and turned off his siren as they approached the guard station. He lowered his window and held out his ID. The guard looked at it, then at Ray.

"How can I help you, Detective Sands?" he asked.

"Just passing through, looking to spend a nice Saturday with our neighbors to the south."

"This wouldn't have anything to do with that report of a truck filled with missing girls from LA, would it? Because the Border Patrol has jurisdiction over that now."

"Not at all," Keri said from the passenger seat. "We're just a couple of frazzled LAPD cops looking to blow off some steam at the jai alai matches. You know how it is."

The guard looked skeptical.

"Next time, please use the civilian lanes if you're not on duty," he said sourly. Without any official reason not to, he waved them by.

"Wait until we're through the city before you pick up the pace again," Keri reminded Ray as he wended his way through the mass of cars headed into town. "We don't need to be pulled over by a Tijuana cop who might tip off Holiday."

They were at the southern edge of the city when the Tile suddenly stopped moving. The last signal was just south of La Joya.

"What does that mean?" Ray asked.

"I'm not sure. I think it could be that they're in a more isolated area now, where the Community Find function doesn't work. Or they could have just stopped moving."

"But that's right near the highway," Ray said, looking over at her. "Would this Bad Place really be in such a high-visibility area?"

"I don't know Ray but…look out!"

She pointed at the curving road in front of them. One of the lanes had been coned off and there were multiple police cars cordoning off the area.

Ray slowed down and switched into the remaining available lane. As they slowly drove by, Keri looked out the window to see several officers standing around what was obviously a dead body under a blanket tarp. There was blood and what looked like human remains scattered everywhere.

"What the hell happened here?" Ray whispered.

Keri looked over at him.

"I've got a really bad feeling that it's connected to our case."

Neither of them spoke for the remaining fifteen minutes until they reached the location of Tile ping. They pulled over to the side of the road.

"There's nothing here," Ray said.

"Yes, there is," Keri noted, pointing in the direction of a metal shed a few hundred yards away across a dried out ravine. "Look, there's a small dirt road that cuts across the ravine. If the big rig had pulled down along there, it wouldn't have been visible from the road."

Ray followed the road, crossing over the ravine, and pulled up next to the shed. They got out and both unholstered their weapons. After circling the exterior of the shed and finding nothing, Ray kicked in the door and Keri stepped inside with her gun raised.

"No one move!" she shouted as she burst in.

But the shed was empty. At least it was devoid of people. But there were lots of discarded clothes lying all along the walls. And the stench was overwhelming.

"What is that smell?" Ray asked, scrunching up his nose. "It's like a sewer in here."

Keri walked over to some clothes in a corner, blinking through her watery eyes.

"It looks like all of this stuff is drenched in urine and crap."

She kicked at various items, trying to locate Sarah's stuff.

"Aren't you supposed to hit a button and the Tile will make a sound?" Ray asked.

"Right, I forgot." Keri pushed the button and they heard a pinging noise from the far wall. She walked over and lifted a soiled blanket to find Sarah's sneakers underneath.

Her heart sinking, she looked at Ray. He was equally crestfallen.

"How are we ever going to find her now?" she asked. "She could be anywhere."

Ray opened his mouth to respond when they both heard a faint moan from the other end of the shed. They whirled in that direction, guns trained on the area where they'd heard it. But there was no one there.

They edged carefully toward the noise, which was soft but persistent. They eventually reached a clump of clothes that was slightly bigger than the others. Clearly the moaning was coming from underneath it.

Ray bent down, grabbed a clump of the clothes, and looked up at Keri. With her gun aimed at the pile, she nodded. Ray yanked the clothes away to reveal a shallow pit underneath. In it was a man lying on his side, facing away from them. He seemed barely conscious.

Keri slowly rolled him over onto his back. He groaned louder at that. He was completely naked. It was hard to tell his age because his face had been beaten so badly. Almost every inch of his body and face was covered in blood, bruises, and open, gaping wounds. He was missing most of his teeth. It looked like someone had tried to partially scalp him. And the area around both eyes was swollen and black. The eyes themselves were mere slits.

He tried to open one of them and Keri suddenly gasped. She knew who this man was. It was the person who'd set this entire nightmare in motion.

"What?" Ray said anxiously.

"Don't you recognize him?" Keri asked. "It's Dean Chisolm."

CHAPTER TWENTY SIX

Dean was almost completely unrecognizable in his current condition. But Keri knew she was right when he tried to open both eyes and nod at the sound of his name.

"What the hell happened to him?" Ray asked.

Keri started to hazard a guess when Dean opened his mouth.

"Holiday…punished me…for… Sammy," he wheezed softly.

"He must have decided to make an example of him after his brother gave up Chiqy's warehouse location," Keri said.

"So he just dumps the guy in a pit in the middle of the Mexican desert?" Ray said. "That's cold, even for this piece of crap."

"Dean," Keri said, turning her attention back to the broken creature before her, "what did Holiday do with Sarah Caldwell and the other girls? Where did he take them?"

"Had them…hosed down. Left… in vans. All went… in different… directions. All decoys but…one."

"Do you know where the real van with the girls was going?" Keri asked.

"Bad Place."

"Where is that?" Ray demanded.

"Bad…Place…" His voice was a weak, raspy whisper now.

Ray looked frustrated and was about to try again when Keri noticed something she'd overlooked before. The left side of Dean's abdomen wasn't just bloody. It was actively bleeding. She looked closer and saw what appeared to be a bullet hole. Glancing into the pit where he'd been lying on his side, she saw that a sizable pool of blood had formed.

She pointed it out to Ray and shook her head. Even if there was a hospital right next door, she doubted they could save him. He had lost too much blood. She was surprised he'd lasted this long.

She slumped down on the ground beside him, out of ideas. She wasn't sure if she should try to press Dean a little more in his remaining moments or if she should just sit with him and offer some soothing words. He was a bastard. But he was dying a death she wouldn't wish on almost anyone.

She noticed his body seize up and thought he was about to go. But then she realized he was girding himself to say something else. He parted his lips and she leaned in close.

"Hurry," he murmured quietly. "Holiday… hates her. She …fought…back. Said… he's going to…break her. Then kill her…today."

Dean took a gulp and Keri thought he was going to say more but he didn't. It took her a second to realize he was dead.

*

Sarah sat on the small twin bed in the room to which she'd been assigned. She wasn't restrained in any way. But a man with a machine gun stood at the door, facing her, his expression blank.

She looked down at herself and couldn't believe that she was clean, having showered and been ordered into a white sundress. Less than hour ago, she'd been naked save for a blanket and sneakers, covered in cow feces in the undercarriage of a truck.

But things had moved quickly after the police cars backed off. The truck had pulled off the road and she and the other girls were yanked out and forced into a shed. They were ordered to strip down.

Sarah had tried to keep her sneakers on but they hadn't allowed it. She hadn't realized that she'd been clinging to the hope that someone might find her through those shoes until they were gone. It seemed like any hope was tossed away when they were.

Holiday's guards had ordered them all out of the shed, hosed them down, and shoved them all in a van far too small for so many of them. As the van pulled out, she thought she saw a battered-looking Dean Chisolm being pulled out of the trunk of a sedan.

The van had traveled for about a half hour before arriving at what looked to be a charming hacienda. That is, if one ignored the concrete walls topped by barbed wire and the armed guards wandering the grounds.

The van drove around the back and the girls were shuttled into the house through a side entrance that led directly into a locker room. They were ordered to shower and wash their hair before finding a sundress that fit snugly from among the hundreds folded on the shelves against the wall.

Sarah did as she was told. After she was clothed she was escorted down a long hallway. She could hear crying from behind some of the doors, screaming from behind others and from one room with a metal door, she heard a strange metallic sound she couldn't identify. Even in her diminished state, it sent a shiver up her spine.

The guard brought her to a room where a man sat at a desk with a pen and sheet of paper. He looked at the number on her forehead and matched it with a room number. Then he pulled out a black marking pen and traced over the slightly faded number on her head once again. Before she left, the man gave her a nasty smile and spoke for the first time.

151

"Mr. Holiday has something special planned for you." Then he turned to the guard and said something in Spanish that she thought sounded like "room fifteen."

She turned out to be right. The guard walked her to room 15, pointed at the bed, and retreated to his spot by the door. That's how things had remained since. That is, until the door opened and Mr. Holiday walked in.

"Hello, Number Four," he said, smiling broadly to expose his gleaming white teeth. His lips curled unnaturally, as if smiling was a conscious, unfamiliar act for him. He had changed. Instead of a track suit, he had on slacks and a way-too-tight white T-shirt meant to show off his bulging muscles.

He nodded for the guard to step outside. When the door closed, he grabbed the one small wooden chair in the corner of the room and brought it over so he could sit right in front of her.

"First of all," he said as he settled in to the chair, "I wanted you to know that you look lovely in that dress. No one would have any idea what atrocities have been perpetrated on your body based on how unsullied you look right now."

Sarah stared back at him, refusing to avert her eyes. He looked annoyed for a second but quickly got over it.

"Unfortunately, this is the last time you'll feel so clean. In a moment, I'm going to walk you through the rest of the day in great detail, so there aren't any surprises. But up front, sort of the headline, if you will, is this. You have been disobedient. And the other girls know about it. So I have to make an example of you. That means that before the sun sets, you'll be dead."

He watched her closely for any reaction. What he said registered in her brain, but Sarah was so tired and sore and hopeless that couldn't muster anything approaching fear. He was clearly expecting a response, but getting none, he continued.

"But I won't kill you before you've been wrecked in every way a young girl can be. I've got a cavalcade of fellas coming your way. And you'll be awake and drug-free for every second of it. And when they've finished with you, I'll end you. But I'll be doing it bit by bit, taking you apart in chunks with my favorite long knife. And I'm going to record the whole thing to show to any other recalcitrant gals. How does that sound?"

She swallowed hard with what little saliva she had left and when she was confident she could speak, she answered him.

"It sounds like a 'roided out sadist is scared of a teenage girl," she said calmly, her eyes blazing.

If this is it, I'm not going out meekly. I'll fight, even if I only have words for weapons, until I have nothing left.

Mr. Holiday's nostrils flared and she could tell she'd hit a nerve. This time it took him several seconds to regain his placid demeanor. When he was sure he could keep his voice level, he spoke again. The acid in his voice was palpable.

"Let me tell you about a few of the gentleman callers who will be visiting you shortly."

CHAPTER TWENTY SEVEN

Keri sat quietly in the passenger seat of Ray's car, trying to keep Dean Chisolm's brutalized face and his last words out of her head. He had said that Mr. Holiday was going to kill Sarah today.

Keri had always felt like they were on a ticking clock to save the girl from a life of degradation. But it turned out that they were literally in a race to save her life.

They were back on Mexico 1, headed southeast in the same direction the big rig had been going before it reached the shed. With nothing to go on, it just made sense to keep going along the same route.

They had left Dean's body in the shed's shallow pit. They didn't have time to bury him and neither was inclined to do it anyway. They couldn't call the local authorities for fear someone might tip off Holiday. They'd have to wait until this was over to retrieve him.

As they drove in silence, scanning the horizon for a van or anything else to go on, Keri's phone rang. It was Jamie Castillo. Keri picked up immediately.

"What have you got for me, Jamie?" she asked hopefully.

"Good news, I think," the officer replied. "I just got off the phone with my uncle. He's never heard of anyone named Holiday or the Bad Place. But he has heard rumors about something called el Malas Vacaciones, which translates as the Bad Vacation."

"I don't get it," Keri said.

"He says it's sort of a sarcastic joke because el Malas Vacaciones is supposedly a posh estate called Hacienda de Los Angeles that caters exclusively to wealthy clientele. No one knows exactly what goes on there besides horseback riding, drinking top-shelf tequila, and smoking Cuban cigars."

"It sounds pretty tame to me," Ray said, "at least on the surface."

"It does," Castillo agreed. "There's never been any illegality discovered there. But my uncle suspects that the owner pays off the Rosarito cops not to ask questions."

"Who's the owner?" Keri asked.

"Officially it's a local rancher. But my uncle thinks he has unofficial American backing."

Ray looked at Keri skeptically but she was more hopeful.

"It's a lot of innuendo," she admitted. "But it does fit the profile. And the name seems like a strange composite of the terms we've been hearing. Where is this place, Jamie?"

"It's in an unincorporated area off Highway 1. I'm texting you the address now."

Keri plugged it into her GPS.

"That's less than ten minutes from here," Keri exclaimed. "In fact, the exit is only a few miles up the road."

"Can your uncle provide backup, Jamie?" Ray asked.

"He can. But it might be a while. There are only four officers on duty today and two are working a speed trap south of town. He's calling in the whole force—eight men—and then they'll meet you at el Malas Vacaciones. He estimated it would take about an hour to get there. His name is Chief Carlo Castillo."

"I appreciate his support," Keri said. "But I don't think we have that kind of time. We learned that Holiday is planning to kill Sarah Caldwell today. I don't know if that's right now, in an hour, or at midnight. Regardless, I'm not willing to wait to find out."

"You're not thinking of going in there alone?" Castillo asked incredulously.

"I'm not alone," Keri said, glancing over at Ray, who was pulling off the highway onto the dusty road that supposedly led to their destination. "I'm with my partner."

*

Twenty-five minutes later, at 11:52 a.m., a respected Rosarito physician named Paolo Moreno drove his Lexus onto the Hacienda de Los Angeles, the official name for el Malas Vacaciones.

Sitting next to him in the passenger seat with a well-hidden gun pointed at his abdomen was Detective Ray Sands. In the trunk, curled up under both a reflective windshield visor and a windbreaker, was Detective Keri Locke.

"I told you already," the nervous Dr. Moreno said for the third time, "they are only expecting me. They will be suspicious that I have a passenger."

"And like I told you," Ray growled, "it's your job to convince them I'm your buddy from LA down for a good time on a Saturday. If they don't buy it, *you* pay the price."

Keri could hear them through backseat and hoped her partner was especially convincing. After all, it was out of her hands now.

She'd done her part a few minutes earlier by pretending to be a damsel in distress, having engine trouble on the side of the road. When Moreno got out to help, Ray had snuck out from behind the car with his gun pulled.

After getting in the trunk and covering herself, and doing her best to ignore her throbbing knees and unrelenting headache, Keri listened on the drive over as Ray explained what they needed from the doctor: "Get us in, don't cause suspicion."

He had protested to them that he was only there to have a drink with friends but seemed to know that he was in an impossible situation. After a few minutes he'd given up denying the purpose of his visit and focused on pleading that the plan wasn't going to work. As they pulled up to the guard house, Ray gave him a little jab with the gun as a friendly reminder as to what was at stake.

The guard offered a friendly greeting and Dr. Moreno responded in kind. Clearly, he was a regular. Through a tiny crack between the trunk and the backseat, Keri could partially see the guard lean down and eye Ray suspiciously.

"What's up?" her partner said to him casually.

"This is my old friend from Los Angeles, Raymond," Moreno said in English. "He's staying at the beach for the day and I promised to show him a good time."

The guard asked something in Spanish that Keri couldn't understand.

"I know it's last second," Moreno replied, again in English. He obviously wanted Ray to know he wasn't secretly ratting him out. "But he leaves tonight and I didn't want him to miss out."

The guard was quiet for a moment, then said something else Keri couldn't understand. She pointed her weapon at the door of the trunk in case they checked it and she had to act quickly.

"He's okay with that," Dr. Moreno said reassuringly. "Any available girl will be more than acceptable."

The guard grunted and waved them through.

"What did he say?" Ray asked.

"He said all the quality girls have appointments. You'll have to get one from the dregs."

"Lovely," Ray said disgustedly before snapping back into focused mode. "Find a parking spot as close to the rear entrance as you can and back in so no one can see my partner getting out."

After a minute the car stopped and Ray called out to her from the front.

"Keri, can you hear me?"

"Loud and clear."

"I'm going to pop the trunk before we get out. There's a rear service entrance thirty yards to the left of the car. I don't see any guards back here but keep your eyes peeled. Wait sixty seconds after we leave so I can text you any additional intel."

"They'll take your phone once we enter the main building," Moreno warned him.

"Good to know," Ray said, then shouted back to Keri. "So I'll text you anything important before then. After that, I'm shutting down the phone so they can't access it. I have the time as eleven fifty-five a.m. Let's say we both do recon and aim for a twelve ten p.m. meet-up. Sound good?"

"Sounds like a plan," Keri said. Then she had a thought. "Hey, Dr. Moreno, where's a good, out-of-the-way place for us find each other?"

Moreno was silent for a moment and she could almost hear him thinking.

"There's a small dining room on the first floor, just off the middle of the main hallway. It's secluded and it's only used in the evenings. At this hour there shouldn't be anyone there. You can identify it by a red velvet curtain at the door."

"Of course you can," Ray said sarcastically. "You good with that, Keri?"

"Yup," she answered. "See you in fifteen."

The trunk latch popped and two doors closed. She heard footsteps crunching away on gravel as she silently counted to sixty. Ray didn't text during that time, which she considered a good sign that there was nothing pressing to share.

Keri put her own phone on silent and slowly pushed the trunk door open a few inches. The whoosh of cold air that rushed in was bracing and made her already prominent goose bumps even more pronounced.

She eased slowly out of the trunk and crouched down behind the car so she could get the lay of the land. The estate was huge, with multiple smaller building encircling the larger main house. A five-foot-high adobe wall surrounded the entire complex as far as she could see.

There were no guards in sight but she knew they had to be around. Maybe they didn't do perimeter sweeps or maybe they were just overconfident because the Rosarito cops were on the take. Either way, they were armed and Keri didn't want to run into them.

She saw the rear entrance Ray had been referencing. There appeared be a delivery truck in front of it and the door was propped open. Zipping up her jacket to fight the bitter chill in the midday air, she scurried from car to car until she was close enough to make a move for the door.

As she was about to move she saw a shadow in front of her and crouched back down. Looking up, she saw a guard on the roof with a machine gun dangling from a shoulder strap. He was facing her direction, but looking in the distance beyond the wall. After about ten seconds he turned his back and disappeared from view.

She wasn't sure when he would return but she didn't have time to wait and see. Her watch read 11:58. She was supposed to meet Ray in twelve minutes.

It's now or never.

She took a deep breath, trying to allow her body to shed some of its anxiety. Then she stepped out from behind the protection of the car and started across the exposed area between her and the building.

CHAPTER TWENTY EIGHT

With her gun stuffed in her jacket pocket and her fingers gripped around it, Keri casually ambled the last ten feet to the door, waiting for the sound of a shouted warning or a gunshot. None came. She stifled the powerful urge to run. If someone was watching, she didn't want to look suspicious.

After what felt like forever, she stepped through the open door. She sighed in relief, then looked around. She appeared to be in the kitchen, which was large and tricked out. It looked like it was intended for a full-service restaurant. Her eyes darted around the room, looking for any sign of movement.

Seeing nothing, she moved quickly over to what looked like a small map of the facility on the wall, complete with room numbers. Everything was in Spanish but she got the gist. One room in particular got her attention: Vestuario – Mujeres. She'd been in enough gyms to know that meant the women's locker room. It was as good a place as any to start and it happened to be right next door. She snapped a quick photo of the map with her phone and peeked through the kitchen door.

The hallway was empty so she darted quickly to the next room and slipped through the door. It too appeared to be empty. The place was bare bones but clean with a huge shower room and towels. She noticed that it wasn't actually a locker room in that there were no lockers.

No personal belongings allowed for these girls.

She moved toward the back where she found a shelf with stacks of white sundresses.

Is this the official uniform of the Bad Place?

She was pretty sure it was. The grotesquery of turning a brothel into a place where the women had to wear the proper attire in order to be violated made her sick to her stomach.

Fighting the urge to retch, Keri stepped over to a sink and splashed cold water on her face. There was a mirror but it was dull and gave back a warped, funhouse reflection of her.

As she stared at the strange but familiar version of herself, an idea stirred in her head. She glanced back at the shelf of dresses and checked the map she'd taken a picture of on her phone. After a moment of studying, she typed a phrase from the map into her translation app. The phrase, *sala de evaluacion,* came back as "evaluation room."

Keri glanced at the time. It was 12:01. She had to make up her mind fast. It only took a second. She decided to go for it. Moments later she was wearing one of the white sundresses and her clothes were hidden in the corner of the shower room.

She picked a dress that was loose so she could keep her gun, Taser, and phone holstered around her waist. She took her small ankle backup weapon and strapped it to her upper arm. She took her hair out of the ponytail and combed it with her fingers so that it fell into her eyes and covered part of her face. It wasn't especially impressive but there wasn't much more she could do in terms of disguising herself.

After one last useless look in the faded mirror, she stepped out into the hall and, with her head down, walked in the direction of the evaluation room. She was barefoot and the gray linoleum floor felt chilly under her feet.

The hall was empty apart from her and she found the room quickly. The door was open and an armed guard with his back to her was standing by a desk, talking to a man seated with his head down, studying a paper in front of him.

For the briefest of seconds, she considered shooting them both on principle. The thought almost made her chuckle. But apart from the noise issue, she reminded herself that it wouldn't help her find Sarah.

Instead she pulled out her Taser and, after taking a moment to marvel at the fact that she felt no nervousness at all, she moved. Without giving herself time to reconsider, she walked quickly toward them, using the guard to keep herself out of the seated man's line of vision.

Being barefoot helped. She was able to cross the ten feet to the guard silently and tased him in the kidney before he knew what was happening. He started to fall backward but she pushed him the other way so that he collapsed on the desk. The other man was so shocked that he didn't see Keri until she was on him, jabbing the Taser into the side of his neck. He slumped in his seat, conscious but incapacitated.

Keri turned her attention back to the guard, who was also conscious and moaning softly. She removed the machine gun from around his shoulder, took the plastic cuffs from his waistband, and tied his own hands behind his back before easing him to the ground and dragging him to the corner of the room. Then she tased him again, this time in the chest.

She glanced back at the man at the desk and saw that he was sloppily reaching toward his own waistband, trying futilely to grab the gun resting there. Keri stepped back toward him and zapped him in the chest. He slumped again, his arms dangling at his sides.

She took his gun out of the holster and set it on the far corner of the desk. Then she hurried over to the door, closed it, and locked it. She had been lucky no one had walked by. Glancing at her watch, she saw that it was 12:06. She was supposed to meet Ray in the dining room in four minutes.

Keri returned to the desk and looked at the sheet of paper the man had been reviewing, hoping to see Sarah's name. It wasn't there but there were room numbers on the left side with other numbers to the right.

Keri remembered how Sergeant Henriksen had said Holiday wrote number on all the girls' foreheads. She remembered seeing Lanie with that big "11" staring back at her. She rifled through the other papers to see if there were any that matched names to numbers but none did.

The man in the chair stirred and she looked over at him.

I don't need a sheet of paper. I've got the human equivalent right here.

She grabbed his gun from the desk and took a step toward him.

"Which room is this girl in?" she demanded, holding up a photo of Sarah on her phone.

"*No habla inglés,*" he muttered.

"That's too bad. Because if you can't speak English, you're no good to me. And since I can't have you getting in my way…" She didn't finish the sentence, instead just taking the safety off his gun and pressing it against his forehead.

He broke immediately.

"Okay, okay. She's in room fifteen."

"You know I'm going to knock you out, right?" she warned him. "And if it turns out she's not there, I'm going to come back and shoot you in the head while you're asleep."

"She's there. I swear."

Without responding, Keri set the safety back on his gun and whacked him in the side of the head with the butt of it. He collapsed in a heap. As with the guard, she grabbed his hands and tied them behind the chair with his own plastic cuffs. Then she grabbed a few of the tissues from the box sitting on the edge of table and jammed them in his mouth. She repeated the process with the guard, who offered no resistance.

It was 12:11. She was a minute late. Poking her head out of the room, she still saw no one and began to suspect that the girls were being held on the second floor, which would explain why there were no other guards down here.

She hurried down the hall and rounded a corner. The dining room with the velvet curtain was up on the right. She scampered in with her gun raised. The room was empty. Then she heard a creak to her right and swung in that direction. She was close to pulling the trigger when she realized it was Ray, who had been crouching behind an anteroom wall that jutted out.

"I almost shot you," she hissed.

"That would have sucked."

"Yes—in more ways than one. Where's the doctor?"

"He had to take a little 'nap.' I left him lying on a lounge chair by the hot tub in the men's locker room with a washcloth over his face. He looks like he's having a spa day. I've been hiding in one of the bathroom stalls until a few minutes ago so I wouldn't get discovered. You have any better luck?"

"As a matter of fact, I did. I found some sort of scheduling guy and convinced him to tell me which room Sarah is in."

"Which one?" Ray asked excitedly, louder than he meant to.

"Fifteen. And I know where that is in the house."

She showed him the map on the phone. Room 15 was almost directly above their current location. Ray shook his head.

"Unfortunately, it looks like there's only one way to reach it— the main stairwell in the central foyer. And that had guards at the top and the bottom of the stairwell. I saw them when I came in."

"There has to be some other way up there," Keri insisted. "After all, some of these perverts are really old. They can't take the stairs."

"You know, now that you mention it, I did see some old dude in the locker room go into what looked like a closet and never come out. Maybe it's some kind of elevator."

They looked at the map but it wasn't definitive one way or the other.

"Can we get in there to check it out?" Keri asked.

"It would look awfully suspicious to anyone in there, especially with you in that sundress. What's that all about anyway?"

Keri was about to answer when she had an idea.

"I think I know how we can get upstairs but we'll have to move fast."

Five minutes later they entered the locker room. Ray was wearing the uniform of the guard Keri had knocked out in the evaluation room. He had the machine gun strapped over his shoulder and held Keri tightly by the forearm, as if she was his prisoner.

She was still wearing the sundress but now she walked with a pronounced, fake limp. She hoped no one asked questions because neither knew enough Spanish to answer convincingly.

Several men stared as they went by, but none said anything as they stepped into the closet and shut the door. Sure enough, it was small, old-fashioned, cage elevator with a pull-across gate. Ray hit "2' and the metal contraption shook violently before climbing slowly.

When it reached the second floor, they stepped out and realized they were in a smaller lounge area. Two men sat in easy chairs. One was reading a paper while sipping a drink. The other was watching a soccer game on television. Neither gave them a second glance.

They moved to the door and Ray stuck his head out. Stepping back, he leaned down and whispered in her ear.

"There are four guards; the one at the top of the stairwell and three standing outside rooms. How do you suggest we take care of them?"

"We could shoot them all," Keri suggested jokingly.

"That would take care of them," Ray agreed. "But it might get the attention of the half dozen other guards I saw downstairs."

"Okay, so no shooting then. The Taser worked pretty well for me in the evaluation room. Want to try that?"

"Sure," Ray said. "How do we want to play it to get them close?"

"I was thinking we could go with the trick we used in the Harwood case."

"I like the way your mind works, partner," Ray said, smiling broadly despite their situation.

Keri noticed the guy reading the paper look up curiously.

"We better get moving," she said. "The natives are getting restless."

Ray nodded. They stepped out into the hallway. The two of them hadn't taken more than a couple of steps before Keri collapsed on the floor.

CHAPTER TWENTY NINE

As the guards drew closer, Keri's body seized up and began shaking uncontrollably. Ray looked over at the other guards as if uncertain what to do.

As one of the guards knelt down to get a closer look at her, through squinted eyes she saw Ray back away, looking frightened. The guard at the top of the stairwell looked confused and asked the fast approaching Ray something in Spanish.

"*Qué pasa?*"

"*Qué pasa?*" Ray repeated back to him, getting closer.

The stairwell guard, suspicious of that response, grabbed his radio and was just about to speak when Ray tased him in the shoulder. The man's knees buckled and Ray caught him just before he slumped to the ground. In one swift motion, he punched the guard in the face and the man went from woozy to unconsciousness.

Keri saw this and made her move. She reached up and grabbed the collar of the guard hovering over her, as if grasping desperately for help. But before he knew it, she had yanked him down. As he toppled over her, she lifted her knee and made sure it collided with the side of his head. He crumpled in a heap at her feet.

The other two guards weren't sure if what happened was accidental or not. Their indecision was costly. Keri shot her arm out again, as if having another seizure. But this time she had the Taser in her hand and jammed it against the closer guard's ankle. He dropped to the ground and she got him again in the neck.

The last remaining guard, now finally aware he'd been duped, raised his machine gun and started to aim it at Keri. But he hadn't completed the motion before Ray was at his side, pressing his Taser into the guard's shoulder and easing him to the ground before hitting him with a second jolt in the chest.

"Were we too noisy?" Keri asked as she got to her feet.

I don't think so, but we better move quickly. We can shove them in an empty room but who knows when they'll bring another John up? And if they see the whole floor unprotected, they'll send out the alarm pretty fast."

"Well there's room twenty-two," Keri said pointing. "Let's get Sarah and put them all in there."

"Agreed," Ray said. "You ready?"

"Are you kidding? I've been waiting a long time for this."

Ray smiled and slowly twisted the doorknob. It gave and the door opened easily. They could hear the strains of what sounded like the Def Leppard song "Pour Some Sugar on Me" coming from inside. He opened it more and Keri stepped in the room.

It took everything she had to stifle her horror. Sarah was indeed lying on the bed. Both her arms and legs were tied to bedposts. Her eyes were squeezed shut. Her body was covered in red welts.

A man stood above her on the bed. From the back it was hard to tell his age. But he was tall and skinny. He wore a long black cape and nothing else. In his hand was a large candle holder with a lit candle.

Keri and Ray stood frozen, unsure what to make of the situation. Then the man tipped the candleholder to the side.

"Here it comes," he giggled as a splash of hot wax landed on Sarah's stomach. She flinched but didn't make a sound.

After that, it took barely a second for Ray to reach him. He rushed the man and clipped him in the back with his forearm. The man dropped the candleholder as he lost his balance and careened to the right. Somehow, as he started to fall, Ray sprinted around the side of the bed and caught him in his arms before he hit the ground.

Once he had him securely, he pinned the man against the far wall with his left hand as he repeatedly punched him in the face with his right. As he did, Keri hurried to the bed and snuffed out the candle flame before it erupted.

The man, all rubbery legs, sagged to the floor. But Ray grabbed him and physically moved him to the window, which was closed. He opened it and started to push the barely conscious guy out.

"Ray, stop!" Keri hissed, afraid he was going to ruin their plan. "A guy falling from the sky isn't going to help us get Sarah out of here. Just knock him out and bring those other guards in the hall in here. We've got to hurry."

Ray seemed to come to his senses. He gave the skinny guy one last punch. Then he gingerly placed the now-unconscious man on the ground and hurried back into the hall to collect the others.

Keri turned her attention to Sarah, who was staring at her with wide eyes.

"Is this real?" she asked. "Did you really say my name?"

Keri forced herself to ignore the girl's battered body and focused on her eyes instead.

"I did, Sarah. My name is Keri. I'm a detective in Los Angeles. That's my partner, Ray. Your parents reached out to us because they were worried. We've been looking for you since yesterday afternoon. And we're going to get you out of here."

Sarah started to cry but forced it down. Instead she swallowed and asked the question that had been eating at her for hours.

"What about Lanie? Is she okay?"

"She's okay," Keri answered as she pulled out her Swiss Army knife and began cutting the ties holding the girl's arms in place. She didn't mention the smeared number "4" on her forehead. "We found her at the motel where you all were being held. All the girls there are okay."

"Did you catch Chiqy?"

"We did," Keri assured her and nodded at Ray as he dragged another guard into the room. "That guy put him in the hospital. He'll be going to jail from there."

As she untied Sarah, Keri tried to give the girl's body a once-over without being obvious. She was covered in wax burns. Otherwise, she seemed bruised but okay. They had caught her in time, she realized, in a wave of relief.

"Did you catch Mr. Holiday yet?" Sarah asked, trying to keep the fear out of her voice but failing.

"Not yet. Our first priority is to get you and the other girls to safety. We'll get Holiday but it's not our focus right now. Do you think you can walk?"

Sarah nodded and Keri helped ease her up to a sitting position. The sundress was lying neatly folded on the table next to the bed. Keri grabbed it and helped ease it over Sarah's head.

"I might need a little help standing up," the girl whispered, as if she was embarrassed. "I've been lying in that position for hours and my hands and feet are pretty numb."

Keri forced the rage she felt rising in her gut back down. This wasn't the time for that. Right now she needed to be a caretaker, a protector, a source of understanding and support.

"No problem," she said, easing Sarah upright and helping support her weight as they hobbled to the door.

Ray dragged the last guard into the room and then stood up and gave Sarah a broad grin.

"Hi. I'm Ray. It's nice to meet you."

"Hi, Ray," she replied, smiling wanly.

"We're leaving this place," he assured her.

"But not without the other girls, right?"

"We'll get them too," Keri promised. "Do you know how many are up here?"

"When they brought me up, there were five others too. But they have over twenty more they took out back to a place they call the stable. Who knows how many girls they're keeping back there."

166

"Okay, we'll start with the girls up here," Ray said. "They're unguarded so there's no better time to get them than right now. We'll move on to the others once you all are safe. Good plan?"

"Good plan," Keri agreed as she grabbed one of the guards' machine guns and slung it over her shoulder, then turned her attention to Sarah. "I want you to stay in this room and peek out at the stairwell. We'll be subduing the men in the in the other rooms. If you see anyone coming up the stairs, give a high whistle to warn us. Can you do that?"

"My mouth is pretty dry but I think so."

"If that doesn't work, just call out my name, got it?"

Sarah nodded. Keri and Ray moved as quickly as they could after that, quietly entering rooms, tasing unsuspecting johns and freeing the five girls also tied to bedposts. They were all in bad shape but none had been brutalized as much as Sarah. They all huddled together in a small group.

No one came upstairs but just as they were all preparing to return to the lounge room, a crackling voice came over one of the guard's radios.

"*Informe!*" ordered a loud, authoritative voice.

"I don't know what means," Ray said. "But it can't be good."

"That's Mr. Holiday," said a waifish girl with "28" written on her forehead. She couldn't have been older than thirteen. "He's asking for a report."

"We better get moving," Keri said urgently. "It won't be long before he sends others up to check on things. We need to be out of the building by then."

"Back the way we came?" Ray asked.

"I think so," Keri agreed. "Why don't you go into the lounge? Those two guys won't pay you any attention. Tase the newspaper guy first. Then go for soccer-watcher. I'll come in after a five-count to help with him when he's looking your way."

Ray nodded and walked through the door.

"Stay here. We'll get you in a moment," Keri told the girls, before taking a deep breath and stepping into the lounge.

She quickly took in the situation. The man who'd been reading the paper was slumped in his chair. The guy watching soccer was staring at the fast-approaching Ray with saucer eyes, unsure what to make of the situation. Keri rushed to him, reaching him just as he started to open his mouth.

She and Ray got to him at the same time. She jolted him in the back as Ray got him in the shoulder. He keeled over and dropped lazily to the floor. As his body landed on the ground, they could hear more chatter on the radios in the other room.

"I don't think we have much time. Get the girls," Keri said without hesitation as she hurried over to open the elevator gate. Ray brought the girls over and they all squeezed in. Keri hit the "1" button and prayed the rickety contraption could hold all their weight.

The thing hummed to life, vibrating like a dog shaking water out of its fur. As it finally started descending, they could hear loud footsteps and shouted voices in the hall outside the lounge.

It seemed to take forever to reach the ground. When the elevator finally stopped, they all piled out, Ray leading the way with six girls behind him. Keri brought up the rear.

As they stepped out into the locker room, eight men—most wearing only towels or completely naked—turned to stare at them. They all looked shocked but it was only when they saw Keri, wearing the sundress uniform but with a machine gun slung over her shoulder, that they knew something was horribly wrong.

Some scurried off to the shower area. Others rushed to their lockers. One of them, without any clothes, turned and ran out into the main hallway.

"We've got to get out of here," Ray said. "They'll be here any minute."

It didn't take that long.

CHAPTER THIRTY

Only a moment later, two men burst through the door, machine guns raised. They looked around wildly.

"Get back," Keri ordered the girls as she stepped forward.

As the six young women in sundresses dove back toward the elevator, the two Los Angeles detectives stepped forward, raised their guns, and fired at the still disoriented guards. Both men dropped instantly.

"Keep your eye on the door," Keri told Ray. "There'll be more of them any second. I've got to move these girls out of the line of fire."

Ray nodded and Keri turned her attention to the group that had piled in the elevator. Glancing around, she saw a man peeking out from behind the tiled wall of a shower.

"This way," she ordered and the girls ran out, following her the short way to the stalls. She found one that was unoccupied and hurried them into it. She was about to pull the curtain across when Sarah grabbed her wrist.

"I want to help," she said more firmly than Keri expected. Suddenly the sound of gunfire erupted from the main part of the locker room.

"Help by keeping them safe. Stay here."

Then she pulled the curtain across the stall and hurried back. She saw Ray pinned down behind the steam room wall. He looked to be unhurt but he couldn't take a shot without exposing himself.

"How many?" she mouthed to him silently.

He held up three fingers. She held up her left hand to show five fingers of her own, then made a fist and held up one finger, then two. Ray realized she was counting down and nodded again.

When she got to four, he fired off a few shots, not so much hoping to the hit the guards as to distract them.

On five, Keri stepped out from behind the wall she'd been using as cover, locked onto a guard, and fired. He fell to the floor as his cohorts turned in her direction. She moved back behind the wall as a spray of bullets sent tile chunks flying by her head.

Ray took advantage of the moment to lean out and fire at the men. Keri didn't know the result but figured their attention would be away from her so she stepped out again to fire, only to find the remaining guards lying on the ground. Ray had gotten them both.

Keri immediately ran to the door and locked and closed it. Then she pushed one of the guards' bodies up against it to slow the entry of anyone else about to enter. Refusing to think about the larger meaning of what she was doing, she rolled another body on top of the first.

Ray saw what she was doing and joined in, tossing the bodies of the remaining three guards on top of the first two so that they created a kind of human blockade.

"Hold them off," Keri said as grabbed one of the machine guns lying on the ground, "I'm going to give this to Sarah as a precaution. Back in a sec."

Ray nodded and assumed a position behind a locker to the right of the door. Keri ran back to the showers. She saw several men poking their heads out of stalls. A soon as they saw her, they darted back in.

She pulled back the curtain to find five girls cowering at the back of the stall. Sarah was standing in front of them defiantly, holding a bottle of shampoo like a weapon.

"I've got something better for you," Keri said. "You're only to use it as a last resort. Keep the curtain closed. If someone pulls it back and it's not me or Ray, start firing, okay?"

Sarah nodded. Keri gave her the twenty-second primer on how to use the weapon.

"This is a converted AK-47 automatic rifle; simple to use. Take the safety off here. Use the sight to fire. You understand?" she asked.

"I think so," Sarah said uncertainly.

"Just don't fire until you know who you're shooting at. And be careful. This thing has a serious kick."

Just then, they heard what sounded like an explosion.

"Stay here!" Keri ordered before running back to the locker area.

The room was smoky and it took her a second to get her bearings. After a moment, she realized what had happened. Someone had used some kind of explosive to blow the door, which was now gone. Body parts from the dead guards were strewn everywhere. The walls were covered in blood and worse.

She looked around for Ray but couldn't see him. She did see someone carrying a machine gun step through the smoke into the room. She waited until she was sure it was a guard before opening up on him. He fell and she heard two other voices yell in Spanish as they retreated back down the hallway.

There was a grunt from across the room and she looked over in that direction. She peered through the smoke and saw what looked like two men struggling. As she stepped cautiously forward, the scene became clear.

Ray was rolling around on the ground with a muscular man with short brown hair in a tight white T-shirt. She assumed it was Mr. Holiday. The explosion had caused the overhead sprinklers to go off and they were being drenched in water. Neither had a gun and neither seemed able to get the upper hand as they slipped on the slick tile floor.

They were in such close quarters that Keri didn't feel confident taking a shot amid all the smoke and water and general carnage. Suddenly she heard gunfire outside the room and turned, waiting for someone to burst in on her. No one did.

She turned back to the fight. She was less than ten feet away now and saw that Ray had gotten the advantage. He had Holiday pressed up against a locker with his left forearm and was punching him hard with his right hand.

Holiday tried to squirm loose to no avail. But as Ray adjusted his feet to keep his traction, one of them slipped on the wet floor and he tumbled forward to the ground. She heard a thud as his head hit the floor. He didn't move.

With a clear line of fire and without a second thought, Keri lifted her machine gun and pulled the trigger. It jammed.

Holiday, oblivious to her, needed only a second to regroup. As he caught his breath, he reached down to his ankle and Keri saw him pull a knife out of a sheath attached there. He raised it high and Keri saw the four-inch blade glimmer in the lights.

Without hesitation, she ran at him and leaped as he started to bring the knife down toward the back of Ray's skull. He was halfway there when she landed on his back, sending him careening forward into another locker.

She heard the knife clatter to the ground as she wrapped her legs around his waist and her arms around his neck. She yanked up hard under his chin and felt him grunt in pain. With her left arms squeezed tight around neck, she jabbed at his eyes repeatedly with her right thumb.

Even as he tried to swat her arm away, she knew she made contact at least once as her nail plunged into soft tissue and she heard him cry out. She held on for dear life as he swung back and forth, trying to dislodge her from his back. And then suddenly, he stopped.

She knew immediately that something was wrong but couldn't figure out what it is. And then she heard him speak in a wheezy growl filled with malice.

"I'm going to make you cry before I kill you," he snarled.

Without warning, he threw himself backward, falling toward the tile floor. Keri, suddenly underneath him, knew she was about to take the brunt of the collision and of his weight landing on top of her.

She braced herself, wrapping her arms around his torso and hunching her shoulders forward so her back would hit the floor before her head did.

She landed hard, feeling the crush of the tile under her shoulder blades and then Holiday's body against her ribs. The air shot out of her chest and she gasped desperately. The back of her head hit the tile but not as hard as she feared. She felt Holiday start to roll off her and tried to keep a grip on him. He shook her off easily.

She looked up through the water splashing her face from the sprinkler above and saw him slowly pulling himself to his feet. He was hunched over and breathing heavily. His right eye was in bad shape, as blood ran down from it, covering the right side of his face and dripping off his jaw.

She remembered her gun in the holster under her sundress but knew she couldn't get to it. She was having trouble just breathing.

After several seconds of just standing there, staring at her with his one good eye, he spoke. His voice was surprisingly calm and quiet.

"I know who you are. You're the cop who saves missing children. The one who couldn't find her own daughter. Locke, right?"

Keri willed herself to slowly inch her right hand across her body so she could grab the emergency ankle pistol hidden under the sleeve on her left arm. But she couldn't do it. Her body wasn't responding. She was totally exposed, too weak and short of breath to do anything. Ray still lay unconscious, only feet away from her. Holiday continued, slightly louder and more confident now.

"Such a sad story, your life. And now it's about to end. I wonder, will the last thought in your head before I smash in your skull be of how your little girl is suffering the same fate as all my little whores here? Will it be of the degradation she'll endure until it's finally just too much and she decides to end it all? Will it be how you died a failure? Or will that last thought just be 'ow' as your brains turn to pulp?"

He took a step forward and raised his knee high. His steel-toed boot rose above her head and seemed to hang there in suspended animation.

"You're the one who's going to be saying 'ow,'" said a voice from behind her.

172

Holiday looked over to see who was speaking and Keri saw genuine shock on his face.

"Number Four?" he said, his voice a mix of surprise and fear.

Suddenly Keri heard a hail of gunfire and saw Holiday fly backward and hit the ground. She glanced over to see Sarah Caldwell, machine gun held high, walk slowly past her, carefully sidestep Ray, and stand right over her tormentor.

Lying on his back, he tried to wriggle backward, even as blood sputtered from his lips.

"You were going to kill me, Mr. Holiday," Sarah said in a soft voice, almost a whisper. "You were going to wreck me. You were going to take me apart in chunks. You were going to make an example of me. But look, I'm still standing, Mr. Holiday. You didn't break me. I'm walking out of here, head held high. And guess what? You and your fake tan and your shiny white teeth are leaving here in a body bag. How does it feel to know it was a girl who did this to you, Mr. Holiday?"

He opened his mouth to speak but before a word came out, she sprayed him with bullets, keeping her finger on the trigger until she'd emptied the magazine. His body tensed and then slumped back down to the ground.

The locker room became strangely quiet. The sprinklers had shut off. There was no more gunfire. Keri thought she heard voices in the distance but she couldn't be sure as her ears were still ringing from the explosion and gunfire. She stared at Holiday's unmoving body. Blood oozed out of him.

Sarah dropped the gun on the ground and sat down next to Keri, a vacant look on her face. Keri was about to speak when she heard a commotion from the doorway and looked over. Sarah started to reach for the useless weapon.

"Don't," Keri yelled at her. "They're the police."

Four men entered the room, all carrying handguns and wearing uniforms that bore the words "*Policia de Ejido Morelos.*" One of them, a short man in his forties with a thick mustache and a barrel chest, stepped forward.

"Detective Keri Locke?" he asked far more calmly than one might expect under the circumstances.

"Yes. Chief Castillo?"

"I am," he said in strongly accented but meticulous English. "I am sorry we are late. My men have secured the area. May we render you assistance?"

"You may," she said, swallowing hard and trying to ignore the odd dizziness she suddenly felt before proceeding. "My partner over

173

there needs to be checked out. He hit his head. This is Sarah. She needs medical attention as well. She's been subjected to…a lot. There are five other girls hiding in a shower back there. Be careful. There are men back there too. Clients, unarmed, I think. Are the other girls okay?"

"Yes, Detective," Chief Castillo assured her. "We found over sixty young women in a warehouse out back. I have men with them and we are calling in medical assistance for them from both Rosarito and Tijuana."

Keri watched as another officer knelt down next to Ray and gently began examining him.

"Do not worry," Castillo said, sensing her concern. "All my men have emergency medical training. We live in a small town and wear many hats. May I examine you?"

"Her first," Keri said, nodding at Sarah. "I'm worried her cuts will get infected."

"Of course. And may I say you are exactly as my niece described you."

"How's that?" Keri asked.

"Very stubborn. Very tough. And very devoted."

"Oh, that's nice," she replied lazily, her dizziness turning into full-on light-headedness. "You know, I may need to get checked out after all. I hit my head earlier and I'm feeling a little woozy. Can someone…"

And then everything went dark.

CHAPTER THIRTY ONE

Twenty-four hours later, flanked by Jamie Castillo and Manny Suarez, Keri walked into the lobby of Hospital Angeles Tijuana after checking out just hours before. Her body was one big bruise and her head still ached. But at least she was mobile.

After spending the night there for observation, she'd been released this morning with a stern warning from the neurologist: get an MRI in Los Angeles. He was worried that so much head trauma in such a short period of time might have permanent effects.

Lieutenant Hillman had stayed in Los Angeles to handle the remainder of the case and sent Castillo and Saurez down to help out there. They'd picked her up and taken her back to the hotel room they got so she could clean up. Jamie gave her some clothes she'd collected from her apartment.

When she stepped out of the bathroom, Jamie was sitting on the bed.

"Where's Manny?" Keri asked.

"He went downstairs to get some waters. He'll be back in a minute." She had an odd expression on her face.

"What's wrong?" Keri asked her. "You look like you're going to be sick."

"No," Jamie answered. "I just…I was wondering…are you and Detective Sands ever going to tell each other how you feel?"

Keri's mouth dropped open. For one of the only times in her life she was genuinely speechless. Just then, Manny opened the door. He could tell something was off.

"Did I come at a bad time?" he asked.

"No," Keri said quickly, giving Castillo a clear "keep your mouth shut" look. "It's actually a perfect time. I'd love a water."

Refreshed, moderately functional, and desperate to avoid any more uncomfortable conversations, she insisted on returning to the hospital as soon as possible to check on the others. So they headed out. Manny drove and Keri made sure to sit in the front seat with him.

"What room is Ray Sands in?" she asked politely to one of the hotel receptionists when they arrived.

The lady looked at her skeptically. Jamie said something in Spanish to which the woman replied warmly. Castillo turned to Keri.

"He's on the fourth floor—room 414."

"Do I look that bad?" Keri asked as they walked to the elevator.

"Nope. I'm just that charming," Castillo answered.

When they got to Ray's room, the door was open and he was sitting in a chair next the bed, tying his shoes.

"Should you be out of bed?" Castillo asked as they all filed in.

Ray looked up to reveal a big bandage on his forehead.

"Oh jeez," Saurez said, taken aback.

"It's not as bad as it looks," Ray insisted. "They just had to give me some stitches and they want me to keep this on until tonight."

"Stitches in your head doesn't sound great, man," Suarez noted skeptically.

"I'm not as bad off as this one," Ray said, pointing at Keri. "How many blows to the head have you had in the last day?"

"Hey, the doctors gave me an all-clear to leave this morning," she lied. They'd let her go but it was far from an all-clear.

"Knowing this town, I bet you paid them off," Ray muttered.

"Nice to see you're back to your old self, Detective," Castillo said sarcastically.

"Always," Ray said, flashing her a big grin. "Now let's get out of here. By the way, where's your uncle? He was gone before I woke up and got to thank him."

"He had to get back to Ejido Morelos last night. With so few officers, he couldn't afford to stay away for long."

"He really saved us," Keri told her as they all walked down the hallway together. "Thanks for reaching out to him."

"No problem. That's what Castillos do, no matter which side of the border you're on. He was pretty impressed with you guys. Apparently you two took down over a dozen of those assholes by yourselves."

"With a little help from Sarah Caldwell," Keri noted quietly.

"Where is she, by the way?" Ray asked as they reached the elevator. "I was hoping to check in on her."

"I asked," Keri said. She's down a floor. Her parents are with her. They got in last night and stayed in the room with her. They slept on cots."

"Have you been to see her yet?" Suarez asked.

"No. I wanted to give her time with her folks and to just decompress, you know? She's been through so much. And she had to kill a man. I don't know what kind of state she's in."

"I think we'll let you and Ray do that without us," Castillo said. "We'll wait downstairs for you. We collected Ray's car and we can all drive back when you're ready. I know Hillman wants you back so you can do that interview with Downtown Division tomorrow."

"Ugh," Keri said. "I was hoping that after all this, I'd get a pass."

"You may still," Suarez said. "Because it's so high profile, Hillman has to go by the book but I get the sense this is a formality. Considering who died on that parking ramp, I don't think anyone's going to push too hard. Besides, those postcards you found led to twenty-nine girls being rescued. They're actively seeking twelve others. That's a big deal. You may get a reprimand but not much more."

"I hope you're right, Manny," Keri said, less confident than he was.

The elevator arrived and Ray hit "3" followed by "L." When the doors opened he and Keri stepped out.

"See you in a few," he said as the doors closed to take the others to the lobby. Then he turned to Keri. "Which room?"

"303."

They walked down the hall in silence for a bit, neither sure what they would say to Sarah, both a little uncertain what to say to each other.

"Have they been able to identify Holiday yet?" he asked.

"Not yet. He burned off all his fingerprints and those pearly whites were fake. Edgerton's going to try to do facial recognition but he's not optimistic. We may never know who this guy really is."

They walked silently for a few more awkward steps.

"Did someone collect Chisolm's body?" Ray finally asked.

"Yeah, Manny and Castillo helped the locals find it. He's being shipped back next week after they do an autopsy. I'm worried that his brother might do something to himself out of guilt when he finds out."

"Out of our hands, Keri. We can't save everyone."

She nodded and stopped walking.

"I know. But I like to try."

"I know you do, Tinkerbell."

"Aw shucks, Gulliver, you're gonna make me blush," she said, and before he could respond added, "This is her room."

She knocked on the door softly and the voice of Mariela Caldwell responded.

"Come in."

They stepped into the room to find Ed and Mariela sitting on chairs on either side of the bed where Sarah was propped up.

"Do you mind if we say hi?" Keri asked hesitantly.

Mariela responded by getting up, walking over, and hugging her so hard that she worried she might cry out from the pain. When she finally let her go, Ed, who had been embracing Ray, took her place, wrapping his arms around her and squeezing tighter than she thought possible.

"Thank you, thank you. Thank you for saving our baby," Mariela said repeatedly through hiccupping sobs.

Keri couldn't think of anything to say so she merely nodded. Sarah, who was looking at her with watery eyes, waved them over.

As Keri approached, she took the girl in. Almost every inch of her exposed skin was covered in bandages.

"How are you doing?" Keri asked.

Sarah took her hand and gave it a little squeeze.

"A lot better than I would be doing without you guys."

"Thank you," Ray said. "But from what Keri tells me, neither of us would be here if not for you."

Sarah nodded but didn't respond. Keri sensed that she wasn't sure yet how to feel about what she'd done.

"When do you get to go home?" she asked, changing the subject.

"In two days," Sarah said, brightening. "That's Tuesday, right? I kind of lost track."

"Yep, that's Tuesday. What about the other girls?"

"Most everyone should be able to go by the end of the week. At least that's what they said in the meeting."

"Meeting?" Keri said.

"Um, yeah," she said a little shyly. "I kind of organized a meeting earlier today. So we could all sort of talk and stuff. I also wanted to create a contact list for anyone who wants to stay in touch."

"You know the prosecutors will have a list of everyone," Ray said.

"This is something different. It's just for us. I figured that we're going to need each other over the next few months. You know, as we try to get past this. I'm hoping to create a support system, especially for the girls who might have lost hope. I want to create a community, like a family almost, that they can turn to when they need it."

Keri wiped away a tear and smiled.

"Sarah, you are just about the most amazing person I've ever met," she said. "And I've met some pretty amazing people."

"Likewise."

Keri gave Ray a glance and, knowing exactly what it meant, he stood up.

"Well, we're going to get out of the way of the Caldwell family reunion. We're expected back in LA. But please, you have our numbers. If there's anything you need, don't hesitate to call."

"Even if it's just to talk," Keri added.

They survived another round of hugs before heading out.

"You think she's going to be okay?" Ray asked as they headed back down the hall to the elevator.

"I don't know. The things she's been through...I don't know how someone moves beyond that to recreate a normal life. The scars she has on the outside are probably nothing compared to what she's dealing with on the inside. But I think that if there's any girl I've met who could come out the other side of this okay, it's her."

When they got to the lobby, Castillo was waiting for them.

"Where's Manny?" Keri asked.

"He's bringing the car around," she said. "Oh, I almost forgot. Now that it's been twenty-four hours since you almost died, I'm giving you your phones back."

"What?" Ray demanded.

"Hillman ordered me not to return them until now. Something about giving yourselves time to recover," she said as she pulled their phones out of her handbag.

"To be honest, I hadn't even thought about it," Keri said

"I don't know if that's a good or a bad thing," Castillo replied.

Manny pulled up and they got in the car. As they drove to the hotel, Keri felt herself starting to drift off. Ray was next to her in the backseat and she rested her head on his shoulder. He glanced down at her and smiled, but said nothing.

She had just closed her eyes when they hit a bump and she was jarred awake. Glancing at her phone, she saw that she had four messages.

May as well check them.

There was one from Keith, the mall security guard who'd helped them out. He wanted to know how things had gone with the case. He also said he had definitely decided to apply to the police academy and was hoping for some advice. He said he was too afraid to call Ray. She chuckled to herself at that and made a mental note to call him after she'd recovered a bit.

The next message was from Susan Granger, the former teen prostitute living at the group home. She too wanted to know how the case was going and if her information was helpful.

Keri didn't feel up to talking to her just yet either. But she texted her back saying the info had been very helpful, that the girl was safe and that she'd call her tomorrow after she'd had a day to recover from her bumps and bruises. She ended by writing, "Thanks, Nancy Drew!"

The third message was from Hillman, saying he needed her to be at the station tomorrow afternoon for her interview with Downtown Division. He said he would accompany her, as would her union rep. He also said she should let him do most of the talking.

Is that a good sign? He sounds like he's got my back but I never know with that guy.

The last message was from Mags. It was short and to the point.

"Call me back when you can."

Keri didn't think it was possible after everything her body had been through, but she felt a pit in her stomach and a surge of adrenaline at the same time.

When they got to the hotel, she excused herself and went into an empty conference room, where she called Mags. Her friend picked up on the first ring.

"Are you okay, darling?"

"I'm fine. Just a couple of concussions, a shot back, crushed shoulders, bruised ribs, and some swollen knees. What going on? It sounded urgent."

"I'm afraid it is. You know that ad I put on Craigslist, the one intended for the Black Widower?"

"Of course."

"He's responded."

Even as a chill ran down her spine, Keri forced herself to stay calm. She stood there, frozen, for a long time. Slowly, she allowed a feeling to grow inside her, one that she thought had permanently disappeared the other night when she'd watched that brown van turn the corner and drive out of sight with her daughter inside.

It was hope.

A TRACE OF CRIME
(A Keri Locke Mystery—Book 4)

"A dynamic story line that grips from the first chapter and doesn't let go."
--Midwest Book Review, Diane Donovan (regarding Once Gone)

From #1 bestselling mystery author Blake Pierce comes a new masterpiece of psychological suspense.

In A TRACE OF CRIME (Book #4 in the Keri Locke mystery series), Keri Locke, Missing Persons Detective in the Homicide division of the LAPD, follows a fresh lead for her abducted daughter. She winds her way through a twisted underworld, and step by step, she gets closer to finding her daughter.

Yet she has no time. Keri is assigned a new case: a dad calls from an affluent community and reports that his teen daughter vanished on the way home from school.

Shortly after, ransom letters arrive. Twisted, filled with riddles, they make it clear that there is little time to save the girl. They also make it clear that this is the work of a diabolical killer who is toying with them.

Keri and the police must scramble to find the kidnapper, to understand his demands, to decode the letters, and most of all, to outwit him. But in this master game of chess, Keri may find herself up against a foe even she cannot understand, and for the missing girl—and her own daughter—she may just be too late.

A dark psychological thriller with heart-pounding suspense, A TRACE OF CRIME is book #4 in a riveting new series—and a beloved new character—that will leave you turning pages late into the night.

"A masterpiece of thriller and mystery! The author did a magnificent job developing characters with a psychological side that is so well described that we feel inside their minds, follow their fears and cheer for their success. The plot is very intelligent and will keep you entertained throughout the book. Full of twists, this book will keep you awake until the turn of the last page."

Book #5 in the Keri Locke series will be available soon.

BOOKS BY BLAKE PIERCE

RILEY PAIGE MYSTERY SERIES
ONCE GONE (Book #1)
ONCE TAKEN (Book #2)
ONCE CRAVED (Book #3)
ONCE LURED (Book #4)
ONCE HUNTED (Book #5)
ONCE PINED (Book #6)
ONCE FORSAKEN (Book #7)
ONCE COLD (Book #8)
ONCE STALKED (Book #9)

MACKENZIE WHITE MYSTERY SERIES
BEFORE HE KILLS (Book #1)
BEFORE HE SEES (Book #2)
BEFORE HE COVETS (Book #3)
BEFORE HE TAKES (Book #4)
BEFORE HE NEEDS (Book #5)
BEFORE HE FEELS (Book #6)

AVERY BLACK MYSTERY SERIES
CAUSE TO KILL (Book #1)
CAUSE TO RUN (Book #2)
CAUSE TO HIDE (Book #3)
CAUSE TO FEAR (Book #4)

KERI LOCKE MYSTERY SERIES
A TRACE OF DEATH (Book #1)
A TRACE OF MUDER (Book #2)
A TRACE OF VICE (Book #3)
A TRACE OF CRIME (Book #4)

Blake Pierce

Blake Pierce is author of the bestselling RILEY PAGE mystery series, which includes seven nine (and counting). Blake Pierce is also the author of the MACKENZIE WHITE mystery series, comprising six books (and counting); of the AVERY BLACK mystery series, comprising four books (and counting); and of the KERI LOCKE mystery series, comprising four books (and counting).

An avid reader and lifelong fan of the mystery and thriller genres, Blake loves to hear from you, so please feel free to visit www.blakepierceauthor.com to learn more and stay in touch.

CPSIA information can be obtained
at www.ICGtesting.com
Printed in the USA
LVOW10s1544130717
541255LV00011B/461/P